Grimm Retold

Speculation Publications

ISBN-13: 979-8986887982

Reprinted Work:
Alba by Erica Ruppert first published in *Another Realm*, April 2016.
The Forbidden Room by TT Madden first published in *Remapping Wonderland: Classic Fairytales Retold by People of Color*, 2021
The Princess and Her Future by Tanith Lee first published in *Red as Blood, Or, Tales from The Sister Grimmer*, 1983
Prized Possessions by Ell Huang first published in *Awkward Mermaid*, 2018
Sickly Sweet by Ephiny Gale first published in *Black Apples*, 2014

Original Illustrations: Brian Lally
Cover Art: LCW Allingham
Copyright © 2024 Speculation Publications LLC

Vectors: Vecteezy
Fonts: Alert Covid, Century 751, Book Antiqua, High Tower Text, Anarchy, Augusta
Published by Speculation Publications
No part of this book was created by AI

For More Information go to www.speculationpub.com

Content Warning

The stories that follow play on the most dark and depraved themes of the original Grimm Fairy Tales.

There is abuse of all types, and some particularly challenging depictions of sexual abuse, graphic descriptions of torture and gore, sexism, slavery, racism, homophobia, and hate.

Please proceed with care for yourself.

A Horror Collection

of Dark Fairy Tales

Edited by LCW Allingham and River Eno

Speculation Publications

Table of Contents

FOREWORD

Cecilia Dart-Thornton

Welcome to a collection of stories offering tantalising glimpses into arcane worlds. Each tale is like a dark jewel; a glittering gem with smoky depths into whose dizzying, splendid and appalling depths you'll willingly plummet.

Prepare to be captivated by weird, enthralling, edgy narratives, often with clever twists.

Be warned, you'll confront violence between these pages! As the editors cautioned me from the beginning, "There is sexual assault, a lot of gore, murder, graphic descriptions and abuse." But you're here because you like the horror genre, so this is what you'll be expecting! Besides, the Brothers Grimm were certainly not averse to a little maltreatment, homicide, cannibalism etc. in their original "grim" tales!

Within these pages there's a recurring motif of hunger, and the dichotomy of eating - how it can be both nourishing and life-giving for the eater, and yet for that which is eaten, it's the opposite.

The tales explore the fine line between a kiss and a bite, between a caress and a blow, or a promise and a betrayal; the perilousness of falling in love. "Be careful who you trust" they seem to say. "Salt and sugar look the same..." The illusion of love may mask treachery—as so many victims of domestic violence have discovered.

Despite scenes of savagery, a moral thread can be found running through these beautifully told stories; a theme of justice, retribution and reclamation of power. And the prose is simply elegant.

Erica Ruppert's "Alba" is a subtle masterpiece, a retelling of the "Snow-White" fairytale, in which the protagonist triumphs over those who would wrong her, using not bladed weapons, but her own ingenuity and initiative.

J.R. Harlow's evocations of wetlands, ponds and marshy places in "No-One Need Ask" are a masterclass in sensory immersion. Every shadow and ripple hints at mystery lurking beneath the surface.

I was charmed by the touches of humor in Eleanor Cooke's innovative retelling of "The Crystal Ball" and intrigued by the dexterous plotting of Liv Strom's delightful "A Wished-for Wife," a retelling of Cinderella.

And it was a delight to re-read, in all its eerie, surprising, gruesome splendour, "The Princess and Her Future: A Retelling of The Frog Prince" by award-winning fantasy author, Tanith Lee.

Stunningly original, this collection will keep you hooked from start to finish.

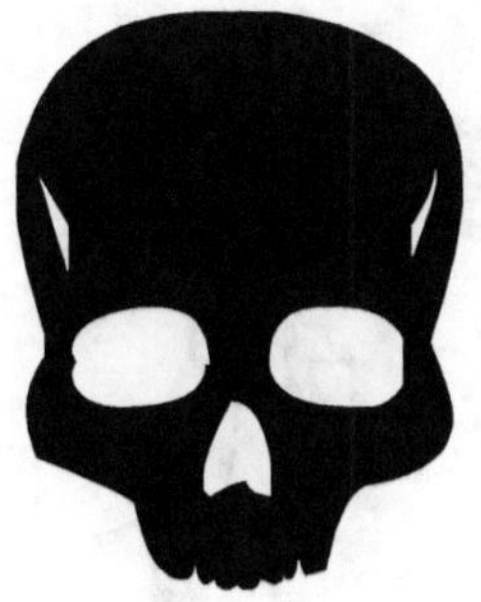

"Rapunzel, Rapunzel, Let down your hair to me."

RAMPION (THE HUNGRY GIRL)
F. Ffrench

Once upon a time, there was a husband and wife. They lived modestly in a little cottage neighboring a great witch and her lovely garden. One fine day, to the delight of husband and wife, they found themselves expecting a child. It would be their first child. They were elated. All the same, they feared for the child's wellbeing.

For you see the husband and wife were both quite poor and had little to eat. The pregnant wife needed far more nutrients than that which could be provided. She told her husband each day of all the fresh fruits and vegetables she longed for. As the pregnancy carried on, slowly her cravings consumed her. Her desire for fresh greens became the only occupation of her mind. More than all of them she longed for the taste of rampion.

The husband wished so badly to fulfill the wish of his wife. He paced back and forth late at night after she fell asleep, thinking up schemes of how he might feed her. Most nights either ended with him collapsing in prayer for a miracle, or collapsing in a hopeless slump. The neighbor witch's garden had such lovely vegetation, no doubt some of which inspired the wife's fantasies. But the witch was a very powerful being, and the husband feared her. One day, in a state he could not parse between desperate and brave, he approached the witch.

"Oh, witch," the husband begged, "your garden is so lovely and full, and yet you never take a single bite from it. Please may you spare some greenery to feed my pregnant wife?"

"I will gladly give my crop to you, for a price."

"What is your price, witch?"

"That firstborn child of yours on the way must become mine on the day of its birth."

"No. I am sorry but that is not possible. There must be another way."

"I have given my price. The choice is yours."

The husband came home defeated, his wife still hungry. She smiled at him and told him it was all right, but he could see the hunger in her eyes. Her appetite became so massive that the husband could no longer gather enough crummy food to keep her from starving.

In his desperation, he put a new plan into motion. In the dead of the night, he rose from his bed and ventured out. He snuck into the old witch's garden and pillaged her crop. He tried to take a little of every plant in the hopes that his theft would go unnoticed. After all, who would miss just a little parsley and a little squash?

However, he made one exception. He ransacked the entire stock of rampion. This was the crop his wife longed for the most, and he wanted as much as possible. He brought the loot of his heist back home to his wife.

The next morning she ate the most magnificent breakfast she had ever had. She marveled at how he could have possibly acquired such a feast. He told her that the prayer had paid off, and the miracle had arrived. This answer seemed sufficient enough for the wife, although the husband was uneasy for the rest of the day. He shook from the lies he had told to his wife and from the fear of the witch barging in and catching him.

But the witch did not come. And the next day when his wife ate again, the witch did not come. And after enough days without sight of the witch passed, his fear relaxed. He slowly became confident that he had successfully tricked the old wretch. He had fed his wife and protected his firstborn. Soon after this, their baby was finally born. A beautiful, healthy baby girl. Her skin and hair seemed to shine with the blessings of the miracle crops. The husband and the wife were overjoyed. But on the night of the baby's birth, after the family had fallen asleep, a knock came at the door. The husband awoke and opened the door without hesitation, having forgotten all about the witch. Until there she was.

"I have come to collect my payment."

The husband and wife turned cold. The witch rolled in like a fog. The husband could not stop her any more than he could stop a thunderstorm or a river flowing. She was a force beyond his strength. The wife went to hide the baby. But when she ran to the nursery, there was the witch. The baby was already in her hands

The parents pleaded, "You cannot take our child! We made no deal."

"I gave you my price, and you chose." The witch's voice sounded like a soft yet persistent wind.

"But why? What could you possibly want with our precious girl?" The parents cried.

"The same thing you wanted with my rampion. She is one of my crops now, and I think she will grow to be a fine meal." The witch cackled and reveled in the horror this news brought the young parents.

The couple made one more attempt to plead with the witch, but she had already disappeared into the night. All that was left was a cradle and a trail of mist.

The witch locked the child up in a high tower with no stairs. She named the child Rampion, because that was what she was. She raised the baby like she was her own.

Every day the witch collected food from her magical garden and brought it up to young Rampion to feed from. She grew stronger by the day on these magical meals.

Rampion came to understand the world little by little. As she became aware of her surroundings, she understood that the entire universe consisted of a single room and that there were only two people in it. It was the room she lived in. The top of the tower. And the two people in all the universe were her and the witch. She came to understand the view from her window as a mirage, something visible in the distance but inaccessible. Something that would vanish if she tried to reach for it.

As she grew older and began to wonder beyond the question of what the world was, she constructed a scheme for why the world was. She observed the entire universe, and the two people in it, and deduced logically sound conclusions.

She determined that the witch created everything. She determined that the food the witch provided Rampion grew from the witch's very body. Everything grew from her body. The tower came from the witch's body, her bed, her clothes, the mirage, everything. All of her joys and wonders were the product of the witch. Rampion's only mother was the mother of the world.

Over time, in her isolation, her hair grew longer and longer. It grew at lengths and speeds completely unnatural for a girl. The witch knew this was the magic food doing its work. The witch let it grow long as a kind of measure of how much had been poured into the girl. Rampion kept it long, because it was long, and she was the only girl, so it must be true that a girl's hair ought to be that long.

The hair kept Rampion occupied. She spent all day every day maintaining it. This was convenient for the witch. Rampion would never have time to consider escaping if she was so distracted by her hair. However the witch noticed even without this distraction, Rampion seemed content with the reality she came to believe in. She never questioned the world further, even as she aged.

One day, when Rampion was a bit older, without any warning, the witch went out for food and never came back. Rampion waited and waited, but there was no sign of her. Rampion became the only person in the entire universe.

At first, she prayed that the witch was still alive and would someday return. But as the days passed, and her hunger grew, she lost all hope. God was dead. God whose body the world grew from. The creator of everything disappeared into thin air. She knew it was the end of all existence.

She was at the beginning of the slow and painful decay of reality. She saw herself withering away to nothing, the room collapsing, the mirage fading into a black void. With no more magical greens, she grew desperate to survive.

She needed to prolong the inevitable. She ate her clothes, or rather she tried her best to. It made her sick. She tried to stretch her portions out and make them last, but she ran out. She licked the stone walls of the tower. She ate her bedsheets. And then there was nothing left. She watched the contents of the universe disappear around her as she ate it. Until the only thing in the world was her, stomach empty, body empty.

Then one day, a figure approached the tower out from the mirage. A strange creature came to the base of the tower and called out to Rampion

"Oh! Rampion! Rampion! Let down your hair! The witch is slain! I've come to rescue you! Rampion! Rampion! Let down your hair!"

From oblivion, this creature came into existence. It was almost like one of the witch's gifts. Rampion's stomach groaned loud. *Winter is over,* she thought to herself.

Rampion let her hair fall down the tower. The tip of her locks floated just above the ground. *Almost like it was planned,* she thought. The knight climbed her hair up to the top. He climbed through the window and broke the mirage. When he reached the top, he took Rampion and kissed her.

Rampion bit off his mouth.

She started with his face. She ate his mouth, his nose, his ears. She sucked his eyeballs out of his skull with only her mouth and chewed them like grapes. Through his face, she found his insides. She sucked little bits of brain out from his eye sockets. But she wanted more. So she laid his limp body on the ground and smashed through his skull. She ate her way down. She tore his skin to shreds with her teeth. She ate her fill of his meat. And when it was still not enough, she tore open his ribcage and ate from inside out.

She ate him down to the bones. She licked the bones dry.

Rampion was full and healthy again. At that moment, she knew the witch was out there, sending her more food. The world grew again, so it must grow from something. From that day on, now and then, a new morsel would arrive at the tower, just when Rampion's hunger was beginning to hurt her. She did not let a single bite of these gifts go to waste.

Every knight that came to save her met a gruesome end. She devoured them each alive like an animal, no, like a pack of animals.

She never bathed and lived in layers upon layers of dried blood and bile. She slept on piles of hair ripped from the heads of knights. She created beautiful things from the remains of her meals. She made bone shell monuments to the witch. Her likeness from the ligaments and the skull shrapnel of her meals. She made jewelry that would dazzle royalty. A crown constructed of ribs. Earrings made from teeth. A necklace designed of tiny finger bones. Her home became a gallery, a shrine, and a palace. Every bit of it was human remains.

Just as she destroyed the universe with her consumption, she built it back up the same way. The universe became a thing of Rampion's creation. Every detail of it was her design. And she was happy.

The more knights that failed to save Rampion, the more knights there were eager to prove their valiance. Although the witch no longer came to her, she could feel her love.

With every knight she swallowed, love. The red that now painted her walls was the red of love.

And the little girl never went hungry again. Happily ever after.

"'Dear father, do with me what you will.
I am your child,' and with that
she stretched forth both hands
and let her father chop them off."

SICKLY SWEET

Ephiny Gale

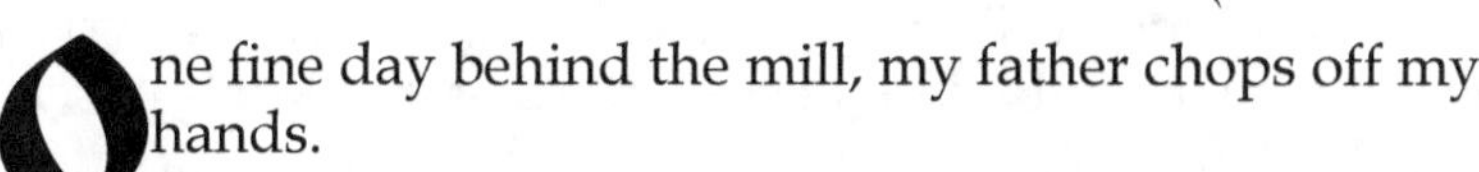

One fine day behind the mill, my father chops off my hands.

He does it with an axe, on a tree stump. He says the devil is coming. That he promised the devil my hands, in exchange for his life.

I do not believe in the devil. My father has been hearing voices for some time.

There is a lot of blood, but no pain. I have heard stories of soldiers, those with their arms sliced off who screamed, not because it hurt but because of the shock of seeing their shoulder and limb separated. The pain is so great that your body snuffs it out. For a little while.

I yell, too. I shriek. I clutch my bloody wrists to my dress and back away, sprinting, stumbling into the forest. My father does not pursue me; the devil can find me anywhere, if I am still wanted.

I curl up at the base of a tree, nesting in its roots. The pain arrives like a delayed traveller. I think I am going to die.

◦◦—

I do not die. I wake with my wrists attached to my dress, the brown of dried blood mixing with the brown of the fabric. They stick, knitting with the cotton, where I'd pressed them tightly to stem the blood flow.

I shift my torso and feel the dried blood cracking on my stomach.

My wrists are swollen, ballooning, fiery things, far more vicious than the worst burn I have experienced. I am loath to upset them further. With effort, I push myself up the tree trunk by my feet, and the bark scrapes sharp against my back.

I begin to walk.

It is a long walk. Several seasons change. My wrists heal, as much could be expected, turning into knots of scar like the knots on an old tree. I take pleasure in small, animalistic activities; biting into a sun-warmed peach and letting the juice run down my chin, diving to the muddy bottom of a river and propelling myself up with jack-knifed legs.

In spring, blood appears between my legs and again, I think I will die.

I do not die.

Later, it comes again, many times.

I do not die then, either.

In the heart of the second autumn, I stumble through a pile of leaves into a clearing. Low, golden sunshine illuminates the charred ruins of a house. And within the ruins, beneath the powdery ash and grey, brittle wood and occasional brick, something glints, metallic and inviting.

I step gingerly over the rubble and peer at my treasure. Nestled safely and perfectly, impossibly intact: a pair of silver hands.

I drop to my knees.

With infinite care and precision, I wipe each hand along my tired, tattered brown dress until the dirt disappears. The joints in the fingers swing back and forth, more or less like a real hand. There is no rust, no squeaking. When I slip the metal cuffs of the hands onto my wrists, they fit exactly, as if they have been made especially for me.

I have avoided people, for the most part, since my hands were stolen. Now I feel buoyed, lighter; I jog to the nearest town, contented simply by the burbles of conversation, the currents of humans flowing past each other in the shopping district.

So many man-made shapes and colours make my head spin. I wander past shops selling thick, salty-looking ink in glass flasks; stalls with glazed, salmon-coloured hams suspended from ceilings; doorways with silk jackets, the colour of morning dew and encrusted with dozens of precious stones.

"You!" A booming masculine voice hits me in the ear, not three paces away. I stop, glance around. He is looking directly at me. "Are you going to pay for that?"

My heart hammers in my chest. I look down, and see a large bag of flour, and a slightly smaller bag of brown sugar clutched in a silver hand. Adrenaline pours into my veins. I am a criminal. I am mortified. I feel about to faint.

The other silver hand curls, reaches into my pocket and pulls out three gold coins. I stare. I have never had any money of my own, and this does not feel like mine, either.

The merchant huffs and holds out his own sweaty hand.

"I'm sorry," I whisper in my rusty voice, dropping the coins down into his palm. He nods like he doesn't believe me.

I take off along the cobblestones, down the streets into the forest. I make a nest in some tree roots, place down the flour and the sweet, caramel-smelling sugar and examine the silver hands.

They do not feel like my hands anymore. I cannot move the fingers of my own free will, and yet they have moved. They have curled and grasped and extended without my consent.

I shake, pressing one hand between my knees, pulling back my arm to wrench the hand away like an unwanted glove. I grunt. But no matter how hard I press or pull, the hand always stays a part of me. It slips out between my knees like it's melded to my skin.

I try again with the other hand to no avail.

When my tears fall, I let them fall on the silver, and I wish fervently that it will rust.

I take the flour and sugar to the clearing, to the ruins of the house. I remember a formation of low bricks, sticking out amongst the wreckage, which gave me the impression of an oven.

I search through the rubble for any other bricks, stacking them together, interlocking them with the remnants of the old oven. The silver hands grab everything easily, nimbly, more skilled at construction than I was ever with my own flesh. They are clever, these hands. They fit the oven together like an expert puzzle.

At the end, the finished oven sits there, red and swollen, and reminds me of my bleeding wrists.

I am ashamed to say I go back to the town. More than anything—food, love, justice—I feel I am starved of opportunity.

The hands have made me ravenous.

From the stalls they pick jars of cinnamon, towers of sea salt, butter wrapped in golden cloth, cloves and ginger in wooden boxes, eggs in woven baskets, and each time, a silver hand dips into my pocket and fishes out gold coins. I never see the coins fall in, but I learn to recognise the slight weight in my pocket, the almost imperceptible clink as the silver hands pilfer someone else's pockets or bags.

I return to the clearing laden with parcels.

I sit in the rubble and press the cinnamon and ginger to my nose, inhaling deeply. I rub the exquisite, perfectly smooth egg against my arms, face and neck. I tip a little of the salt onto my tongue and revel in it, my eyes sliding shut.

And then the hands really get to work.

Deep in the woods, though not that deep, stands a house made entirely of gingerbread. The walls and roof and floors are gingerbread, as are the chimney and single iced door. If you licked the windows you would know them to be sugar, and if you bit into the windowsills you would know them to be thick, fresh marzipan.

The house does not age, or rot, or melt. Encrusted in the gingerbread are hard candies of every flavour and colour, liquorices which seem to sparkle, candy-covered chocolates in the shapes of hearts and stars and clovers.

Inside the house there lives a woman, though she was only recently a girl. They say idle hands are the devil's work, but how fervently I wish mine would stop.

The silver hands are always moving, like mechanical spiders desperate to get out of the rain. Sometimes they clean and scrub and tidy. Sometimes they play over my body, prying open my mouth and feeling my tongue, the ridges of my teeth. Sometimes they crawl between my legs and play me like an instrument, running their intelligent fingers inside me and warming with my body heat.

Sometimes I don't mind.

Mostly, they like to cook. They like sugar. They like ever more elaborate desserts, which never seem to go off and pile in towers, gathering on most surfaces of the house and in ever-expanding nooks and crannies. They cook shelves and cupboards for more cooked treats.

They cook another room for the house.

Often, at night, I suffocate the hands beneath my mattress and feel them struggle, twisting, beneath my body weight. After a little while they give up. Alone, unmoving, quiet washes over me. Bliss.

There are usually scars from this ritual when the hands break free; long scratch marks across my torso, legs or back, one or two or five in a row, but they're always worth it.

And then, one day, a gap in my wall appears, and on the other side a chewing child.

They freeze when I open the door; a boy with his mouth stuffed with gingerbread, and a girl with her lips wrapped around my windowsill. They are short, sickly pale and bony, their wide blue eyes protruding too far out of their skulls. I suspect they're not much younger than I am.

The boy swallows hastily, the girl detaches her lips.

"You must be very hungry," I say.

The girl smiles and digs her fingernails into her other arm. "We've walked for three days," she says, "with very little food, and are lost in these woods, and our parents can't feed us anymore."

A dozen competing emotions swim inside me like a school of fish.

Eventually, I say, "If you believe you shall starve if you don't come in… you may."

The children's faces relax with joy. A silver hand pushes the door fully open, and with barely restrained hunger, they dart inside.

I feed the children like they've never eaten in their lives.

I bring them: sticky date puddings drenched in hot fudge; towered chocolate cakes with sparkling shards of sugary caramel; raspberry and mint strewn in three layers; macaroons in twelve different flavours; cupcakes containing huge chunks of cookie dough; scones with jams and the fluffiest creams and melted chocolates.

When they've eaten their fill, groaning with pleasure on my wooden benches, I make them a bed of marshmallows in the corner of my living room. They curl up on the soft, rubbery pillows and are asleep within minutes.

I clean for some time to delay my own sleep. The hands have been delighted all evening, practically dancing off my wrists, and the guilt eats me up like acid. I should send the children on their way after breakfast tomorrow.

Later, under my blankets, the hands do not want me to rest. They want to play.

I decide I won't put them under the mattress tonight, won't make them angry with the children in the house.

I will send the children away tomorrow.

I am still half asleep when a third hand appears on my shoulder. I pay it no more attention than my own breathing.

"Are you alright?" asks a female voice.

My eyes snap open. The girl's blonde hair, inches away, is almost iridescent white in such early dawn. Unaccustomed to either company or shame, I throw my arms to either side of me.

"You were making noises."

I try to control my breathing, try to restrict the bile rising up my throat. "Noises?" I whisper.

"Murmurs, mutterings in your sleep… you were having a nightmare?"

I consider the girl's open face. A small glob of melted marshmallow is stuck to the side of her forehead.

"Always," I say.

We pad through the front door and around to my back garden; little more than two fruit trees and a small hill of seeded soil. The girl stares at every fruit and every leaf, cataloguing and greedy.

I hold out my arms. "You're very welcome."

She falls to her knees before a dozen strawberries, shovelling them into her mouth with dazzling efficiency. I sit nearby, my hands drawing meaningless patterns in the damp dirt. In the end she leaves three on their stems, wiping the crimson juice from her lips. Her hunger seems to still.

I suspect it's rude to ask, but the children will be gone in a matter of mouthfuls. I ask, "Do you despise your parents for letting you down?"

The girl's eyes widen. "Why would I despise them? They did their best."

"They almost killed you."

"They sent us away because they couldn't bear to see us starve before their eyes. I can't hate them for that." She picks a fat lemon from the tree and peels the skin with a combination of fingernails and teeth. "We aren't starving anymore, thanks to you."

She comes and sits next to me, too close; my hands may damage her. I scoot back. In the dull light I'm uncertain, but I think her face falls.

"It's not personal," I say. "I lost my hands a long time ago."

She studies the patterns on the ground. "They seem to work well enough."

"They're not…" I'm afraid, suddenly, that the hands can hear me. "They're not really mine." The last word morphs into a gasp as a sharp silver finger digs into the flesh of my side. A tiny darker patch appears on my brown dress.

Perhaps the hands can hear; perhaps they simply sense intention.

The girl is up on her feet. She hesitates for a moment, rocking back on her heels and then kicks the offending hand away from my side. With her right knee, she pushes my shoulder to the ground and pins the hand with her left boot. It convulses like a dying spider.

My other hand is blessedly still.

The wind has been knocked out of me. I lie with my head in the dewy grass, staring up at the frightened girl. Her shin is warm along the side of my torso. I can't remember the last time I touched someone.

"Do you need bandages?" she asks. "Something else?"

I shake my head against the grass. "I don't think it's deep. It will heal like the others."

"Others?"

The hand stops its convulsions after one last spasm, but the girl doesn't move away.

"There's a town to the east of here," I say. "A bit less than half a day's walk away. You should head there. Take as much food as you want, I insist."

She doesn't respond. Instead, she looks over her shoulder at an empty wire cage. "Is that for meat?"

"Chickens," I confirm. "But years ago." I'm hit with old memories of the hands snapping their necks.

She nods. "Are we safe to go to breakfast?"

I take several moments considering the frozen hands. They are playacting, surely, but I suspect they'll behave until their next calculated moment of rebellion. "If we behave," I say. "Though they shan't like you leaving."

"I'm not planning to leave," says the girl.

⊚⸺

Breakfast passes in relative silence. At one point the boy reaches over and scratches the marshmallow off the girl's forehead. She smiles at him and crinkles her nose, and I feel a stab of jealousy for that kind of easy companionship. This morning, the hands have refused me any liquid but melted chocolate in a mug. I take tiny sips; sickly sweet.

With a couple of short, insistent gestures the girl directs the boy to my back garden. She follows, announcing she'll be back in a minute, and either I believe her or the silver hands do, because they make no move to cease scratching patterns into the wooden sides of my mug.

The girl does return shortly, without her brother but with a strange sort of smile. She tosses a second lemon in the air between alternating palms. "We should do it," she says. "What you were talking about in your sleep."

I feel instantly naked.

"We should eat the boy," she says. "Cook him."

The only sound is the lemon thumping in her hands.

She presses on: "I mean, not even chicken for years. You must be starved for meat. I've locked him in the cage." She points needlessly to the garden. "Go and see."

I hear the blood beating in my ears. I step outside; the cage has not moved. The boy is curled against the far corner, one blue eye open and fixed warily on me.

I take another step, and he cries out. I am speechless.

"Not any closer!" he yells. "I know what those hands can do!"

I hold them up, clear in front of me. The silver fingers wriggle.

"You put them away!"

The venom in his voice makes my throat constrict. I tuck my hands tight behind my back, which is the best I can do. I venture another step.

Like a well-practiced magic trick, he reveals a rusty key — the key to the cage — and winks. It disappears again.

I take out the silver hands.

"Are you going to eat me?"

I realise with relief that the hands can't reach him while he's caged.

"Not now," I say, to buy some time. "I have to fatten you up first. You're so thin; it would hardly be worth cooking you now."

His tears come right on cue, and when I return inside to his sister, she's sitting cross-legged on my dining table and squeezing lemon juice onto her tongue.

⟡

"Do you have an axe?"

My hands pause in the middle of kneading lemon-scented cookie dough. "No," I tell her, and the hands start up again.

"How do you chop firewood, then?"

"No firewood." I push a lock of hair out of my face with my shoulder. "I use oil."

The girl's mouth cracks open.

"It never seems to run out," I confess, and find I can't meet her eyes any longer.

Her footsteps retreat towards the front door. "It's just—I've been looking at your knives. We'll need something hardier to chop up a boy. A cleaver? I'll go to the town you talked about. Be back just after nightfall if I leave now."

I nod, not entirely sure what I'm agreeing to. "There's some money in the cupboard to your left, the one with…"

The silver hands have raced across the table and are climbing up my torso, digging painfully into my flesh as they crawl. I try and wrench them away, but my arm muscles are weak from this angle and the fingers sink into my stomach and breasts too deep.

Within two seconds the cold metal is wrapped around my neck, still covered in traces of cookie dough.

The thumbs are pressed tight into my oesophagus. My lips open in a continuous gasp. I struggle, bashing the hands against the edge of the table, but they hold fast. My vision blurs.

The last thing I see is the girl, her arms prying at my wrists. She calls my name like she means it.

When I wake, it is surreal. Under any other circumstances I would freeze completely. At this very moment I am too wrung out to care.

I am lying on top of the bed, the woollen blanket scratching against my naked back. My arms are wrenched to either side of the mattress. The silver hands are out of sight, and tugging confirms that they are both tied securely under the bed.

The girl has removed my dress and is straddling my hips, wiping my cuts with a rag soaked in green liquid. The rag stings like being sliced up all over again.

Absinthe, then.

There are perhaps two dozen cuts staggered over my torso. The girl attends to one just next to my nipple and my chest shudders. She glances up, registers I'm awake and immediately averts her gaze.

"Apologies. There was…"

"You don't have to apologise." My voice comes out hoarse and scratchy, followed by a minor coughing fit.

The girl leaves to fetch a glass of water. As she goes, her thigh brushes over my hip. My mind feels ill and unanchored, like I've come down with a fever, but I don't think I have. Thoughts arrive as if through a fog.

Sipping is awkward, with her hand behind my head and the cup at my lips. I take tiny, restricted swallows and trails of water run down the sides of my mouth. She wipes them aside with her thumb.

"What did you tie them up with?"

"I found rope in a kitchen cupboard," she says.

"It won't hold them for much longer. An hour or two, maybe. They'll slice through it. They've hollowed out chunks of my mattress."

Her face falls, her hand holding the cup shakes. A couple of drops escape, falling onto my skin and running down the cleft between my breasts. She turns away to gather her composure.

Three long, fresh scabs run down her forearm.

Eventually she says, "Well, what else will hold them? Anything here?"

"Chains would," I say. "I have none. The mattress might for another hour, longer if they thought that wasn't going to be permanent."

She plays with her fingernails while she considers this. Glances under the bed, then climbs on and reclaims her position over my hips. "I was going to..." She leans forward, biting her lip and touches my elbows, making a sawing motion with her fingers. "But there's no time."

I nod. The axe. The cleaver. "How did you tie them up at all?"

"Oh. I wasn't planning to. But once you passed out, they went limp for a while. I don't think they want you dead." Her blue eyes bore into mine. "Really dead."

When she doesn't get a response, the girl picks up the rag and the absinthe again. "I know it seems a bit redundant. But may I?"

My mouth feels too dry. "Alright."

Her wipes with the rag are gentle and precise. She rests her other hand on my arm, my shoulder, my ribs for balance. Her skin feels twice as soft and warm as my own. Sometimes, she traces my many scars with an absent fingertip.

Despite myself, my tears start to fall.

She kisses them from the sides of my face, her lips like velvet. The light fabric of her dress grazes my stomach, my breasts, my nipples. My skin breaks out in goosebumps. My breath comes out in tiny sighs and shudders.

She kisses my forehead, my cheeks, my lips. I feel like I'm floating up out of my body, and the stinging fades to background noise. There is no mattress, no rope, no silver hands.

Then her own tears fall onto my collarbone.

"Is there anything we can do for you?" she whispers. "Anything at all?"

When the words finally come, my voice is cold and composed. Not quite my own.

"We have to cook the boy," I say.

Inside the oven, the fire blazes. Flames of a million different yellows and oranges lick at the bricks. The boy has been fed and watered. The girl has prepared the lemon-scented cookie dough for baking.

The hands are largely behaving themselves, almost humming in anticipation.

I will my pulse to slow and turn to the girl. "It's time."

She looks me straight in the eyes, so blatantly that I'm worried a silver finger will impale me. "Are you sure?"

"Yes. Check that the oven is hot enough, will you?"

She tugs open the oven door. The heat is noticeable even from here. The girl peers inside, the flames playing over her lovely face. "I don't know how to," she lies.

I blurt out the first curse I can think of. "Let me, then." I shuffle over and take her place, my heart inside my mouth.

I stick my head clear inside the oven. Farther than necessary. So close that the fire sparks in my hair, and I can feel my face beginning to burn.

"It's ready," I call.

And she shoves me inside, where the world is white hot.

My last thoughts are a series of cluttered imaginings: that the girl and her brother run home, their arms full of candies and treasures and coins.

That they leave the remains of the gingerbread house behind them; a smoking pile of powdery ash.

That they arrive, safe, to loving parents.

And that somewhere, the devil appears to a father who bargains a daughter he forgets could be behind his mill.

It's a small comfort. To know I'm not the only one.

And the silver hands don't burn at all.

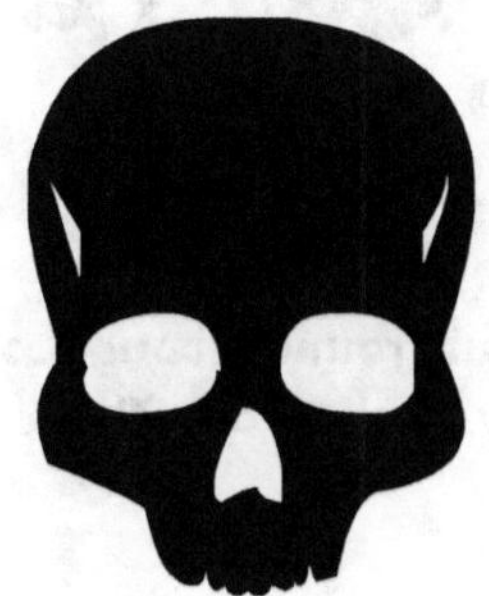

"Round about, round about, Lo and behold!
Reel away, reel away, Straw into gold!"

IN THE HOUSE OF THREAD AND SHADOW

Shehrazade Zafar-Arif

There is a house, deep in the heart of rural Sindh, coated in layers of history and open to an unforgiving sky. Those who know steer clear of it; even fresh meat won't tempt the stray dogs across its threshold. Only crows make their homes in the buried spaces of its rooftops. Only crows.

Deep in the stones sleeps a creature that exists only in the embers of long-forgotten fires, in the shadows cast by moonlight-drenched trees. A creature of stories and wishes.

It stirs at the sound of voices.

⊚⁓

Under the baking sun, a man begged for his life.

All over the country, men begged — for life, for food, for money, sometimes for death. Pride and honour died in the merciless dust. Men who never bothered to prostrate themselves before God had no trouble going on their knees before the feet of the powerful. And who could blame them? God's eyes were elsewhere these days.

And so there was always a man on his knees, and a man standing over him.

The man on the ground, a farm manager named Tariq, wore a tattered, sweat-stained shalwar kurta, his face sun-darkened and pockmarked under his beard. A bruise was swelling over one eye, and the fingers of his left hand were bent and broken, pressed to the dirt as if it could protect him.

"Sahib—Sahib, you've always been so kind to us. My family has worked for yours since before I was born, my children think of you as their father."

The man lounging on the cane chair, a servant holding an umbrella over his head to shield him from the sun, didn't look his way. He was preoccupied watching a quail skitter across the cotton field, a blur of feathers and panic, before a well-timed bullet made it drop like a stone. Village children, their bare feet slapping in the sand, waded into the cotton, fighting to be the first one to retrieve the kill. An approving cheer went up from the men gathered around with rifles, the smoke from their cigarettes mixing with the dust rising in the air.

"Sahib…" Tariq began again, and the man standing over him delivered a swift kick to his back, making him squeal like an injured animal, doubling over until the man in the chair was ready to give him his attention.

Javaid Mirza, dressed in clean brown slacks and a button down shirt, surveyed the farm manager from behind sunglasses that cost more than his tenants saw in a month. Like his father and grandfather, he was ruler of this miniature kingdom of cotton and eucalyptus, landlord of these two thousand acres of farmland that sprawled on either side of the house. He preferred it here to his other house in Karachi, where in the big city he was just another rich man among rich men. Here the farmers and orchard managers and district officials fell over each other to flatter him, and the labourers crowded around his car whenever it came up the driveway. He was a father to them, allowing them to live on his land, paying off their debts in the form of successful harvests, giving them allowances for their daily expenses. Here, he could condemn a man to death with a snap of his fingers.

God was not needed here, Javaid Mirza thought. "You stole from me, took money that was meant for the farmers and lined your own pockets."

"Sahib, I was desperate! I didn't have enough to feed my children. I'm a poor man, think of my burdens. I have no sons, only daughters, all unmarried. I'll pay you back every rupee, I swear it."

Tariq was weeping now, and Mirza was almost embarrassed by his tears. He looked away again, as one of the hunters came to his chair, holding out a dead quail by its slender leg. A drop of blood trickled between its glassy eyes and splattered on the ground next to Mirza's polished shoe.

As if he saw his own death prophesized in the bird, Tariq burst out: "I have a daughter. She's a gifted tailor. Any design you give her, she can stitch it for you in a single night. God has blessed her. She could spin straw into gold!"

The men gathered around the field laughed scornfully at his bold, desperate claim, but Mirza leaned forward, his interest piqued. His wife, who had been sulking ever since he had dragged her down here from the city, had a fondness for clothes. He doubted the girl was as talented as her father claimed, but she could be useful to have around the house, and collateral to make sure he paid back his debt.

"Very well. Have your daughter sent up to the house tomorrow."

Every man had his price, thought the creature, as Tariq bowed down and kissed the ground at Mirza's feet, babbling his thanks. *After all, what was a daughter, but a burden to be passed on to another's hands?*

Mona's father could not meet her eyes as he told her she was being sent away. She squatted in the courtyard, her hands prune-dry with the soapy water she was washing their clothes in, and all she could think was that this never would have happened if her mother were still alive. Her father would have never dared steal from the landlord who owned their lives, and he would never have been allowed to sell his daughter to pay off his debt.

But her mother was gone, and so it was Mona who managed the house and made sure her younger sisters were fed and dressed before they were sent to the school in the next village, the one she had been made to drop out of when she turned sixteen. Now there would be no one to stand on the roadside to make sure they were safely boarded into the van that came to pick them up.

There was no time to grieve, and even less time to rage. Mirza's driver came for her in the morning. Her sisters cried and clung to her, and she mopped their eyes and made them promise to focus on their studies.

"I'm going on an adventure," she told them. "Just like in the stories Mama used to tell us."

In her smile there was sunshine, and something mysterious and cunning, and the girls' tears dried up. In the stories, adventure was always a wonderful thing, inevitably destined for a happy ending, and to them their clever, beautiful sister made the perfect heroine.

She held her own tears in check, sitting in the backseat of the jeep that rattled over the pothole-ridden road. Instead she looked out the dust-smeared windows at the endlessly rolling fields of cotton and sugarcane, the stalks of wheat rippling in an occasional breeze. Here and there were houses just like the one she had grown up in, wooden shacks as rickety and precarious as their owners' claim to the land that surrounded them. Tractors rumbled over the soil, labourers squatted in the fields with scarves wrapped around their heads to protect against the sun, and women crouched along the banks of the river to fill buckets with leaf-strewn water.

Everything she saw, Mona knew, belonged to the man to whom she was going: every blade of grass, every weed to be yanked out, and every man and woman whose bare feet sank into the loamy soil. Her soul was forfeit.

They passed a guava orchard, where the skeletal arms of the trees seemed to strain towards the sun even as they were weighed down by swollen yellow-green fruit and then turned onto a narrow dirt road lined with misshapen eucalyptus trees. The landlord's house loomed over the fields, a menacing hunchback shape silhouetted against the lightening sky. Mona thought it looked like she imagined the old Mughal palaces had in their heyday, arrogant in its opulence. But it was a fallen beauty. The russet brown stones were cracking, strained by time and the elements. Tall weeds grew around its pillars, and cobwebs wove through the wooden lattices of the jharokhas that protruded from the front wall.

The tenants who lived on Mirza's land claimed that the house was haunted, that terrible things had happened there since it was first built, shortly after Pakistan became an independent nation. As Mona watched, crows lighted on the roof, a warning in their inkblot eyes and ruffled feathers: *turn away, turn away.*

She knew the cruelty of this land as well as anyone, and it had nothing to do with spirits or hauntings, but with the greed of men.

The servants of Mirza's household observed as the new girl climbed out of the jeep. She was beautiful in a wretched sort of way, too thin, long-faced, sombre eyes and a severe mouth. Her dark hair was long and braided down her back, and her eyes were wide and brown like a fawn's, offsetting severity with innocence. *Braised innocence,* they thought. *This house would eat her alive.*

Mona walked up the driveway, carrying a plastic bag with all her belongings, knotted around her fingers and ripping from the bottom. Her chin was tipped back, trying to take in as much of the house as she could. There was a neem tree at the edge of the garden, its roots ripping free of the ground as if they strained to reach the sky.

She was met on the patio by an old woman with steel-grey hair pulled into a sharp bun and a deep, gruff voice who introduced herself as Zainab, the housekeeper. She led Mona into the house, which could have fit her own home comfortably three times over. It was dimly lit by an assortment of lamps that did little to beat back the shadows, and a fine layer of dust lay sleepily over the furniture.

They passed a large, filthy kitchen, where a round-bellied man barked orders at a boy who was chopping vegetables with dirt-stained fingers, the air swampy with the smell of frying meat and sizzling garlic, and through a door that led into the servant quarters. Zainab showed Mona the charpoy bed she would be sleeping in, and the bathroom shared by the women, with a mouldy bucket that could be filled with cold water.

Mona got the sense that the housekeeper had led her through the house instead of going around it to get to the servant quarters not as a shortcut but in order to remind her of her place in this fragile ecosystem.

She did not meet the masters of the house until later that evening, when Zainab enlisted her to serve them dinner in a dining room with tall windows that looked out over the cotton fields. She had never met Javaid Mirza before. He was a coldly handsome sort of man, with a thick moustache and perfectly white, straight teeth. His wife, Farida, was a bored beauty, hair shiny and straightened, fanning herself with a delicately embroidered paper fan, but her eyes lit up when she saw Mona.

"So you're the tailor! I'll be putting you to work soon enough, once you're settled in."

She spoke in a tenderly maternal tone, even though she couldn't have been more than ten or fifteen years older than Mona. Mona inclined her head and stuttered a thank you for the opportunity to be given work, and then looked at Mirza Sahib. He looked back with an appraising smile, the kind that made her feel like he was trying to look through her clothes.

She imagined herself picking up the steaming pot of lamb stew and dumping it in his lap, imagined laughing gleefully as he flailed in pain, the look of horror on Farida Begum's vacantly pretty face. She hid the fantasy behind a smile as he said, "I hope you'll feel at home here."

Home, it was not. She missed her sisters squirming and snoring in the bed beside her, as she tossed and turned in her new room. Around her, the house seemed to sigh and settle on its foundations, a bone-weary creaking running through its stones. As she drifted off to sleep, she thought it seemed to take a breath. It never let it out.

On her third day in the Mirza house, Zainab took Mona to the top floor of the house, unlocking the door to a small room with a low ceiling and a square window with wooden shutters. A bare light bulb dangled from the ceiling, shining a spotlight on the sewing machine set up on a narrow table, along with fabric scissors and measuring tape. Spilling out of a chest of drawers were mounds of fabric: slippery silk and heavy velvet, soft pastels and deep jewel tones.

"This was Mirza Sahib's mother's sewing room," said Zainab, lurking just outside the threshold of the room, as if held back by an invisible barrier. "Farida Begum says it's to be your workroom."

Mona had never had a workroom before. Her hands itched to reach for the gleaming masses of fabric, but she held herself back. "What am I supposed to be doing?"

"Your father said you were a gifted seamstress. She wants you to make her clothes." Zainab's tone suggested that this was a simple command, and Mona was equally simple for not grasping it immediately.

Mona's mother had taught her how to stitch. In order to make extra money, she had taken up tailoring jobs, mostly mending clothes for people in their village, but sometimes sewing shalwar kameezes for daily wear or, occasionally, formal clothes for Eid or weddings.

Her mother's gift had been forged into a tool of survival rather than an instrument of joy, but as a little girl assisting her, Mona had discovered an inescapable beauty even in the drab fabric of a shirt that needed its seams loosened for a man who had gained weight in old age. She would try to persuade her mother to let her embroider the collar or add a colourful lining to the sleeves, would dream up and sketch out designs on her school notebooks.

But whatever the landlord's wife was demanding would clearly be beyond her skills, no matter how much her desperate father had embellished her talents. And if she failed to live up to those standards, it was her family who would suffer. Her gift had become her prison, a prison of fabric and thread.

Zainab left her and Mona stood alone among the dust motes catching the dying rays of sunlight through the gaps in the shutters. She pulled fabric out of the drawers and let it spill around her, swallowing up the floor. It was beautiful, more beautiful than any material she had ever worked with, but she couldn't bring herself to touch it.

Outside, the sky billowed with stars, and moonlight washed over the silent fields, creeping into the room where Mona sat surrounded by beautiful, untouchable fabric, her tears catching like sequins on velvet and silk. She wasn't sure why she was crying, whether it was the gut-wrenching longing for home and the injustice of being ripped from it, or sorrow over this abandoned room, a dead woman's workshop, so much beauty left to gather dust and rot, so much left unfinished. Unremembered, as she would be.

"Why are you crying, girl?"

Mona's head snapped up, but the room was empty. Only moonlight and shadows, and yet in the darkness the shape of a man materialised from nothing. She hadn't heard him enter, and her heart hammered. She didn't recognise him as any of the servants she had seen around the house. He wore a plain black shalwar kurta and his skin was sun-darkened as though he worked in the fields. His beard was neatly trimmed, but his hair, inky black and curly, hung in a mane past his shoulders.

"Who are you?" she demanded.

"That's an interesting question," he said, crossing the room, his steps as silent as though he was gliding across the floor, and coming to a stop in front of the window, so his silhouette was traced in moonlight. "I am many things, and have been called many names. But tonight, I am your servant."

In the faint light, she could see his eyes. At first glance they appeared black, but as she gazed into them, she saw twin flames devouring his pupils and irises, so that they were not simply black but the colour of dying embers.

She had grown up on stories of jinns — creatures of fire, said to exist between one world and another, sometimes tricksters and other times friends. Always mercurial, capricious and dangerous. Her hands came together, and automatically she began whispering the words to the prayer every child was taught, the one to protect against jinns.

"There's no need for that," the jinn said. His voice was melodious, somehow simultaneously like the tinkle of wind chimes and yet raspy as if he had inhaled smoke. "I'm here to help."

The strangeness of his words, and of this night, shattered her paralyzing shock. Jinns were only stories, and Mona had never belonged in a story, not even her own. She sat back on her heels and lifted her chin. "Why?"

He crouched, trailing a hand over the mounds of fabric. "Nothing you make will ever be good enough for them, and they will punish you for it. Allow me to level the playing field."

Mona's fingers curled, nails digging into her palms. The sharp pain was a realisation: it wasn't fear she was feeling, but fury. The fury of a prisoner clawing at the walls, trying to dig her way out. Between despair and resignation, there could only be anger.

"Yes." The word spilled out. "Help me."

The jinn smiled, a knife-edged smile, all teeth and no mirth. "I'll require payment."

Mona tensed, drawing away from him, suddenly acutely aware of how utterly inhuman he was, a spirit of air and night, while she was fragile flesh and earth. "What kind of payment?"

"Something precious to you." His eyes dropped to her neck, predatory. "The necklace will do."

The necklace was hidden under her kameez, and Mona untucked it now: a slender gold chain with a pendant inscribed with the name of God in Arabic. She wore it for protection, from things like this.

Then again, it hadn't protected her from being sold like a cow for the slaughter. God hadn't answered her prayers, but this creature had. With trembling fingers she undid the clasp and let the gold pool on her palm. When she passed it to him—his own palm, she noticed, was smooth and unlined like a statue's—it felt as though she was surrendering a piece of her soul.

"Sleep, Mona," the jinn murmured. "When you wake, all will be well."

Mona's eyes were heavy, already swollen with crying. "You know my name, but you haven't told me yours."

The jinn laughed, and the house shuddered with the sound, as if the night itself was recoiling. But there was something painful in the laugh, silk tearing itself into pieces.

"If I had a name," he said, "I have long forgotten it."

Mona woke, curled up on the hard floor, neck stiff and head aching, convinced it had all been a dream, until she saw the clothes.

The entire household gathered on the landing, peering incredulously into the workroom. Sunlight drenched the room, proudly exposing the clothes that dangled from hooks on the wall: pink silk transformed into a sari embroidered with delicate gold lace, royal blue velvet into a sweeping lehenga and matching choli decorated with copper roses, green chiffon into a shalwar kameez with a sheer, gauzy dupatta.

Farida Begum cried out in delight, but what Mona felt instead of amazement and wonder was a surprising blaze of jealousy. She could have worked for hours and never been able to create such beautiful clothes, so precisely stitched, each design as unique as it was dazzling.

Since she was a little girl, the satisfaction of watching thread and fabric turn into something tangible had filled her with a kind of power. God was the Creator after all, and therefore in creation was the greatest kind of power.

So it made sense, then, that a jinn would have this kind of power. Mona shivered.

"But how did you manage to make all these in one night?" Mirza Sahib asked, his sharp eyes bewildered.

Farida Begum was less concerned. "They're beautiful! Oh, I can wear this one to my sister's wedding next month. You're a genius, girl. It looks like they're my size too!"

Mona hadn't realised that. She had thought they were *her* size, but she supposed she and Farida Begum were of similar builds.

She noticed Zainab watching her nervously, lips moving in silent prayer, as if she could sense the unnaturalness that still lingered in the room, the electric crackle of a storm about to break.

Of course, she didn't expect to see the jinn again, considering that to be the end of the story. But the story, like loose thread, kept unravelling.

Mona spent most of her days in the workroom, though Zainab occasionally pulled her into other duties around the house, like helping Shoaib the cook in the kitchen or sweeping the floors or serving meals to the Mirzas at dinner. She noticed that Mirza Sahib tended to request her services when he had guests over, usually men who eyed her with greedy appreciation.

She was happier in the workroom, but Farida had begun giving her designs, rough sketches in the pages of a glossy, leather-bound notebook. They were complicated, sometimes impossible to manipulate into reality, but Mona tackled them with grim determination. Hard calluses formed under her fingers, and her eyes burned from squinting.

Despite that, Farida Begum wasn't satisfied, complaining that the finished products didn't match up to her designs, or the images in her head, that they weren't as good as the clothes Mona had made the first night. And of course all Mona could do was nod and say she would try harder, even as her throat burned with a hundred unspoken vicious retorts.

She could tell Farida Begum hated it out here in the countryside, that she missed the city in the same way Mona missed her home. Every piece of her recoiled against the dusty fields and the endless stretches of sky where the stars were painfully visible, the night-time silence stretched like a hangman's rope.

More than that, she was bored. Bored in a way only the rich had the luxury of being, without the worries of money or work to occupy them, allowing room in their minds for an absent-minded sort of sorrow. She and her husband had been married for almost ten years, Mona knew, and yet they had no children. She wasn't sure whether that was misfortune or choice, but given the way Mirza Sahib ignored his wife, flirting shamelessly with the female servants and any women who visited the house, she knew love had nothing to do with it.

And so Farida had seized this obsession with designing clothes as if it was the key to her salvation, and Mona was her tool.

She also began observing things in the house that she hadn't noticed before, as if a door had been opened in her mind. Paintings fell off the walls. Meat rotted in the fridge even if it came from a freshly slaughtered goat. Lamps spluttered and died, shrouding rooms in darkness. It was as though the house itself was at war with its inhabitants, an unbroken stallion determined to make life difficult for its rider.

"Is it true this house is haunted?" she asked Shoaib the cook one day, as she stood helping him in the kitchen.

Out of all the servants in the Mirza household, Mona liked Shoaib best. Rafiq, the driver who had brought her here, was always sullen and scowling. Zainab looked at her as though she was cursed. But Shoaib was always cheerful, flirting with the farmhands and singing old Bollywood songs as he stirred a pot of biryani.

"Most places are haunted," he said, flippant as always, navigating his heavy girth through the kitchen as gracefully as a dancer. A pot was bubbling on the stove, and he tipped into it the coriander Mona had cut for him, so the pieces quivered for a moment on the hunks of chicken before dissolving into the stew.

"But this house has always been strange," he continued. "I've worked here since I was a boy, and I remember when Mirza Sahib's parents died. You know how it happened? His father fell off the roof one night. No one knew what he was doing up there; they just found his body in the garden in the morning. And his mother, she hanged herself in her bedroom, using the material of one of her saris as a noose. But she was troubled even before her husband died. She used to wake up screaming in the middle of the night, claiming she heard a man's voice at her window."

The other servants had their own horror stories to share about the house. "I heard Mirza Sahib's grandfather called a pir to repel the evil spirits from the house," said Rafiq, who stood by the gate smoking as Mona hung up the washing to dry. "The holy man prayed in every room in the house, and when he was finished, there was blood coming out of his ears. He told Mirza Sahib's grandfather that there was an old evil in the house, something which hated their family, and that he should tear the house down to its foundations and rebuild it. He didn't, of course. No one was going to chase the old man out of his ancestral home, not even a jinn."

Mona flinched at the word *jinn*. Only stories, she told herself, and focused on her work. After hours in the workroom, she felt as though her eyes were filled with needles and threads, distorting everything: a shadow on the wall became a face, the light streaming through the shutters became grabbing fingers, and a nightingale's call in the evening a cry for help.

One smouldering hot night, when she woke, she was no longer in her bed. She had never sleep-walked in her life, but now she stood under the enormous neem tree at the edge of the garden. Her mother's voice rippled through her mind, a whispered warning heard by all young girls: *don't stand under a tree at night with your hair open, or a jinn will take notice of you.*

"I come when you call," a voice said from the leaves above her, and when she peered up, she thought he had branches curling out of his hair, like antlers, as if he and the tree were becoming one.

Mona folded her arms, feigning bravado. "I don't remember calling you."

"I felt your despair," the jinn said. "I could taste it in the wind. And your anger. Anger is more interesting than despair. And why shouldn't you be angry? They have made you a prisoner."

The ugly bitterness in his voice, a disrupted melody, made her remember Rafiq's story, and the pir's warning. "Why do you hate them?"

"Perhaps I am a prisoner too," the jinn said. "Nameless, confined to this house and the land that surrounds it. There is freedom in anger. Would you like me to help you again?"

She scowled. "I suppose it'll cost me?"

"Nothing in this world is free." The jinn cocked his head, owl-like. "How about one of your sisters? I'll let you pick which one."

The words spliced through her, filling her with cold terror. "No. Absolutely not."

"Your father, then? He sacrificed you, for the sake of his own greed and weakness."

She was still angry at her father. He never called on the house, or asked her to come visit, as if by pretending she no longer existed he could hide from his own shame. But still she shook her head.

Instead she adopted the tone her mother used to take when she was negotiating with vendors at the market, equal parts disinterest and skepticism. "If it's a sacrifice you need, I can get you one of the goats from the farm."

He scoffed. "What would I do with a goat?"

Mona thought quickly. "Shoaib made some halwa today. It's still cooling in the kitchen." She had heard jinns liked sweet things.

He laughed, shaking his head, enjoying their game. She frowned. "Last time you asked for jewellery. Farida Begum has whole boxes of jewellery on her dresser. I can steal you something. She won't even miss it."

"It needs to be something precious," he said, "to you."

Mona's hand crept to her right wrist, the bangle hidden under the sleeve of her kameez. It was the only piece of jewellery she wore now that the necklace was gone. A plain gold bangle, one of a set of four that had been gifted to her mother on her wedding day, distributed among her four daughters before she died.

It was worth enough that she could have sold it to feed her family for a month. But selfishly, she had clung to it, hiding it from her father in case he tried to take it from her. It was all she had left of her mother, besides the face she saw in the mirror and the deftness with which she held a needle and thread.

In the end, it wasn't fear of retribution from the Mirzas, of what they might do to her family, that made her yank the bangle from her wrist. It was hunger, for a taste of the magic she had witnessed that night, the satisfaction of seeing shock and wonder in the Mirzas when they had discovered the clothes the jinn had made.

She held out the bangle to him, and then paused. It felt as if they were the only two beings left in a silent, dead world, empty of all souls. In his eyes she could see the ashes of a volcanic world, the only light on this moonless night.

"I have another condition," she said, in her negotiator's voice. "You teach me how to make the kind of clothes you made that night. I don't want to just be a tool anymore."

The jinn surveyed her curiously, and she had the sense he was sizing her up. Then he smiled, and once again it was something alien and unfathomable.

"For that I must have payment too."

"I have nothing else to give you."

"Then how about a wager?" He plucked the bangle from her hand and retreated back into the branches, swallowed up by darkness, and the tree groaned as if under some painful weight. "If you can guess my name, I'll not only share my gifts with you, but I'll also give you your freedom."

As spring rolled into summer, Farida Designs became one of the most electric and popular fashion brands in Pakistan. Throughout Karachi, and even Lahore and Islamabad, the clothes were worn by wealthy socialites to dinner parties and weddings. Actresses wore them to give television interviews and models posed in them on the runway. They exploded across the covers of fashion magazines, each design eagerly dissected by journalists and influencers alike.

It wasn't only the clothes themselves that drove this frenzy—although each piece was unique, some drawing on traditional Sindhi colours and patterns, others mimicking the sleek modernity of Western clothing—or the way their beauty seemed to defy reason itself, like the famous sari worn by an actress to a Hollywood premiere that appeared to change colour in different lights, or the kameez that seemed to be made of starlight. No, it was also the story behind the brand, advertised proudly on its website. While the fashion line was the brainchild of Farida Mirza, wife to businessman and feudal lord Javaid Mirza, the actual clothes were stitched by a poor village girl from interior Sindh.

What was more, the girl claimed that she had designed and stitched the clothes with the help of a jinn. It made people chuckle, gentle amusement at the imaginative fabrications of an innocent but illiterate girl. It was a good marketing ploy, for sure. Though those who wore the clothes often found themselves wondering if there was a grain of truth to the story, if there really was magic woven into the fabrics wrapped around their bodies.

Mona was largely oblivious to the excitement her clothes had stirred up all across the country, though Farida Begum had proudly showed her the brand's website, with clothes being sold for dizzying amounts of money. She never saw a single rupee of it.

Her world had shrunk into the four walls of the box-like workroom. She took her meals there, even slept there sometimes on a mattress set up in the corner. She barely had room to move among the clothes that hung from the racks that Mirza Sahib had ordered for them, fluttering in an unlikely breeze as if they were teasing her. She would fall asleep to the sound of cloth rustling against the wooden floor. She had become a mechanical thing, and even in idle moments she found her fingers mimicking the motions of the sewing machine.

It was her hands, her body that spun gold from straw, her mind that pulled designs from thin air and sometimes conjured up fabrics that didn't exist. But it was the jinn who worked through her, invisible hands guiding her own, a silent voice whispering in her ear. The thought troubled her sometimes, that she was still an instrument to another force, but the thrill of creation was too addictive to put aside.

As Eid approached, orders for clothes piled up. The other servants went home for the holidays, and the Mirzas went down to Karachi, but Mona remained. She had too much work to do, and it had become difficult to go home. Her sisters seemed to have grown up in her absence, no longer needing her the way they used to, and her father still couldn't meet her eyes. Perhaps they could see the hint of madness in her, the touch of supernatural influence. She felt like a stranger among them.

She was bent over her sewing machine when the jinn appeared. By now she had learned to recognise his presence, as subtle as the first patter of raindrops or a cat's paws on dew-damp grass.

"Hello, Kabir," she said, without looking up.

He sounded bemused. "Incorrect."

She looked up and grinned. It had become a game between them. She would try to guess his name, cycling through a random list of men's (and sometimes women's, because who knew if jinns had genders?) names, and he would tell her she was wrong. Sometimes she amused herself picking ridiculous and outrageous names.

"How about Abu Kawwa?" she said lightly.

"Father of Crows?" he asked, and she could've sworn he wrinkled his nose.

"The crows seem to like you. They're the only animals who'll come near the house. I don't even see lizards or spiders." Mona rubbed her eyes. Her eyesight had worsened over the past few months.

"Come," the jinn said. "It is a night of celebration. Let us leave this miserable house."

Mona squinted at him. "I thought you were trapped here."

"I am a being of air and fire," he said. "*Trapped* for me does not mean the same thing as it does for you." He held out a hand, the same one with which he had taken her necklace and bangle. She wondered what else he would demand from her.

It was the night before Eid, when the new moon had been sighted signalling the end of the holy month of Ramadan, and there were celebrations throughout the country. If she had been home, Mona and her sisters would have dressed up, and she would have applied henna to their hands, scolding them as they giggled and squirmed. But tonight, the strange, wild creature she had become covered herself with a black niqab and stole into the night in the company of a jinn.

They went to the city of Sehwan Sharif, where the shrine of the Sufi saint Lal Shahbaz Qalandar was wreathed in colourful lights all along its proud minarets and the gleaming gold of its dome. In the courtyard below the shrine, under crisscrossing strings of orange blossoms, there were stalls selling bangles and henna, steaming jalebis and gol gappay and frothing cups of tea.

Mona held a warm cup of tea between her palms and watched the streets pulsate with vivid colour and light, people dressed in their finest, bangles clinking around the henna-painted wrists of women. She felt curiously removed from this world, although she looked for all intents and purposes like an ordinary woman out enjoying the festival. Next to her, the jinn, in his disguise as a human man, could have been her brother or her husband.

"Marid," Mona said aloud.

"Incorrect," he said, without looking at her, his bored gaze fixed on the teeming crowds, though she thought she glimpsed a hint of longing in those ember eyes.

"No, it wasn't a guess. That's what I've decided to call you. I heard the word from one of my schoolteachers, long ago. She said a marid was a type of jinn. She also said it means 'rebel' in Arabic. I think it's appropriate, don't you?"

He turned to her, startled. "You are naming me?"

She shrugged. "I'm tired of just calling you 'the jinn.' I'm never going to win our wager."

He was silent for a moment, the glitter of lights from the shrine playing on the inky darkness of his hair. Among all these ordinary people, he had never looked so alien to her. Finally he said, "I promised you power. Let me act through you, and we can take it together. Revenge and freedom both. Destroy those who have wronged us and escape our prison."

The tea suddenly felt cold in her hands, as if his words had sucked the warmth from the night. The stories she had heard as a child flooded through her mind. Jinns possessing unsuspecting victims, contorting their bodies into torturous shapes, destroying their minds. Jinns preying on young girls. *Don't stand under a tree at night with your hair open, or a jinn will take notice of you.*

"Is that why you brought me here?" she demanded. "You thought a kind gesture would get me to agree to become your slave?"

His eyes flashed, and she continued, "I won't give you my soul. I've given enough. I'm sick of being an instrument, and I won't exchange one prison for another."

He seemed to grow in size, swelling up to fill the courtyard, his eyes so large and burning she could have been looking into twin suns. The lights in the courtyard flickered, and yet no one seemed to notice, as if they were invisible, or had been all along, or as if this whole night had been an illusion.

His fury blazed over her like a hungry fire. "Ungrateful wretch. After all I have done for you!"

"I don't want your gifts," she whispered.

He bared his teeth, a wild thing, a creature of storm and rage. "Then you will suffer."

The day after Eid, all the mirrors in the house melted, their glass turning into sizzling sludge in puddles along the floor.

The next day, twenty dead quails lay across the garden, not a mark on their little bodies.

"You've angered it," Zainab said to Mona.

It was the first time either of them had ever spoken to each other about the jinn, as if by naming it Zainab was afraid to give it power over her. Mona wondered if he had ever visited any of the others. Not the Mirzas, whom he hated, but the other servants, those who were as much at the mercy of the house as he was.

She didn't go into her workroom anymore, refused to touch the sewing machine. Farida was enraged. They had a backlog of orders, and the clothes Mona had made before Eid had fallen apart on their hangers, silk and chiffon crumbling into ashes, their colours bleeding away.

Javaid Mirza summoned her to his office, where the walls were adorned with the gaping, glassy-eyed heads of animals from his various hunting trips. They seemed to watch Mona mournfully as she stood before the landlord's desk, in the same way her father had knelt before his chair in the field, a dozen lifetimes ago.

"I hear you haven't stepped into your workroom for days," he said. "What, did you and the jinn have a fight?"

From his smirk, she could tell he was mocking her, that he alone in this house didn't believe the stories. Mona kept her head bowed and her voice monotone. "I told Farida Begum that I can't make clothes for her anymore."

"Of course, I understand. It's tiresome work. Perhaps you need a break. Maybe you should go home to visit your father and sisters."

Mona's head snapped up, her heart pounding. There was something in his voice, a coldness that made the invitation sound like a threat. Throat dry, she stared at him.

"I could send some of my boys ahead to let them know you're coming," Mirza Sahib said, smiling blandly. "Perhaps tonight. But I warn you, they can be a bit boisterous."

The threat grew louder, became deafening, laced into the deceptive softness of his words and the faint half-smile on his cruelly handsome face. Mona dug her hands into her sides, trying to keep herself from shaking. She was like a quail, she thought, fleeing across the fields, the terror in its tiny heart telling it that it could never escape the predators that chased it. Weak. Always weak and powerless.

"How dare you," she said quietly.

Mirza's face twisted, the smile morphing into an ugly thing. He rose from his chair. "What did you say to me, you little bitch? Have you forgotten your place? I *own* you. You and your wretched father. Now you will get back to work, or I'll have you beaten until you can't hold a needle."

Mona met his glare with her own, fury writhing in her chest, and bared her teeth. Mirza recoiled from her snarl, startled and disoriented, but she just turned and walked out of his office. She climbed the stairs, through the cursed house that had built a prison around her soul, and went into her workroom.

Mona surrendered to the darkness. Locked away in the workroom, she stitched and stitched for what could have been hours or might have been days. The sun rose, or maybe it set. The shadows deepened, or perhaps it was her vision blurring. She heard Zainab knocking at the door, and then Rafiq trying to kick it down, but she couldn't have responded to them if she'd wanted to. The sewing machine seemed to have become a part of her body, an extension of her hands, and all around her the piles of clothes grew and grew, writhing creatures given life by her rage.

Mona closed her eyes, but all she saw were endless, looping, tangled threads. "Marid," she choked out.

He appeared to her, melting out of the shadows as he had the first night he had come to her workroom. He appeared more inhuman than ever, his skin stretched taut over a skeletal face, those twin flames filling up his eye sockets and casting beams on the floor like a car's headlights.

"Mona," he said.

She bent her head over the sewing machine. "I'm so tired, Marid."

"Let me help you."

She peered up at him. Her body felt like a slab of meat, empty and hollow. Her vision was so blurred that he looked like a writhing mass of shadows. She smiled. "I think I won our wager."

The shadows recoiled.

"I called you by the name I chose for you, and you came. I know you were tricking me. I never could have guessed your name correctly because you didn't remember it. You told me so yourself." She smiled faintly. Even that felt like an effort. "But then I named you, and that became your name. So I won."

Silence, and then Marid answered, his voice soft as the silence before a storm. "Then I owe you your freedom."

"And your revenge." Her eyes fluttered shut. She whispered, "Not the servants."

The darkness kissed her cheek. "As you wish."

Every window in the house shattered, glass raining out over the fields like a mockery of the rain that the farmers had been praying for all summer. Flames licked their way across the carpets, hungry and gleeful. All the fabric in the house seemed to come alive, from the clothes in the wardrobes to the curtains hanging from their rods, living things full of wrath and vengeance.

In Javaid Mirza's office, the stag's head on his wall snarled, and the landlord toppled over against his desk, choking in the grip of an invisible hand on his throat. In her bedroom, Farida Begum screamed as her body became tangled in the sheets on her bed, trapping her as the flames raged across the floor.

The servants fled across the courtyard, escaping into the cotton fields where stray dogs barked frantically, and the tenants of the Mirzas's lands rushed out of their homes to gaze in horror at the blaze that swept through the house. Zainab thrashed in Shoaib's strong grasp, struggling to break free, shouting that they had to go back for Mona, that she was still inside.

A crowd gathered in the fields, faces tipped back to watch as the glow of the fire turned the sky a hellish orange and smoke billowed across the trees. Zainab, still weeping, thought she saw a lone figure in the window of the workroom, looking back at them. But then she blinked, and it was gone.

There is a house, deep in the heart of rural Sindh, coated in layers of history and open to an unforgiving sky. Those who know steer clear of it; even fresh meat won't tempt the stray dogs across its threshold. Only crows make their homes in the buried spaces of its rooftops. Only crows.

So the house sits empty, its russet walls and once-beautiful jharokhas ruined by a fire that occurred long ago, leaving it a charred husk of house, a shadow of a house, the imprint of what once was.

Sometimes the village children dare each other to get as close to the house as their fear will allow, and sometimes they see a figure in the window on the top floor, a slash of colour against the bleakness: a woman wreathed in so many layers of cloth, her eyes burning with the glow of undying embers. They run home and tell ghost stories, jinn stories, stories that distort over time, blurring into each other like paints mixing, but always remembered.

Deep in the house walks a creature that exists only in the gossamer spill of thread and the whisper of shadows against deadened walls. A creature of dreams and memory.

"Tell me, glass, tell me true!
Of all the ladies in the land,
Who is fairest, tell me, who?"

ALBA

Erica Ruppert

Alba, princess, only child of a dead wife. What hope for her? Docile, dreaming, her own wants leading her away from her purpose. She knows. Desire and obedience cannot inhabit the same heart. Not without consequence. But still, she wants.

Alba is a soft girl, the early loss of her mother compensated with toys and luxuries. She is her father's souvenir, her dead mother's mirror, tall and narrow in a stark sketch of black hair and ivory pallor. But her father's new wife Irina is dark, small and ripe, as if to blur the memory of the other. Her body promises sons. Alba cannot compete with that in her father's affections. His memory of her mother is already washing away.

But not Alba's. She looks in the mirror each morning and misses the woman she never knew.

Irina has no time for daughters not her own, especially those who could be her sister. Alba becomes almost forgotten in her father's house, still coddled, still a pet, but now overshadowed by the new wife's lure. As a daughter she can only be offered in alliance; she cannot be his heir.

Alba watches her father's new wife obliquely, and sees the script of her own fate as a royal daughter. She sees tension begin to pull at Irina's mouth as one month after another goes by in barren blood. Then Irina is at last pregnant, and Alba watches the way the ripe woman is treated in her father's house, coddled too like a favorite bitch until the day she miscarries, birthing a stillborn girl. The disappointment in the house makes the air almost too thick to breathe.

Alba is not a stupid child; her mother left her depth as well as surface, and Alba thinks long on Irina's circumstance. They are after all close in age. Alba tries to be warm toward her father's wife, to create a common ground out of sorrow. She is lonely, too.

"Sit with me, mother," she says, laying a pillow on the wide sill of the tower window that looks over the late summer gardens. But Irina rejects her in the face of other concerns.

In Irina's country in the wild north, the child that kills its mother in childbirth must die too, for it has shown itself greedy for life. Irina knows Alba's past, and knows that the girl's greed is what keeps her own womb empty. She knows Alba is unnatural, and she knows what magic will end her.

But such magic costs dear. It costs the days she longs to spend as her own. Those still are fewer days than what she will forfeit if she does not bear an heir. Irina weighs her possibilities, and decides. She casts her magic, listens to the old wisdom. She makes her plans.

"Forgive me for my sullenness. Walk with me in the forest," Irina asks, and the lonely girl agrees. Alba hopes this will be the thin seedling of amity between them, but her hope is ignorant and without roots. Irina has made the required sacrifices, that she should have Alba's heart to eat, and let wild beasts take the rest. Alba's days will be hers, an intimacy Alba could not imagine. Irina's possible children will be safe.

But when they reach the place Irina has chosen and consecrated, Irina pauses. Her predator's instincts rouse. Her fingers tap the butt of the knife sheathed up her sleeve, knowing it is already too late to draw it. There are eyes among the trees that watch their every step, every breath, eyes glinting like fractured mirrors where they catch the sun. Leaves tremble without a breeze to stir them. Shadows do not fit to the trees from which they spring. This is magic, too, far different from what Irina wields. Irina cannot see the watchers but she knows she will not leave the forest unmarked in flesh or memory if she keeps on. Alba, calm as milk, seems not to notice.

"What is there, girl?"

Alba looks sweetly at Irina, a smile on her lips. There is such comfort here, for her.

"I know you know. Tell me!" Irina demands.

Alba closes her eyes, then, scents the air. "I do not know them," she says, "yet they are no strangers."

In the dim light the shadows gradually move and take form, arms and legs straighten to reveal manikin shapes with bright, black eyes in their dust-brown faces. Not animals, not men. They wear rags and leaves and skins, hold short knives and carry spears; they are prepared to hunt. Irina grabs Alba's wrist to hold her where she stands, although Alba makes no motion to run. Irina gestures with her free hand and whispers a single word to ward the manikins away. It has no effect. Sweat stands out on her face.

"Make them go," Irina hisses in Alba's ear. "Tell them you don't need them."

Thin rumors have long echoed that Alba's mother had been so protected, that the charm was in her blood. Even Irina had heard them. She had hoped they were exaggerations.

Alba stares at the creatures, wondering, unafraid. These creatures love her. She knows this, does not know how, but their love is a thing to which she is entitled. They will not let her come to harm. She knows.

"It is all right," Alba says to the dusky creatures. "We are friends."

The manikins seem to fade into the tangle of the forest, only their sharp eyes still visible. Irina pulls on Alba's arm to steer them back the way they had come. She can read the warning. Now is the wrong time. The wrong place. There will be another time, when she is better prepared.

Soon Irina is pregnant again. The house fills with tense anticipation rather than joy.

While this new child grows in his wife's belly, the king negotiates a match for his Alba. It is past time for it. She is well old enough to be useful, to heal an old breach in a once profitable alliance. Alba is told the name of her future husband, and told to prepare for him. She must be pleasing, she must be ripe. She must be worth her husband's father's risk in taking her.

Alba says nothing to her father's command, although she thinks long on it. She sees how thin Irina has become despite her growing belly, how drawn and pale her face is. She watches Irina's fear. She pities her. She does not want this for herself.

Irina knows that Alba watches her. She knows she will not bear a living child until Alba is gone. But Irina cannot raise a weapon against her; the inherited protection about Alba is too strong. But Irina can turn to another way, as old as the old magic and as dark in its wiles. She can disguise the knife.

Irina uses her other skills to make an apple flawless, blushing red, and poisonous. It costs her much, but it will bring her much. Once Alba tastes it, once the poison stops her heart from beating, and her blood lies still in her veins, the creatures will lose all sense of her. Her protections will fail, and Irina will have her heart to eat like some rare fruit, and swallow with it all of Alba's days.

"Let us go into the forest again," Irina says to Alba. "It is so hot in the gardens, and the trees make it cool."

"Yes," Alba says, her thoughts already on other concerns.

Irina fears the forest, but there is no spot secret enough in her husband's house for such a purpose as hers. She veils her thoughts, hoping Alba's creatures will not see past them to her intentions. Irina leads them down a different path than the last time, but the ending will come all the same.

When Irina tires they stop, and she draws from her pocket the beautiful fruit. She wipes a speck of lint away with shaking fingers and holds the apple out to the girl. "We have walked so far," she says. "You must be hungry."

The trees around them own their shadows. It is quiet here, and cool.

Alba knows what she is being given. She has thought long on it, turned the prospects in her mind like a jewel. She sees the pain and starving need in Irina's face, thinly masked with false friendship. Alba weighs the possibilities contained in Irina's plot. She can choose a quick death here in the cool green forest, or a slow one in service to her husband-to-be.

Alba takes the red fruit, turns it in her hand. Irina watches her, avid. Alba meets her stare and lifts the apple to her opened mouth. She bites it, and her eyes grow wide as the morsel falls on the back of her tongue and shuts her throat. The juice of it trickles down, sweet, the taste of the apple following her into nothingness, like a memory.

Irina waits, her own breath held as Alba's stops. Her fingers crook into claws around a sliver of blade. She hopes she has hidden her purpose from the creatures, hopes she will have enough time. The forest is still as a grave. Irina bends over fallen Alba, loosens her blouse, bares her white breast for her harvest. She clears her thoughts to let the memorized chant flow free, but the spell she whispers dies on her lips as Alba's protectors coalesce from the shadows. They come armed with knives and claws and teeth of their own. Irina knows her chance is gone and runs from them, unsated, hot hate in her mouth instead of a warm heart. One possible future is wasted.

The manikins do not care that Irina has escaped. They care only for their Alba. They lift her, a multitude of small hands to bear her slender body away. Under the trees, with them, she is safe even if she does not draw breath. They know she is not lost to them. Irina did not understand her potion's subtlety. The rare poison keeps Alba still, but not ended. Her eyes remain open, reflecting patterns of leaves and shards of sky. Her pale hand still curls around the apple.

The creatures carry her deep into the forest to their home, where they have made a shrine for her in anticipation of this moment. They have carved a coffin of quartz as clear as glass, polished and shaped like the curve of arms to hold her. Fine loam covers the bottom, and moss and thickly scattered leaves, a soft bed for a sleeping princess. They knew she would need such shelter. They lay her in it like a babe into a cradle, tuck the bitten apple in with her and close the case.

Time goes on, days, seasons, at last a year.

It is a year she does not live, a year her great gray eyes look into nothingness and watch it pass. She has become a traveler within her own glass coffin, always between time and more time. Her pale fingers bend around the red, red fruit, cradling it against her still heart. Her coffin's translucence is lost to dust and cobwebs, to a dappled pattern made of rain on the dust. Weeds crawl up around it. She is outside the limits of measure, now, and can extend her life indefinitely, tick by precious tick. She remains unpossessed, drowsing and almost aware.

In the year Alba dreams, Irina loses two more pregnancies. The second is a son born too early who drew breath for an hour before he died. She grows desperate, knowing how close her own fate hangs over her. Her king's mood changes from one of expectation to one of demand. He grows older, his own time slipping away, his opportunity for an heir with it. Even his daughter is lost. Sometimes he strikes Irina, careless in his disappointment, because she means so little to him.

To escape him for brief hours Irina walks alone in the forest. It is safe enough now that Alba is gone. She travels the paths she knows. She wonders if her life is worth another apple for the king.

One day she pushes further into the trees, following the merest sketch of a path. She can feel the age of the mossy trunks around her, the weight of time misting the air. She presses on through a grove of fir trees, sliding past their sagging branches into a dappled clearing. Irina stands for a moment in the sudden sunlight, letting it warm her skin. She has lost much of her color since she has become a wife.

It is a few moments before Irina notices the mottled glass coffin beneath its covering of branches. She walks to it cautiously and brushes away the powdery dust. Inside, blurred as if by water, she can make out the still form of Alba. The girl is unchanged, uncorrupted. Irina draws in a startled breath. The protections on Alba have preserved her even from poison.

Irina's mind is quick. She sees a chance she did not have before. She marks the path she took, and plots for her own survival.

"My lord," Irina says one day after she had thought long on what to tell him, "My lord, I have heard whispers of where Alba may be."

He takes her bait. He has missed Alba, his only child. But she is also still part of his strategy. The discovered child is of far more use than those yet unborn.

The king gathers his rowdy court and makes a party of the expedition. Irina, brittle in bright dress, leads the company into the forest by an indirect path, forcing them to rely on her direction. She will hold what power she can. At times she glances over her shoulder at the loud pageant of lords and servants and the prince to whom Alba is still promised. Irina thinks him vulgar, but she is not his bride. The party laughs and jokes and sings around her, but Irina pays them little mind, leading them on, wary always of Alba's guardians. At last she stops, knowing the nobles are lost, and points to the end of their journey.

"There she is," she says, her voice low and resonant beneath the trees.

The forest is lush around Alba's coffin, but still the glint of crystal scatters through the branches. The prince alone dismounts, and with the king's permission tears away the weeds that have grown up around Alba where she rests. The prince rubs the surface of the casket clean with his yellow velvet sleeve and peers into Alba's wide open eyes. He cries out, and jumps back, shaming himself before the company.

The king laughs hard and comes up beside the young man, looking down at his lost daughter.

"Well, free her, man," he says, and beckons his party forward to help the prince lift the massive lid. Stone scrapes stone, and cool air spills over the sides of the casket. It smells sweetly of apple.

With nothing between them the prince gazes down on Alba, appraising her. Then he bends close and touches her lightly, stroking her dark hair and running fingers over her parted lips. He slips his hands beneath her cool body and lifts her free of her tomb. As he raises her, the bit of apple falls from her between lips, burning the ground where it lands. Alba coughs in a spasm and draws breath again, and her open eyes once more see the world. The company falls back in superstitious caution. Irina watches the resurrection, fascinated and appalled. She has bought herself time.

As Alba comes awake she looks dazedly at the faces around her, until she looks up at her father's wife. Their eyes meet, their gazes hold. Alba sees clearly how tight Irina's face is drawn, the fear there, the pallor. Alba knows she has been bartered again.

Even as she allows the strange prince to lift her high, hold her up and carry her before him on his horse, Alba's heart balks. She does not want this, she will not bear this. But she is weak from her year away, and tolerates his touch and his smell as the company sings out the miracle of her return and chatters emptily of the coming wedding. Alba does not desire the prince who will release her from one stasis into another. How could she? He is a stranger, who loves not her but what she brings. She marries him at her father's will, to bind the kingdoms, to seal their fortunes. Alba leans her head back against this strange man and closes her eyes at last.

Time flies, now. Three months from her awakening is the length of her engagement, three hours long the wedding rite, and three days full of the feasting. The guests grow fat and drunk in celebration.

But Alba is bored by it all, her prince becoming a lout in fine clothing as he guzzles rich wine, and her father a bloated pig. Nothingness is more than what this court can offer. Alba glances at Irina where she sits like a statue beside her reveling king, gray as dust and wasting away, pregnant again. Maybe this time she will bear a live son.

Alba sits at the table as she should and toys with her silver knife, crossing it with her spoon, slicing the grease still smeared on her plate. She is finished with looking at the rejoicing company. They do not matter to her. This is not what she wants. Her eyes, watching the glint of the blade, do not see whose hands place the bowl of fruit close before her. But she does see, nestled among grapes and figs and almonds, a single red apple with dew still on its skin. She glances quickly around to see who else has noticed, but they ignore her. She is not one of them. She is alone with the temptation in the sea of revelers.

She takes the apple from the bowl, the apple so smooth and perfect it can only be a thing of artifice. It fits her hand. It has been there before. Turning it she can see where she bit into it once, a year ago. The flesh is still perfectly white, uncorrupted. Her fingers burn against its rosy skin. Alba lifts it to her lips, smiles around it at her new husband when he leers at her, and once again sinks her small sharp teeth into its flesh.

The next breath Alba draws rattles in her throat, drawing the morsel of apple down to lodge behind her tongue, to bind her again to the space between moments, to take her out of the world. As she falls she hears Irina cry out. She cannot tell the words, only the tone of despair. Then she is gone.

Hands lift her, soft as wings. A shadow, she is moving, but only across distance. Time is done with her. She does not know it. Her protectors carry her gently back to the sheltering forest, to the glass coffin they kept for her should she need its refuge again. They understand the workings of her world. They lay her in it, make sure the apple is still in her hands, brush her tangled black hair smooth again. They touch her, patting her softly, affectionately, with long fingers before they close the lid once more upon her. She slips from memory into myth.

Years pass before her open eyes. She dreams, awake, a slow fever of motion and change, light and darkness, frost and hot sunlight. She has no memory of it. She herself is changeless. She becomes a legend, Alba, the lost girl, the lost tomb with a treasure within it, rubies and onyx, ivory and pearl. She would laugh to hear the young men whisper about her over their mugs, plotting to prove their manhood by finding her and releasing her. She is something to be acted upon, a blank canvas, clear water.

But one young man goes further than bragging. He searches beyond the rumors and bravado for the fragments of truth that straggle through old church records and royal missives. Royal himself, another prince, he has the means and the time to follow each possibility into the forest, a quest that he hopes will win him a legend of his own.

He does not truly expect to find her, not Alba. He expects barren bones. He expects some hollow reflection of the gilded tales. But with effort and a long portion of his youth, he finds the place where she lays, and at last stands in the strangeness of it. The forest clearing is hushed, and lonely, lost rather than abandoned. Vines twine thickly around the glass tomb, the grave so long untended that the form inside is unseeable, her existence an act of faith. Like another prince before him he pulls the heavy growth away, rubs at the filthy coffin to peer inside. There is a figure in there, shadowed and indistinct, still softly female.

This prince runs his fingers along the edge of the casket, feeling for the junction between body and lid. He finds it. He digs a pry-bar into the narrow slot, and wedges the heavy lid up. When the seal is breached a sweet breath escapes, a fragrance of earth and dry grasses and ripe fruit. Straining, he pushes the lid aside, rocking the coffin, rocking the still figure within. The incorrupt apple once more rolls out of Alba's hands. The bite of it once more rolls off her tongue. Her throat again opens. She gasps, and closes her eyes for the first time in ages, letting her memory refill. She has felt all this before. It is no surprise to her.

But he steps back, overwhelmed, overawed. Alba rises without his help, pale within a cloak of loose black hair, and looks at him in slow, chill judgment. His fine clothes and signet betray his rank. He is a man like her father was, like her long-ago husband. Rooted to the earth, consumed with status and rule. She does not want him. She raises one white hand and waves him away.

The prince flees from her, convinced she is vampire, demon, monster. He sought only to rob a grave and prove his own wit, not to resurrect a living myth. She is unnatural, to still live. Her magic is not what was bargained for.

Alba is glad for the rustling silence that fills in the prince's wake. She sits alone on the edge of the glass coffin as the day unspools, adjusting to the sensation of passing hours. It does not matter to her that she is alone, unanchored. She breathes, deeply, evenly, reclaiming her life. She must decide what it will be, now.

The falling sun gilds her, and finally she is able to slip back into the steam of time. She stands, solitary, surveying the quiet forest. She knew this place once. It was safe here.

It is hard to walk, hard to begin to live again. The apple still lies in the coffin, in the cool hollow where her body had been. Alba moves a little stiffly, steps gingerly away from it, uncertain of this new course. It has been so very long.

Among the tall trunks she remembers more than sees the path she must take. She follows the bare memory of a trail to a low, ruined house. She has never been inside it, but she knows what she knows. Her mother left her this, if nothing else.

The door is gone, and much of the roof. The house has been uninhabited for many of the years she lay untouched in her coffin. Inside the crumbled house still are seven small husks, dry scraps of leather and bone, the relics of her protectors. They were faithful to her to the ends of their lives, but they could not live forever. Not like she might.

The thought is too much for her. She turns away from them, unable to alter their fate.

Light streams into the house from many broken places, a lattice in the air. On the sagging mantle a bright thing catches her eye. She lifts it into the light. It is a small statue of a slim young woman, all in white marble save the ruby heart cupped in her carved hands and the smoke quartz glint of her eyes.

Her eyes are open. They knew she would come back.

"Oh! but, grandmother, what a terrible big mouth
you have!'
The better to eat you with!'"

BORN AGAINST TEETH

Tiffany Morris

No trace of winter in
green spring. Birdcalls
sugar the end of a breath:
greetings born
against teeth. Every promise
is a path. Petals of daylight
pasgine'gl *are torn*
from tree bark.

A voice at the door.
A voice from the bed.
The room filled with a mouth
metewjigmit *growling,*
snarled open: snapped shut.

Sunlight blinds as
life begins at the end
of a needle, ugs'tqamuit
comes into the world
at the end of a knife.

Hands red
as her velvet skull, eating winnu
tongue from the wolfwomb —
rebirth is stepping out whole
from that which tried
to devour you.

"She sat down on a stool,
pulled her foot out of the heavy wooden shoe,
and put it into the slipper
and it fitted her perfectly."

A WISHED FOR WIFE

Liv Strom

Dearest,

I cannot change what happened, my fate or yours; only argue ignorance, offer my truth, and beg forgiveness for my role. Everyone knows we are fickle beings, though that's no excuse.

With my fellow sylphs, I danced through the wind when, enthralled by the sweetest notes, I entered the house of man. The master maker's music box sang, mirrors twinkling and pulling me in until a shadow fell from above, a prince with gold on his fingers, jewels on his crown, and emptiness in his heart snapped the trap's oiled jaws shut.

The mirror became a window to the world outside, the music louder, consuming.

"Do my bidding, and I'll set you free," he said, and wound it up once more before my mind could clear.

My heart rode the high tones, plunged at the low. As long as the box played, it would never let me go. "Three wishes, and no more," I swore, for what did I care for the desires of men? Somewhere out there, my sisters rode the air—even through the fog, I knew I did not belong in this plush prison.

Magic's trill married the song, lulling me into unnatural sleep until he called in my vow.

When he let the music still, I awoke and, in spirit form, bowed.

"They say I must marry, so you'll find me the perfect wife," the prince said, this time dressed in crimson velvet and lace. "Find the one who'll always be true; exquisite on the outside, naïve on the inside, to do with as I please."

I shuddered at the darkness growing inside as he contemplated wishes I could never forget.

"I can give you true love," I said. "Someone as wicked as you." Everyone had a match.

"Do as I say," he snapped. "Bring her to the ball tomorrow night. At midnight, I'll claim her and announce our engagement."

The wish wrapped around me, squeezed until I no longer could contain the words, "As you please, so shall it be."

Again, he played the music, and ethereal, I rode it out into the world.

Channelling the prince's dreams, I asked the wind to find me a girl too kind to anticipate what would come, too innocent to see beyond the palace glitter, too scared to run.

On the edge of the wood stood a crumbling manor with three desperate girls, hoping marriage could save them from poverty.

The oldest was too worldly, able to trick any trickster.

The second too argumentative, never meek enough to do his bidding.

But their stepsister, barely old enough to marry, with no parents to protect her or experience of courtly intrigues, fulfilled all the prince's desires—she'd never left the manor, saw the good in all, and became more beautiful each day, inside and out.

If I'd let myself dwell on it, I would have known he would crush you. But the song of the wish lulled me as I waited. Still, when your older sisters dressed in their finest and left for the ball, I rejoiced that they'd deemed you too young — that you were out of bounds. Then a discordant note yanked me down. The wish had to be fulfilled.

Human skin enveloped me for the first time as I appeared out of the air. I took a shape similar to yours, seeking to calm and cajole. Your stepsisters would have known better than to trust a fae, but you gave me a smile, a gift I could not return.

"I'm here to bring you to the ball," I said, testing each word against the wish's constraints.

"Are you my fairy godmother?"

I nodded, because how could I explain? I asked foliage and flowers to tangle into a dress and cover your flesh. The stars to gather in your hair. A million grains of sand to meld into glass slippers around your feet. The prince would be pleased, the melody told me, as I brought you to the palace steps. Finally, the music box called me back; the wish fulfilled.

"Thank you. It's like a dream," you said and spun.

And I knew, before the sun rose again, the nightmare would start.

I plucked the moon and let it cover your face like a mask. Maybe if he did not see your beauty, he would pick another.

The song transformed into an insistent tug.

Trust brighter than the moon-mask's glow shone in your eyes, and I wanted to whisk you away across the now empty sky. Instead, I grabbed your hand in mine as you turned to leave.

"Promise me one thing," I said as the wind rustled the leaves.

You smiled. "Anything."

"Leave before midnight."

The magic, pounding on unseen keys, could no longer be denied. When you entered the ball, I was already back in my velvet prison, knowing I had been a fool to promise magic to a mortal. A fool to think I did not care, because your hopeful eyes and spirit pure enough to fly kept me from the magic's slumber.

Did he pick you right away? Did you dance and talk? Were you happy until, in the gardens' darkness, he took what you did not offer, claiming your innocence as in his cruel dreams? I only know that by the time the midnight bell rang, you kept your promise.

"Don't let her disappear!" The prince shouted as he threw me from the box into a ballroom swarming with guards, and the second wish wrote itself across my airy being.

"So shall it be," my mouth said, while my mind sought any loophole.

Across space, I saw you running down the road, dress torn by his hands, stars escaping your dishevelled hair, moon-mask dissolved by tears.

Your fear enveloped me while the wish commanded. There was no time.

Fall, I whispered to the tree ahead of you. A branch snapped to trap your leg.

"It's done," I said aloud, and the prince rode out at the head of his wild hunt, set on an unmasked bride.

The wish played brilliantly inside me, telling me I was good, though I felt wicked. One more, and I would be free from the affairs of men.

As the box called me back, I fought to appear at your side.

There were rules—my magic was bound, my wishes not my own—but again, I squeezed myself into physical form and used my last strength to shift the branch. You twisted away as the hounds howled, leaving but a glass slipper behind.

This time, the music sounded hollow, tainted by darkness and fear. Had you gotten away? Were you trapped in his arms at this very moment, saying your wedding vows?

My master, surrounded by men and horses, called me again, and I learned only moments had passed.

"Where is my bride? My wish has not been fulfilled," he asked, and the air vibrated with the truth of his words.

The slipper glimmered and wishes pulled. Pain screeched through my being, the wind roared, I must bring him his future wife, keep her from disappearing, keep the bargain.

I listened to the delicate glass, the sand grains calling for their missing neighbors, once part of the same stone, the same mountain, and reluctantly handed the prince the slipper.

"It'll lead you to its partner."

He narrowed his eyes as if he knew I had tried to circumvent his words.

"And until the marriage is final, she will not be able to hide or run, seek help or other hearths."

The final wish sang in dulcet tones—its fulfillment would freedom me from my trap and snap yours shut—but there were limits even to my powers.

"The girl you ask for will have to voluntarily accept the proposal. Magic cannot change minds or souls."

He waved a hand to dismiss my cautions, and I could feel the darkness inside growing. My hope withered. Magic might not be able to coerce; but humans had other means.

"So it shall be." The magic spread with my words.

I reappeared at your manor, knowing your future husband was racing here. With a hand wave, I blocked all doors and windows. I could not help you run again. Could not hide you.

I owed him a bride.

Despite their imperfections, your stepsisters saw your crying face, saw the prince's hurt upon your body, and sought to help. They offered to force their feet into the slipper and go in your stead, but you could not accept. The magic had picked you for your kindness. And even had you tried to accept, the first wish would have rejected them as unsuitable. The third, you from running.

I'm made of music and air, frivolity and fancies, a fickle creature whose wants change with the wind, but regret ate me from the inside as I realized I sold your freedom for mine.

Magic always holds its own undoing. It only requires a change: of perspective, of person, of sacrifice.

I wrapped myself in mortal flesh and strode inside.

He'd wished for someone who would always be true—bound by magic I could never play false.

He'd wished for someone perfect on the outside—I had moulded my flesh to imitate yours. Last night, the moon's beauty had hidden your face. Having only seen my spirit, he would not know which one of us he had taken in the dark.

He had wished for someone who would do as he pleased — still bound by wishes, I could do little else.

In me, each wish could be fulfilled.

I met your fear-filled eyes but knew if he spotted the change, no one could help either of us. When the knock on the door came, I placed myself before you and clenched my frail human hands around the second slippery glass. When the prince entered, and the magic locked your feet to the entry floor, I stepped between you.

"I've been looking for you," he said with greedy eyes and slid the missing slipper onto my foot. The wish snapped like a second trap — and my freedom came and went between one breath and the next as the prince grabbed my hand. The tale had to play out until the end. "You can leave as mine or my men will torch this house with everyone inside."

"I'm already yours," I said, speaking to you as he smiled.

I'm sorry you had to watch as I married him, see him leer and cheer after he violated you. I'm sorry you had to pretend joy, pretend me your sister, and stay at the palace through the wedding night. That I turned away when you hugged yourself, hiding a secret you did not yet know. It was the only way to make it right.

The wishes steered my steps through wedding banquet and vows. To my left sat you and your sisters, claiming me as kin. You squeezed my hand with gratitude I did not deserve, and I became more female than fae, for I knew the barely contained panic when the prince led me away was a thousand times shared.

In bedchamber, he drew on his nightmarish desires — abusing and using despite the cries I could not hold back. Through it, I locked my mind on you, hoping he had not broken your kindness with your heart. On the nightstand, the music box mocked me. Could I be carefree in the sky again after this?

When dawn finally broke, the air once more tried to carry me away. The marriage was complete. The prince had his wife. All three wishes had been fulfilled.

Through wedding and bedding, you would have been forever trapped. But me, they freed. Wilful and wild once again, I whispered in my former master's ear that a deal with the fae often goes astray, and, with a kiss and a wish, I stole all the breaths left in his chest.

While you took my place and grieved even for him who hurt you, I left you in my place and disappeared, knowing the court would take you for me. That no one could look at you and doubt your care or kindness. You had been married until death did you part. And if they did not search too long for answer, the prince only had himself to blame.

The child you bear, paid for by wishes, pains and tears, is a queen to be. No one can promise happy ever after, I offer only a chance in recompense for stealing the fate of someone kind and true. This is not the end of your tale, but the start.

He used me. We used you. I hope, one day, when you're able to forgive my errant ways, you'll wind up this music box and play a tune as sweet as you. Then, perhaps, I'll make your child's wishes true.

-Your fae godmother

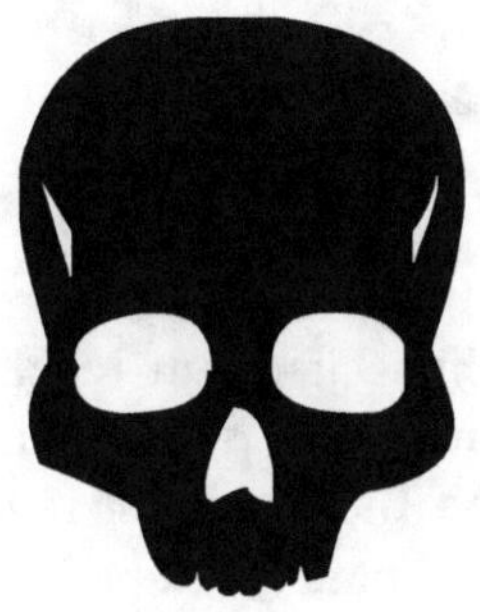

"In the morning
after he had said his prayers,
he sat himself down to his work;
when, to his great wonder,
there stood the shoes all ready made,
upon the table."

THE ELVES AND THE SHOEMAKER
David Kenneth Mitchell

I

Luke wasn't a bad cobbler. In fact, Luke was an extremely talented cobbler. The problem is, nobody really gives a shit about cobblers anymore.

You can scream the virtues of your craft until your face turns blue. *Buy cheap, buy twice. Our grandparents' generation would have made the shoes they were married in last until the day they died, they'd probably be buried in them. Sure, but I bet they weren't made by a nine-year-old in Taiwan.* Hopefully, your moral superiority will keep you warm because the people you're screaming at have already ordered the cheaper option online, oh, and they'll be here tomorrow, and, by the way, your heating bill is overdue.

Luke's customer base was shrinking year on year as another regular traded in their formal shoes, or work boots, for their retirement home issue slippers. Luke was also too weak, and he knew it. The cost of living was spiralling wildly, but Cyril had paid fifteen pounds to have his shoes re-soled for the last decade. Luke didn't have the necessary assertiveness required to tell him the service now cost twenty-five pounds, not including a tip.

In reality, the only thing keeping "Heeling Hands" afloat was Luke's *VIP* customer. A local professional footballer whose grandfather had worked as a mortician. Luke had maintained the undertaker's footwear for the last fifteen years and, fortuitously, as the mortician's health dwindled his wealthy grandson had taken it upon himself to escort the ageing traditionalist around. The footballer, preoccupied by an obsession to be unique, to own something exclusive, something he could parade about on his socials, was fascinated by the workshop and would frequently spend twice the market value on a rarer piece. This was a man who would wear a pair of three-hundred pound football boots once, before mindlessly leaving them in a dressing room bin, the idea of restoring a pair of one-hundred-year-old brogues was completely alien. Luke used the footballer's desires and intrigue to spin a narrative, any basic, flash in the pan, celebrity could model the latest trend from the catwalks, only a real visionary would wear a pair of painstakingly restored 1903 Chestnut brown wingtips. The margins were astronomical and the logic was sound, well, sound-ish.

"No one gave a flying fuck man!" the words had shot across the room before the shopkeeper's bell had finished its quaint chime.

"Mr Bannan, Sir. How can I help you?" Luke responded, through a gritted smile.

"Don't *Mr Bannan* me, mate. You promised me premium. Unique. I wore these to London fashion week and the socials are lit up about me buying clobber off eBay." He slammed down the vintage brogues on the counter, scattering a small pile of red-stamped letters. Luke winced, the heels had been visibly squashed, Mr Bannan clearly hadn't used any dubbing since he purchased them, people have no respect for the finer things.

"I'm sorry people didn't appreciate the quality of —"

"Fuck your *quality*, these could be made out of unicorn ass for all I care. If no one's impressed, what's the point?"

What's the point? He made a compelling argument.

"Look, I won't mug you off, you always did right by 'Pa but when I come back this weekend, you're going to have something good for me. Something that will turn heads. I want the socials to blow up."

"Of course Mr Bannan. I've got a lovely pair of—"

"Yeah, yeah, yeah, I'm sure they're great. Just make sure they're ready by the weekend and they're not…dead like those ones." He glared at the discarded shoes on the counter top, and with no regard for Luke, Mr Bannan had turned and excited the shop. A quick thud, and a little bell chime to sound his farewell.

Bannan's exit was undoubtedly rude; the arrogant behaviour of a man who'd been pandered to his entire adult life, just because he had a skill. Luke could carefully restore torn leather, so seamlessly, that you'd never know there had been any damage at all. That's skill. Bannan could just kick an inflated sack of air. There's no justice, or at least that's how Luke saw things. The abrupt nature of Bannan's departure had at least spared Luke's blushes. In his pathetic *yes sir* snivelling, he had begun to promise some mythical, astonishing pair of shoes. In reality, he had nothing.

Luke lay in bed that night, pondering his way out of this mess, he even debated some fairly permanent ways out. He was so deep in the red, he didn't have any options, so he had to produce *something*. But, rather than give into despair, he did something he hadn't done in years. He prayed. He prayed for help. He prayed to anyone that would listen.

II

Luke awoke at dawn, as he always did. He was fiercely proud of his strong work ethic. *The early bird gets the worm.* At least, that's a lot catchier than: *the cobbler has to wake up early to desperately find a way to satisfy the whims of an overpaid prima donna.*

First things first, a coffee and the morning paper. Luke had a routine, and he wasn't going to let urgency affect that. His nose crinkled as he spooned the instant coffee into a chipped and stained mug. Disgusting, mass produced, swill. It had none of the depth or subtlety of *real* coffee, but beggars can't be choosers. As the lime scale ridden kettle rattled to a boil, Luke walked to the back door to retrieve the morning paper. The paper used to be left on the front step, but Luke didn't like that, someone could just walk by and steal it, no-one ever had, but they could. The paperboy had kicked up quite the fuss about having to walk down an alleyway and up to the back door, Luke even had to threaten to cancel his subscription with the news agents to get them to adhere to his request. This country. The paper *boy* was in his twenties by the way. Covered, head to toe in tattoos. Even those repulsive neck ones. Luke tutted to himself as he opened the back door.

Tangs of copper instantly hit Luke's nose, foul acrid air that permeated all of his senses. His eyes watered slightly and his stomach dropped. Whatever he was smelling was unpleasant on a biological level, an evolutionary level. His mouth began to feel dry and his lips chapped, the scent around him so repugnant he dare not lick his lips, lest it find a way inside his body.

Reluctantly looking for the smells' source, Luke stepped out into the alley. There it was. Suspended from some guttering, above the archway that allowed access back onto the main street, death. Violent death, seemingly ceremonial death, impressive, almost magnificent death.

A large tabby had been flayed from the top of its head to its underside, and hung above the archway. Its fur and skin barely held on at points on either side of its torso, creating the effect of four, fire-orange wings. Luke's lizard brain was screaming danger, adrenaline surged through his veins, and his heart drummed in his chest. He shut that down, he wasn't like the rest, ruled by primitive instincts. Taking a deep breath he stepped closer.

The incisions were surgical. The system of twine suspending the body was sophisticated and precise. A morbid sense of professional appreciation swept over Luke. He avoided looking into the creature's lifeless eyes. He did, however, notice something in its mouth. Tucked firmly in its exposed jaw was a tightly rolled up piece of parchment. Parchment, not paper. Someone appreciated the classics. Luke unfurled the scroll and began to read the note, handwritten in red "ink."

> We are the last of the ancient ones.
> Before people prayed to God, Allah, or Yahweh, they prayed to us.
> Whisper to the darkness, we shall whisper back.
> We are of the old. Alpha. The First.
> We are of the undying. Masters of death. The alf, the alpi, the ailbhin, the ljosalfar.
> We are the elves. Marvel at our creations.

At the bottom of the note was some form of sigil, a sort of eight-pointed star, encased in a circle, the crisses and crosses of the stars' points formed a perfect square at their middle, and in the centre of that square was a simplistic looking eye. Luke was taken aback, but, as he noted, no longer scared. He scanned the area to make sure that no one was watching. Nothing, the only window that looked onto this alley was his own, and no one was coming in through the high street. Only teenagers looking for a place to smoke or drink came up this alleyway, them and that reprobate paper "boy."

Luke had time to think. He took a few steps back, a moment to take in the situation. The craftsmanship on show really was…admirable. "Disgusting," he supposed, but objectively impressive. The fur was all intact. In fact, the skin and fur were completely blemish free. Luke's leather suppliers couldn't provide materials of this quality. No one had material of this quality.

Something like this would really…turn heads.

III

Luke had promptly disposed of the carcass, whilst he was sure some taxidermist might find it interesting, the husk was of no use or interest to him, and neither were taxidermists. The skin and fur, on the other hand, had proven to be exactly what he needed. After a number of treatments, cures and conditioners the hide was ready to be worked and formed into a shoe. The only issue was, it remained a little too supple, it didn't have the rigidity to form a shoe on its own, but Luke could bond it to an existing shoe to completely change the aesthetic. The vintage chestnut brogues. They would be perfect. They were Bannan's size, and there was some poetic justice in the idea of him wearing these shoes, these beautiful shoes, which he'd so readily discarded. Now, with their new finish, their exciting veneer, he would finally appreciate Luke's work. Even if his primitive eyes couldn't fully comprehend the majesty before them, they could at least accept that they were in the presence of greatness.

Saturday morning arrived and Bannan had popped into the store, collected his new shoes, and left. He'd not said a word. It had enraged Luke at the time, but he didn't let it show. The audacity to just nod and go. Whilst smashing his stained mug against a wall, Luke ruminated on his frustration. Did Bannan not realise how much work had gone into those shoes? Not just Luke's work. These shoes had survived over a century, they'd been crafted and moulded by masters, then modified by a genius, clad in the work of…well, Luke didn't truly know whose work these shoes were clad in. Luke didn't believe in elves, obviously, but something had happened. He'd prayed, and he'd prayed earnestly, and on the next day his problems had been solved. Ask and you shall receive, and all that. It was either divine intervention or he was aiding and abetting a psychopath, and that was a crazy idea. Luke was a law abiding professional, a proper gentleman, elves made more sense.

IV

A perky little chime rang out.

"Myyyy fucking maaaaaaaan!!!" An excited voice cried through the building. Luke put down his bowl of coffee—he was struggling to drink it without spilling anyway—and walked through to the storefront. "Have you seen it?" Bannan continued. "We're blowing up. We started trending from the second I got off the team bus, and we we're still in the top ten by the time Match of the Day started."

Luke didn't really know, or care, what any of this meant, but the fact Mr Bannan was jubilant had to be good news, for Luke's financial situation at the very least.

"We've got the Football Writers Awards next Saturday, me and the boys are all going, dressed up to the nines. Black tie thing, so no fur, but we need to stand out. Can you do something, but..." Mr Bannan had paused, scrambling for some polite terminology. "Not those dull old brown things from before. We need to do numbers on the socials. We can't be dressed like old men."

Luke recoiled at every plebeian sentiment but nodded politely. "Of course, sir. We shall make sure you're the belles of the ball, or beaus." He paused for a little laugh. Nothing. "So, how many are in a soccer squad? Thirteen or so?"

Bannan laughed, finally. "Nah man, come on. There's about twenty-three of us going." Luke winced, and Bannan, despite his obvious deficiencies, did pick up on that cue at least. "But don't worry. There's only like eight of us in the inner circle. Ten tops. I'll DM you the sizes in the week. You can do this by next week, yeah?"

Luke was almost certain he couldn't. "But of course, sir." He paused, for dramatic effect, adding a little sigh as a flourish. "But, something this specialist at such short notice? It won't be easy, and it won't be cheap." If he was going to perform miracles, he should at least be fairly compensated.

"As long as the number only ends in five zeros, we'll deal." Bannan stopped, suddenly serious and slightly severe. "And I'm serious. The boys have all been laying it on thick since I broke the internet. They all want in on this, but we'll have eyes on us. This needs to be special. Can. You. Deliver?"

"Without a doubt" Luke replied, smiling from ear to ear, whilst silently screaming inside. To be fair, he wasn't lying. There were no doubts, he was quite sure, he wouldn't be able to fulfil the brief without divine intervention.

"My man." Replied Bannan, extending a balled fist.

Luke, instinctively going for a handshake, encased Bannan's entire hand in his palm. The awkward second lasted for eons. "I'll catch you on Friday, late." Said Bannan.

"I cannot wait." Sighed Luke, to no one, the door had already swung shut.

V

The next few days flew by for Luke, the store was quiet, but he spent every waking moment trying to conjure inspiration for some magical footwear that would make Bannan and his teammates *break the internet,* whatever that meant. One would think that breaking the internet would be bad. The plebs seemed to spend all day on it.

No celestial inspiration hit him, only desperation. By Wednesday Luke was frantically modifying his existing stock. Adding frills, sparkles and other flamboyant flourishes to classic shoes, but nothing felt right. These additions were all without heart, without soul. The problem was that the existing stock was perfectly fine, nice examples of subtle artistry, but the only heads they would turn were connoisseurs, people who understood finery. When Luke tacked these superfluous extras on, they took away from the original elegance rather than adding to it. It was akin to covering a beautiful woman in layers of cheap makeup and false lashes. He had nothing.

So, Luke went to bed again that night, turned off the light and lay in darkness. Whispering hushed prayers. Bargaining with the universe. Sending out an SOS with no way of knowing if the message was being received, and if it was, did the listener care?

VI

On Friday morning Luke awoke at dawn, as he always did. He couldn't have his morning coffee, the remnants of his only mug lay shattered in a small plastic pan next to the kitchen bin. He wouldn't have had the patience to wait for the kettle to boil anyway, he knew he was almost certainly indulging a fantasy, but *what if*, what if his prayers had been answered again.

He paced to the back door and threw it open, not even checking for the morning paper, not noticing its absence. He turned his nostrils to the air and breathed deep. The same metallic aroma that had once stirred a visceral reaction within him now stirred up feelings of hope. Even the bitterness that caused his nostrils to curl at their edges was forgiven. He was excited to see what he had been gifted. As he stepped out his mind raced, maybe a fox, he could work wonders with a pelt from them. A slight niggle in his mind, he had to make ten pairs, a fox wouldn't provide nearly enough material.

Then he saw it, a lack of supply was not an issue.

VII

The basic mise en scene was the same, flesh pulled from muscle and sinew, a body suspended above the dank, red brick archway. Where there had been twine before, now there was thick nautical rope. Coarse dark brown fibres holding the body firmly in place. Tendons pulled taut.

Many years ago, when young master Bannon would still have been a child, Mr Bannon Snr Snr had offered to show Luke around the funeral home, to see the embalming process. The funeral director had proposed that Luke took himself too seriously, seeing a reminder that "no one gets out of life alive" might help Luke gain some perspective. Luke had turned him down, of course. He'd seen funeral homes as something medical, functional.

He stared at the corpse in awe, feeling deep pangs of regret. Not for this former person, but because he'd deprived himself of this experience all those years ago. The human body was a marvel, the epitome of form and function. An amazing piece of machinery wrapped in a breath-taking canvas. He approached the skin, again spread into wings, and ran his fingers along it. This would work. To all intents and purposes this was just another type of leather. The skin was absolutely covered in tattoos. The things he could make with this, true, pure art.

Luke checked the mouth. There was another scroll. He pried it loose with a little force, there was a little pop of cartilage and the bodies' jaw swung agape. Luke tried to nudge it back shut, the slack jaw was less aesthetically pleasing, but it was to no avail. The body would remain looking shocked.

Luke's fingertips tingled with excitement as he unfurled the latest scroll.

> We notice those who notice.
> We appreciate those who appreciate.
> Elves have Long valued skilled craftsmanship.
> The ants marvel at the majesty of the boot
> above their heads, even as it falls to crush
> them.
> Make sure the boot is magnificent.
> The ants deserve that at Least.

The scroll was once again signed with the eight-pointed star. The eye at its centre felt comforting now, like the caring gaze of a parent watching their child learn to ride a bike.

Luke's skin tingled with exhilaration. He'd never felt this important before. This marvel of human taxidermy was a gift for him. These elves, or whatever the hell they were, had noticed his work, and they would notice his next move. This wasn't just clicks, likes and follows for Bannon any more. Luke was serving something higher. Artisanal spirits. Finally, the appreciation he deserved.

He wandered back to his canvas, mentally carving it up. He'd have to be economical. There was plenty of flesh, but he had ten pairs to make, and for them to really make an impact he'd need to ensure each unit contained at least one prevalent tattoo. It was odd, Luke had always hated tattoos, they're cheap, tacky, and for chavs, but in this context they were beautiful. He ran his hand along flesh that would once have been attached to a neck. An alarming feeling of recognition swept over Luke, he hadn't just hated tattoos like this, he had hated *this* tattoo. His eyes darted all over. He'd hated so many of these tattoos before. These were the paperboy's tattoos.

Luke felt uneasy, a level of cognitive dissonance had kept him from accepting that this body was ever a person. It was a canvas, it was clay, it was marble to be shaped into something beautiful. He didn't want to think about the fact the marble once had a family, that it may have screamed out in pain as the chisel struck it. He buried that feeling, he buried it deep. It was the thought of lesser men, of ants.

Luke put on nitrile gloves and disposed of the carcass in several large black bin bags, making sure that each one was light enough that it had no risk of tearing, or drawing attention. Then he set about working on the vellum, preparing it for tomorrow's work. He almost wanted to pull an all-nighter, he'd never felt this enthused for work before, but he needed to be at his best. This deserved the best version of him.

VIII

Luke awoke at dawn, giddy with excitement. The lack of a coffee mug didn't matter, he didn't require artificial stimulation today. He worked for hours and hours without a break. Bonding this glorious patterned leather to classic black oxfords. The old world and the new.

He worked tirelessly, ignoring the blisters forming on his hands and the twinges of cramp that teased his fingers. Each shoe was unique but felt in keeping with the others. Their wearers would shine on their own but also sparkle together. Like stars in the sky. His work had become comparable to the heavens. The evening light was setting in and Luke was applying the final touches, buffing out imperfections and shining the visible old leather.

The door chimed and Luke called out without looking up from his murky, oil soaked rag.

"Mr Bannan, Sir! Ten sets, each more perfect than the last. Will that be cheque or card, I forget myself, at your age you probably don't even own a cheque—"

He was interrupted by a firm cough.

Looking up from his stool, he was greeted with a stern, thick-set and well-dressed man. He wore a crisp, unbranded black suit, and his white shirt looked as if it was set by a ruler. He was completely clean shaven, and his jet black hair was a lesson in geometry.

"I'm sorry sir. We're closed. I'm just awaiting a collection. If you leave a number I can recommend something for you." He looked the man up and down. "Possibly a black Chelsea dress boot, but I digress, as I said, we're closed."

The man reached into his breast pocket and removed a small, engraved badge and a lanyard. "Detective Chief Inspector Harding. Can I ask a few questions?"

Luke's heart raced. Most of the paperboy's remains were sat in black bags, less than twenty feet away, in the alley.

"Are you…of a nervous disposition sir?" The detective continued as Luke fret. Was he giving off subconscious signs of guilt? "The things I'd like to discuss may upset you, but I'd appreciate being able to speak freely and unambiguously."

"Oh, no, it's fine, speak away, Mr Harding."

"Detective." He corrected. "I'm investigating a recent murder. CCTV from a few stores on the high street suggest that our suspect likely came to this area. He was seen carrying what we believe was the body along the high street at about four am. Last night. Then we lose track of him somewhere on the main road that leads off from the alley out back." The detective's stare was severe and penetrating. The cadence of his speech left painful pauses, pauses that willed you to spill your soul. "Have you seen or heard anything unusual over the last couple of nights?"

"No, sir. I mean, Detective."

"I don't mean to be rude." The detective leant in. "but you're taking this news in your stride. You don't seem too concerned a murderer might have been just outside your store." He looked around. "And home?"

"Yes Detective. It's humble, but it's home. I have a small flat upstairs," replied Luke meekly, gesturing to a door that led to his bedroom. "I'm sorry, it is very sad, but don't mistake my composure for a lack of empathy."

"And no fear? At the potential proximity of the crime?" Harding fired back, not missing a beat.

"I've no enemies." Luke smiled in an attempt at friendly. "No one would have any reason to harm me."

A solid thud, and a chime at the door.

"Yewwwww. You better have the goods, or I'm gonna whoop yo' ass, old man!" proclaimed a jovial voice. Bannan was clearly taken aback by the sight of the detective, his instant recognition of an authority figure betrayed a precocious youth. Luke swiftly completed the interaction with Bannan. Although he only peeked into a box as Luke packed them away, Bannan was clearly thrilled, and so he should be. He was quick to present his card, and he barely batted an eyelid as Luke keyed in an astronomical figure into the PDQ machine. More money than Luke had ever had, more money than he had ever seen. If he was smart this could set him up for life.

"I do hope you *break the internet, sir,*" said Luke with a curt smile, and then without waiting for a reply, he turned his back on Bannon and returned to the detective. A chime confirmed they were alone again.

"Sorry about that, where were we?"

"You were telling me you had nothing to fear. An enviable position." Harding's expression remained that of stone. "Have you got any surveillance equipment with eyes on the alley behind? A camera, one of those fancy doorbells?"

"Nothing no, it feels like an invasion of privacy. One never truly knows who's watching."

"Shame. If you don't mind, we'll be attaching some surveillance overnight. You won't be able to see any of them. We'll just be fiddling about on ladders for a few hours. They'll only be looking at the alley, your privacy won't be violated at all. Is that okay." The words were technically a question, but Luke knew that he was being told.

"Of course, can I do anything to help at all?"

The detective handed over a small black card that had his name, rank, and phone number on. "If you hear or see anything suspicious, day or night, you call me. Okay?" As he reached the threshold, he turned back to look at Luke, and inhaled ever so slightly, as if preparing a question. Nothing followed. The detective turned back and exited, disappearing into the increasingly purple light.

The bell rang gently.

IX

The beginning of the week was a euphoric blur. Firstly, the bin men arrived in the early hours of the morning, and the remains of the paperboy were whisked off to some landfill. Luke had to admit, there was some thrill to be had in watching the lawmen assemble their surveillance equipment mere feet and inches away from the body. If the severed parts had been discovered there was nothing to link them to him, but still, even the false jeopardy was exhilarating.

Secondly, the shoes were an absolute hit. Luke didn't bother with all that online stuff, so he didn't know if Bannan and his cohort *trended*, but they had garnered enough attention to make headlines in the paper, not the front pages, that was all dedicated to the ongoing manhunt, but in the sport section they had apparently justified a whole page. "United's feet dazzle on and off the field." He'd had to collect the paper himself though, which was quite the inconvenience. Worth it though, he'd also bought a frame on his trip to town. The page would be mounted above the counter in the store.

Finally, the funds from Bannan had cleared, and Luke wouldn't ever have to worry about finances again. On the way home, he popped into the local coffee shop and ordered a cortado, a lovely single origin blend from Colombia. The smooth and subtle bitterness teased his taste buds. He glided the rest of the way home, savouring every sip.

The next few days were a joy, Luke spent them working on things for himself, vintage pieces, niche items that would probably never sell, but it didn't matter anymore. After all that time spent struggling, he was finally free to make art. His prayers had been answered.

X

His prayers *had* been answered. His thoughts now lingered on this. It was Thursday evening. For the last two weeks this night had been spent pleading for help, begging for interference from a higher power.

Whilst he may never know if what he had found in that alleyway was divine intervention, it had, undoubtedly, saved him. If his unknown benefactors returned, they would be caught on camera. Were the police watching the feed 24/7? Would someone, ancient being or not, be bundled into the back of a police van, or would grainy pictures of them be plastered around town? "Have you seen this Ancient deity? Call 999—quote reference 2073."

Luke was a man of principle. A proper gentleman. Gifts should be returned in kind.

Luke waited until midnight before leaving, he left via the front door and walked down the high street. It was a crisp night, and there was little more than a faint breeze. In other circumstances it would have felt peaceful, but Luke found the silence eerie. Frequently checking over his shoulder for onlookers, Luke walked around the corner, reached the street entrance to the alleyway. He slumped down on his haunches and peered through, making sure he wouldn't be visible in any of the many cameras the police had set up. He was safe, from this crouching position, he could just about see his own bedroom window. The cameras were mounted on the roof so they certainly couldn't record this spot.

With one final look around, he removed a can of red shoe spray from his jacket pocket. Getting up on tip toes he pressed the can to the brick above the arched entrance to the alleyway. He began by drawing a circle. Then, he traced the diagonal lines, slowly forming an eight pointed star. A perfect square emerged at its centre. Within this, Luke drew an eye, wide open. Under the drawing he wrote.

"TURN BACK. THE ANTS ARE WATCHING AND THEIR PINCERS WILL CLOSE TIGHTLY."

Luke walked home briskly. He moved his legs as fast as possible, without the risk of drawing attention. As soon as he got in, he wrapped the spray can in the remnants of the newspaper and sunk it deep into the bottom of his bin. He had planned to go to sleep, but he found himself drawn to the window.

He spent the night there, staring at the small portion of the highstreets he could see from the window. Tinges of cerulean began to annex the black of the night sky, and Luke's eyes grew heavy. A couple of times he was woken by the sudden, dramatic sensation of falling. Just as he'd committed to the idea of sleeping, he caught a glimpse of movement. The silhouette of the bottom of two thick legs, and next to them, a black shape. A bag perhaps? A sack?

The legs didn't move. They stood, facing towards the alley, not turning back but not proceeding.

After what seemed like an age, a hand crept into view, it reached down and into the sack and rummaged around. The outline of something dripped to the ground, and the hand rose back up, out of view. The figure then turned and walked away, taking the bag with it.

XI

Luke woke just before midday. His eyes stung, and his limbs ached. He slowly and awkwardly dressed himself before lurching down the stairs and out into the street.

The light was blinding and the murmur of the busy lunchtime crowds was slightly overwhelming. Luke wasn't suited to crowds, he was suited to quiet moments. Steady hands and calmness. He clumsily paced along the road, around the corner and straight towards the alley's archway. It was mostly intact and unchanged, all except the eye. Where Luke had drawn an open eye, it was now closed shut. Painted over in a dark, glistening red.

Luke reached up and touched the eye. Strands of red dripped from the wall to his fingertips and broke, flopping to the ground. His glistening fingers were sticky with crimson. He could smell the coppery tang before he even reached towards his nose.

The eye was closed. No one was watching anymore.

Heeling Hands continued to thrive for years.

No one was ever charged with the murder of the paperboy.

There was once an old woman, but you have surely seen an old woman going begging before now."

THE OLD BEGGAR WOMAN
Lindsay Comer

There was once an old woman. You surely must know what an old woman begging looks like?

You nod. Yes of course, you know what an old woman begging looks like. Her clothes would be old, faded, and raggedy looking. Autumn is quickly turning into winter, so you decide the beggar woman would be wearing a couple of layers, held together with spiderweb threads. Her hair would likely be a dusty grey, it would be hard to keep white hair white with all the pollution. Tiny eyes hidden behind glass, thin lips, a wrinkled face shrinking in on itself like an imploding star. A blanket for coins, she would gain a lot of money, no one wants to see an old woman stuck on the street. See, of course you know what an old woman begging looks like.

Yes, that is what an old woman begging looks like, but what about <u>this</u> old woman?

You look again at this beggar woman, she is sat on the corner of the busy street. There is no blanket in front of her, no glistening coins. Countless legs pass, but no one stops. You expect to see others sat begging around her, but it is oddly quiet. You take a look at her face, but you see no wrinkles. She opens her thin lips and a long, long, slimy tongue falls out, picking up dust from her outfit of many rags as it returns to her mouth. You blink. That's not right. You focus on a different part of her face, everyone has a nose right? But that's a beak. No, a snout? You shake your head, your eyes must be tired. The creature masquerading as a beggar woman shakily puts out a hand, a ragged sleeve flops over it.

"Arian os gwelwch yn dda."

What strange, squishy words. Definitely not English, you wonder where the words are from. They sound like they come from a place wet and rainy, that you visited long ago. You watch a man dressed in dirty, mismatched clothes walk past the beggar woman. A large coin purse jingling around his waist. He glances at the beggar woman, but ignores her strangely worded pleas. He takes two steps away. You watch as a snake slithers out from behind the beggar woman. No, not a snake. A tail? A hand? You want to shake your head, blink, anything to change the strange image of a human hand headed snake sneaking out from this beggar woman's back, but you feel compelled to watch.

The hand-tail-snake grasps for the man's ankle. The man's leg lags behind him as he tries to shake off the tightening grip of the hand-tail-snake. The man screams and yells. But no one stops to help. You wonder how anyone can ignore those high-pitched wails and shrieks.

Only you can hear him.

You watch as the man is pulled back to the beggar woman. Panicked screams reaching a crescendo, making your heart squeeze and your shoulders ache in a strange anxiety. You want to cover your ears, but you can't. Someone must hear this man's last noises, and it must be you. The thin lips open and the long, long, slimy tongue joins the hand in wrapping around the man's body.

Tightening until the screams cut off, your ears tingle in the eerie silence that follows. The thin lips continue to open, and open, and open. You watch as the creature masquerading as a beggar woman pulls the tongue back and swallows the man whole. You expect to hear the crunch of bones, the squelch of blood, the smack of the creature's lips at a meal enjoyed. All you hear is the clink of coins as the man's coin purse lands in the rag covered lap of the creature.

You need to kill the old beggar woman.

You shake your head. No. You do not kill. Not anymore…at least not without a good reason.

You must. You watched her kill that man. Isn't that reason enough? A life for a life? Wasn't that always your reasoning?

You ponder, yes a life for a life was your mantra, all that time ago. It seemed like good, solid reasoning. Yet, you've grown, you understand that your viewpoint isn't always the correct one. You don't know if that man slighted the beggar woman. You don't know if those coins were taken from another beggar. You don't know what that man's crimes were. Maybe he deserved to die. You can't take a life in return, if today was the day that man was destined to die.

You've grown soft. What if the man had no crimes?

You ponder this new information. No one really deserves to die by eating. A life for a life, you watched a life be taken. By your own logic a life must be given in return. You replay the grab and eat within your mind. The creature masquerading as a beggar woman attacked unprovoked. You know a planned murder when you see one, yet this was too oddly timed. You feel sorry for the poor man, maybe the coins were to clean his dirty clothes. Maybe he was on his way to help some other beggars.

You must avenge him.

You nod. Yes, you must avenge this man. What an odd thought—you've never avenged someone before. You wonder how it would feel. Your precious kills always felt so…exhilarating. No matter the method you picked, hand, knife, sword, spoon, mallet. Each kill made your heart giddy and your body buzz with an addictive pleasantness. You've been chasing a replacement for that pleasantness for a long, long time. A little relapse wouldn't hurt.

You wonder if avenging the man with the beggar woman's death would feel as exhilarating. You've never had a personal stake in your kills. You take another look at the beggar woman. A small child, a long patched up coat covering their thin frame, is stood in front of her. You watch as the child helps the beggar woman to stand. You're afraid this child will be eaten too, but the creature masquerading as a beggar woman behaves. One hand grips the coin purse, the other grips the shoulder of the child. You see the child flinch as the beggar woman's grip tightens, but they do not cringe out of her grasp. Instead they begin to lead the woman down the street.

You need to follow them.

You follow them. You stare at the beggar woman's back, waiting for a peek of the hand-tail-snake. You notice her gait is unusual, leaning to one side as if missing a cane. You look at the beggar woman's feet. Expecting some confusing mirage of hooves and paws, you're surprised to see two left boots, darned polka dot socks poking through holes at the toe and heel.

You stay three and a three-quarter steps behind. No one has ever noticed you follow them. With each step you wonder what method you will use to avenge the man. You don't carry weapons anymore. You will need to do something about the child, you can't have them witnessing such a thing. It's going to be hard enough keeping yourself safe from the hand-tail-snake, the long, long tongue and whatever else the creature is hiding. You wonder if you have time to detour and grab a weapon. You know a man who knows a man who would be able to get you something on such short notice. You're sure they're based somewhere round here.

You won't need a weapon.

You pat your body, nothing you are wearing can be used as a weapon. You wiggle your fingers, skin stretching and tendons flexing as you assess the strength in your hands. Time worn scars pop out as you move your soft hands. You guess you could use your hands, if it came to that. You wiggle your toes, hitting the tough outer of your shoe, you wonder if you have enough strength to cause the damage you need it to. As you try to remember your training, the child stops and leads the beggar woman into a squat little house. You want to follow, but something stops you. So you wait. After three and three-quarter minutes the child steps out. They turn to face you, a smooth face hidden under a hood nods at you before briskly walking away.

It's time.

You push open the mould slimed door, rubbing the grime not away but into your fingerprints. You find yourself in a small room, floral curtains drawn, the only door shutting with a thud behind you. The room is lit by a fire, you watch the marmalade flames flicker and whorl. You wonder what secrets the coals are whispering to the beggar woman as she warms her three hands by the fire. The hand-tail-snake shakes each time it waves too close to the fire. You realise that you do not need a weapon, all you need to do is push the creature masquerading as a beggar woman straight into the fireplace. You take a giddy step forward, but something catches your eye. A flicker of orange, too large for a polka dot, sparks at the beggar woman's foot. You step from foot to foot, your toes suddenly feeling warm, too warm.

Why don't you get closer?

Yes, you must get closer. You cannot let the fire avenge the man alone. You have been chosen for this task, and you have never left a precious kill incomplete. Your leg starts to feel itchy, and you notice the orange spark starts to climb the many rags that make up the beggar woman's legs. Spiderweb threads alight and their dust falls to the ground. You watch as the hand-tail-snake notices the steadily growing flames and tries to pat it out, the beggar woman lets out a yelp-hiss then turns to you.

"Dŵr os gwelwch yn dda."

More squelchy letters, you shake your head. You don't know what the request is, but no, you will not give it to the creature masquerading as a beggar woman. The flames begin to climb up her torso.

"Dŵr…dŵr…DŴR!"

You flinch as the beggar woman reaches out with a hand the colour of an old radiator, rusted cracks of age leap out at you. You can't let her touch you.

Why not?

You don't want to be eaten. You're afraid of catching the flames. They aren't working for you, you don't know what secrets they whispered to the beggar woman. You pull at your clothes, you're feeling stuffy and sweaty. Water, you want, no, you *need* water. Your mouth feels dry, too large tongue filling all the crevices leaving no room for saliva. The room is too hot. You are too hot. You blink your eyes, willing them to cry for the poor coin purse man. A kettle hot tear slides out, the steam burning your eyes. As the steam clears from your eyes, you look at the old beggar woman.

Have you realised who you are yet?

The old beggar woman, she looks like a rickety bonfire. You do not need to look down to know you are her mirror. You can feel the flames burning through your rags, the acrid scent of leftover soap mingling with the bubble of your skin. The hand-tail-snake shakes and shivers as its mighty reach cannot escape the draw of the flame. You feel yourself, you and the creature masquerading as a beggar woman get drawn closer to the flames. You can hear the secrets the coals are whispering as the flame pulls you into a searing hot cwtch. You cannot understand a single secret, too many competing languages. Yet each voice has a strange, almost begging lilt to it. The beggar woman begins her call for dŵr again. Voice raw and distorted from the burns of the flames. You add your own call for water. You start to wish you had asked the child to stay. You wish you had never agreed to avenge the coin purse man. You do not want to join the coals.

A life for a life? Wasn't that always your reasoning?

Yes, but not *your* life. You were never supposed to be caught. You want to call out, to cry and beg for someone to extinguish the flames. Yet no one heeds your call. Your words become strange and squishy, all you want is dŵr. You begin to crumble. You do not want to join the secrets and the flames. For a moment you feel too heavy, too warm. Your ash and bones mix with the beggar woman as you fall into the coals, your secrets becoming one with the fire.

There was once an old woman. You surely must know what an old woman begging looks like? No? Well, listen hard to the next fire you light, and maybe you will hear her last beggar words, but don't listen too close, my flames are hungry.

Translation Notes:
Arian – Money.
os gwelwch yn dda – Please.
Dŵr – Water.
Cwtch – A cuddle or hug, but nicer, cosier, and more personal than a hug.

"When they went to bed,
the doors were shut and locked up;
but every morning their shoes were found to be
quite worn through
as if they had been danced in
all night."

THE SUITORS SPEAK
M. Weigel

The princesses only wanted to dance, they said.
They pursued underground suitors and attended
nightly festivals.
The women lied, and their indulgent father knew
the truth.
He ordered any who attempted the riddle killed as
a way to thin his rivals.
Of course every kingdom would send their sons.

But we have mothers, and they grieved our losses.
They used their magic to learn the king's secrets.
He not only knew of the dancing, he supplied the
sleeping agent
the eldest daughter used on all twelve of us.
He never returned our arms, jewels, or even final
letters to our families.

Our mothers found a path for vengeance.
The second to last suitor was a youngest son from a
small kingdom.
His godmother had helped raise the boy, and
she wept silver tears at his loss.
That old woman found a soldier with a good heart
and a sense of justice.

Through her arts, he resisted the drugged wine.
He followed the girls through forests of silver, gold,
and diamonds.
The man stole a cup, and he did all of this with an
invisible cloak.
An entire royal family was stony faced as their ruse
ended.
Entire kingdoms celebrated their relief when the
wedding was announced.

The mothers held their breath in anticipation.
A newly married soldier turned prince was ready
to begin his work.
He and the godmother plotted, and she trained him
well.
The prince soon swayed his father-in-law that he
would look after the twelve daughters.
He arranged ambassadorships, fake weddings, and
even a trip to celebrate his marriage.

Each princess was already more than old enough to
wed.
All of them knew of and supported their father's
plan, entirely complicit.
They shed no tears when the suitors died, but our
mothers were not cruel.
None of the women were to be beaten or raped.
But they would not live in a world where they
discarded sons.

The youngest found her carriage stuck in a forest.
The coachman had to free the horses,
and then he guided the princess on a narrow track.
The path was too narrow for anyone sitting
sidesaddle,
and a suddenly startled horse threw its rider down
a mountainside.

The twins were sent to visit a realm across the sea.
They were four days on the water when the pirates
struck.
The sailors surrendered immediately, and the
princesses did not understand the
lack of fighting or crashing noises at first, hiding in
their cabin. Only when everyone else
boarded the boats did they realize their ship now
had holes and was sinking.

Three more were sent in a carriage over an ancient
bridge.
The structure had not been safe in centuries,
but royalty rarely cares about history and safety
when impatient
after a morning of countless delays.
The horses and driver became wisps of smoke
when the bridge collapsed.

The next pair of sisters stopped at a luxurious inn.
They were astonished at the fine wines and
delicacies in the middle of nowhere.
Because they felt tired the next morning, they
delayed their travels,
preferring a few more days of indulgence.
The vomiting started on day five.

One sister was touring a nunnery. No one knew
how she
found the way to the bell tower until her blood
splattered the cobblestones.
Another visited a distinguished university and fell
on the stairs.
She landed poorly on her neck. The middle-most
sister was fed shellfish, her nemesis.
Their passings were quick.

But the mothers decreed that the eldest daughter
must suffer.
The soldier took her on a trip to celebrate their
marriage.
One morning, he slipped valerian root into her tea.
She awoke alone, inside an old crumbling tower
with no exits.
She was given 12 days of food, and each day a
mother stood guard until it was over.

Her soldier went back and put a sword through the
father.
Our hero fled the kingdom before the councilors
could act, and
as word arrived of the deaths, the castle soon grew
quite haunted.
Now, an old king, twelve princesses, and twelve
fallen suitors linger.
We stare at each other in hatred for eternity.

We claim to be at rest so that our families heal.
But only anger remains in our hearts.
Each night, we prepare a festival for the thirteen
furious ghosts.
None of us will cross over until the princesses
dance in our arms.
We are fallen suitors for all time.

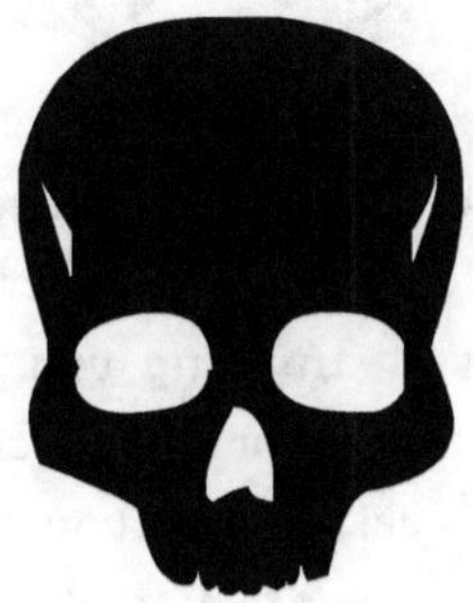

"You may go anywhere
in the castle, unlock everything,
and look at anything you want to,
except for one door, to which this little
golden key belongs. If you value your
life, you are not allowed
to open it!"

THE FORBIDDEN ROOM

TT Madden

Benjamin had always been fascinated by the concept of doors. As a field slave, he had never known doors. Doors were not and never had been a part of his life. Nor did he ever expect them to be. A door meant having the ability to keep someone out, or something in.

And you did not have possessions when you were a possession.

Doors were a part of the big house, though. The world Benjamin could see, but not enter. The world just to the side of his own. The world which he never thought he would be a part of.

Until now.

Steven, a crotchety old house-slave who walked with a light stoop but refused to use a cane, helped Benjamin dress (His name wasn't really Steven, but Benjamin didn't know what name he was born with. Just as he couldn't remember the name he himself was born with. All he knew was that it wasn't Benjamin; that was a white man's name).

Steven was the best-dressed slave Benjamin had ever seen, always impeccable in his suit, and now Benjamin was impeccable just like him.

When he was dressed, Benjamin felt like a completely different person. The suit was tight, and it was hot. The collar stood up and crowded Benjamin's newly-shaven neck and cheeks. So many folds and tucks and buttons. He never liked his old rags—no shoes, pants multiple sizes too big that he'd cinched with a rope belt, and a torso covering that could barely be called a shirt anymore—but he couldn't believe anyone actually enjoyed dressing like this.

Just a few hours ago, Benjamin had been out in the fields. He'd panicked when he heard his name called from the direction of the big house, but he knew better than to lollygag. Steven was the field slaves' only point of contact with the big house, and from the porch he shouted and waved Benjamin over. Benjamin came slowly, tentatively, remembering the years of being told not to go anywhere near the big house, the implications of what would happen if he should. He'd been whipped before, only once, for accidentally breaking eggs. He wanted to tell himself that it would never happen again, but he knew better than to promise himself something like that.

When Benjamin asked what he could help with, Steven looked sad, like something was weighing on him. It was there for just a moment before he sucked it up, and his face returned to normal.

"Benny, you gonna come be in the big house now."

There was an agonizingly long moment of silence, where Benjamin just stood there, waiting for Steven to tell him what he really wanted from him.

Eventually, Benjamin simply asked, "What?"

"You heard me, boy. You gonna come live in the big house now. Master's orders."

Benjamin started to sweat, and not from the Georgia heat. Live in the big house? That...that wasn't the way things worked. You either worked the house or the fields, not both. You didn't switch. At least not that Benjamin had ever heard of. That wasn't the way things worked.

And yet here he was. With Steven tightening his tie. Inside the big house. What was the explanation for it? Why had he suddenly been called up?

"Alright," Steven said, smoothing down the front of Benjamin's jacket. "Miss Margaret is outside waiting for you. Are you ready?"

"Wait, wha—"

But he was already on the move. The bathroom door was opening, and Steven was right behind him and Benjamin was suddenly out in the hall, face to face with a tall woman in a magnificent blue gown. She had long, golden curls, and her skin was pale like a ghost's.

Benjamin had never been this close to one of the masters of the house before. He was panicking, and he knew it.

"Benjamin," Steven lightly whacked him on the shoulder, "say hello to Miss Margaret."

"Hello, Miss Margaret." Benjamin did what he knew he ought to in the presence of someone like Miss Margaret; kept his head low and his eyes lower, averted from her. He was distracted by a strawberry perfume Miss Margaret wore, and when she stepped closer and he got a better whiff, was temporarily overcome with the thought of her spritzing it on her neck and breast.

"Lift your eyes and look at me, sweetheart."

What was happening? Someone like Benjamin wasn't supposed to look directly on someone like Miss Margaret. Of course, the men and boys in the fields all snuck glances upon her or any other woman with the safety of distance. At night, out of earshot, they joked in hushed tones. Aware that, though they had never seen one, there were mulatto children out there, they wondered about the carnal prowess of white women. Benjamin heard another slave once say the lighter the skin the nastier the woman, yessir, and everyone else laughed. Benjamin guessed that because they wanted to keep ahold of that laughter, no one ever questioned how he claimed to know that.

But this close?

He heard Miss Margaret's voice; "Benjamin."

And then she grasped his chin in her hand.

There was lightning on Miss Margaret's fingertips, a power — or rather a power imbalance — that connected her to Benjamin. Terror sent acid surging through his veins and up out of his stomach, and he was sure Miss Margaret could see the sweat break out on his temples. He struggled not to retch, and could swear the entire house could hear his knees knocking together.

It wasn't supposed to be like this. Only hours ago Benjamin had been out in the fields. Only moments ago he had been bathing, and for the first time in something that was not a lake or river. He wasn't sure he liked it. You were supposed to keep all the water in that little tub? The door was closed when Benjamin was bathing, and again he'd marveled at the fact that there were places people could go to entirely shut out the rest of the world.

He wished he had a door right now.

Miss Margaret's fingers clenched tighter on Benjamin's chin.

Benjamin looked at her. He had no idea what to do with his hands, so he frantically gripped the tails of his coat.

Objectively, Miss Margaret was a very pretty woman, but Benjamin could barely move past the fear taking control of his body. Her hair was long and golden, slightly curly. Freckles dotted her cheeks, and her eyes were a vibrant spring green. Benjamin noticed a thickness to her, one he could see in her cheeks and upper arms, feel in her fingers, and he suddenly became envious of the food that must be served in the big house. Was any of that going to be his now that he worked here?

Miss Margaret let go of his chin and said, softly, "It's very nice to meet you, Benjamin." Her voice was breathy, calm. Like how Benjamin would have expected the spring breeze to sound, could it talk. What was this that he was feeling, this lure towards Miss Margaret? Was it just the big house and its illusion of comforts? Benjamin's head was spinning too fast to think.

After a couple false starts, he finally said, "It's very nice to meet you, Miss Margaret."

"There," she smiled, but there was something about it Benjamin did not like, could not identify. Her teeth were much better than any Benjamin had ever seen, and she still had all of them, and yet something told him it was not a smile of friendship. What was it, then? "That wasn't so hard, was it?" She let go of him. "Now, Benjamin, Steven and I are going to give you a tour of the house, tell you about some of your responsibilities. Okay?"

Responsibilities? His responsibilities were supposed to be outside. *He* was supposed to be outside. None of this made sense to him. Benjamin was young. He was strong. Someone like him was supposed to be doing field work. Weren't they? He was the kind of slave who was supposed to help push a wagon out of the mud, like he had last week. Not serving food to the masters. Benjamin wanted to ask why him, why he was here, but he knew better than to ask questions of white people. Especially white women. Especially white masters.

It took a moment for Benjamin to find his voice again. "Ok—Okay, Miss Margaret."

"Good boy," she said, and again gave Benjamin that smile that made him uncomfortable in some way he could not define.

Miss Margaret and Steven showed him the entrance room and the reception room (Benjamin didn't know why those weren't just one room, but he didn't ask), the library and the study (the same applied to those). All of them had doors. They were all open, of course, in the middle of the day, allowing house slaves to head from room to room to tidy up, to transition from one place to another. Benjamin could not believe how many doors there were.

They passed other slaves, women in pretty dresses—but not as regal as Miss Margaret's—and men dressed in suits similar to Steven and Benjamin, none of whom acknowledged them except to step out of their way and bow as they passed.

Miss Margaret said, "Steven, now I think it's time to show Benjamin the most important part of the house, don't you?"

Benjamin almost missed it. If he'd blinked he would have. Steven's reaction was nearly imperceptible, just a flicker of fear on his face before his default expression returned. Eyes widening, a slight puff of his cheeks, and then he was back to being Steven again. Just like the look he gave Benjamin outside.

They took Benjamin to the black door.

He followed Miss Margaret and Steven downstairs, past the kitchen, and into the basement, where Steven needed to light a lamp so that they could see. They moved past enormous selections of ancient wines and stacked boxes, across a dirt floor, wove around and between the foundations of the house. The darkness made Benjamin think of ghost stories told around the cooking fire, of prisoners and madmen, spirits roaming the earth, hunting for flesh. Some of the slaves said that spirits neglected to follow them over from Africa, but that America had its own ghosts to worry about.

When they finally stopped, it was at an enormous, black door in a stone wall.

"This," said Miss Margaret, "is the most important door of the house, Benjamin. It's the one you need to know the most about."

The door looked like it belonged to a house other than this one. Some old, decrepit, haunted place. It was black, and Benjamin could not tell if it was painted that way or if perhaps it had been burned. The design carved into it was horrifying; an old man, but he was crawling around on all fours like a beast. In fact, he appeared to be changing into one; the nails on his toes had turned into animal claws, and some sort of scales or fur was creeping up along his legs and across his torso. Benjamin could not tell whether the look on his face was that of horror, pain, or madness. Maybe some combination of all three. The man's beard and long hair dragged along the ground beneath him, and the light of Steven's lamp cast rippling shadows over the carving in the door, so that the crawling figure appeared to move and wriggle.

Benjamin only noticed it because of the lamplight, but he could see a thick line of what appeared to be salt on the floor just in front of the black door, stretching from end to end of the threshold.

"What is it?" Benjamin asked, trying to hide his disgust. He hoped Miss Margaret didn't want him to be in awe of the door.

"You don't recognize him?" Miss Margaret asked with a slight *tsk.* "Oh, Benjamin, I thought you people knew your Bible."

Bible, Benjamin thought quickly, Bible, Bible. Who in the Bible turned into an animal? If that was indeed what was happening here.

Miss Margaret giggled. "Oh, give him a hint, Steven."

Steven said, "Starts with an N."

"An N," Benjamin echoed. And then, quieter, almost to himself, "Nebuchadnezzar." He remembered, of course. The Book of Jeremiah told Benjamin about when Nebuchadnezzar laid siege to Jerusalem. It called him the "destroyer of nations." He remembered where the Book of Daniel had Daniel interpreting Nebuchadnezzar's dreams. It was not Benjamin's favorite part of the Bible, if he was being honest, but he did not say that aloud. Benjamin much preferred the stories of heroes like Noah and David.

Miss Margaret purred. "Nebuchadnezzar," she said. "That's a smart boy." For a moment, Benjamin thought she would reach out and stroke him gently, like one would a good dog, but Miss Margaret kept her hands to herself. Benjamin was only aware of his tension after he unclenched. Miss Margaret said, "I knew we picked right when we invited you up to the big house."

"Now, Benjamin," Miss Margaret said, "I want you to pay very close attention to me." She wanted such close attention that she turned, looked Benjamin straight on. Benjamin could again smell whatever strawberry scent Miss Margaret covered herself with, and it made the bottom of his stomach drop out. It stirred something inside him, the same thing that awoke when he saw the sweat running down the arms and the backs of the girls in the fields. He wanted to back away, knew this wasn't right, this proximity, this familiarity. They were too close. But something inside him told him that to back away would offend Miss Margaret. Something told him she wouldn't like that. Why was she doing this? Why was she so close?

"Are you paying attention?" Miss Margaret asked. In the humidity of the basement, Benjamin could see a single bead of sweat roll off Miss Margaret's neck. It traveled down her collarbone, and something told him that she moved in such a way to show it to him as it slipped between her breasts.

Stop it, Benjamin told himself. What are you talking about? What are you doing? Don't look there. He told himself it was only because he hadn't been with a woman in years. Such a long time would make anyone stupid.

"Yes, Miss Margaret," Benjamin said, not taking his eyes off hers, "I'm paying attention."

"Good boy," she said. She held her hand out towards Steven without taking her eyes off Benjamin. Steven, apparently knowing exactly what this signal meant, reached into his jacket and pulled out a large ring of keys. He put them gently into Miss Margaret's hand and then she put the keys into Benjamin's.

She said, "You have a key to every door in the house. Every door. Including this one," she gestured to the Nebuchadnezzar door. "But you are to never go through it."

Benjamin did not ask why. With what was carved into the door itself, he had no inclination to see what was beyond. He merely clutched the keys as if they were a talisman. At the very least, they were something to do with his hands.

Miss Margaret said, "I want to make sure you understand fully, Benjamin. No one except the Master or myself is allowed beyond this door. Not anyone. Not even Steven."

Behind her, Steven was silent, but nodded.

"I understand, Miss Margaret."

She stared Benjamin right in the eyes for a long time, undoubtedly to see if there was any lie or misunderstanding. Benjamin knew that she would find none, but what she would find was fear. Questions. Why did he have the key to this door if he was not allowed to enter it? Why was the door carved in such a way? What was actually behind it? Why tell him about it if he couldn't go in? Why was he here at all? If he was so strong, why wasn't he back out in the fields?

In that silence, Benjamin thought he heard something stirring beyond the door, something shuffling, moving. Was it in his own head, or did he hear the sound of grunting? Of loud chewing? There was a sound like a tree branch breaking, and Benjamin spoke so that he would hear something other than those terrible noises.

"I understand, Miss Margaret."

Miss Margaret smiled and stood back. When she spoke again, her voice was as bright and happy as before, as if this door had never existed.

"I believe you, Benjamin," she said. "Come now. We have the whole rest of the house to visit."

⚬

Benjamin quickly learned to serve the big house, but his mind never truly left the basement, the black door, and what he heard beyond it. He felt tethered to it. Benjamin dusted furniture and thought about the black door. He washed dishes and thought about the black door. He followed Steven's orders and thought about the black door. It never truly left his mind, always lingered back there, ready to pounce, like the crouching Nebuchadnezzar. He became more and more certain that there was something alive behind it.

While Benjamin was uncomfortable in his suit, he was glad to be inside, out of the heat. The big house was not easier work, exactly, but it was different work. He was away from the physical exhaustion of field work, even if it was replaced with mental exhaustion. There was something simpler about field work, though. Fix this, tend to that. In the big house he felt pressure, that any mistake he made would be instantly witnessed and punished. But Benjamin made no mistakes. Even with the black door on his mind, he listened and obeyed, did everything he was told.

One of his daily duties was to bring Miss Margaret her meals. She ate afternoon snacks or took tea wherever she pleased, but her big meals were always alone in the lavish dining room. She often asked Benjamin to stay with her. He did not sit down, of course, but waited silently at the edge of the room in case she asked for anything from him. Occasionally Miss Margaret spoke to him. Sometimes she did not. When she did, she asked him how he was liking it in the big house. A couple times she asked him to sing for her, and she seemed to appreciate it even though he didn't think his voice was very good. All he knew were religious hymns and field work songs.

The more time Benjamin spent inside the big house, the more he realized he was constantly by Miss Margaret's side. Almost all of his duties were related to her. Benjamin often found Miss Margaret staring at him out of the corner of her eye, enraptured. Like he was the first black man she'd ever seen. Miss Margaret often came physically closer and closer to Benjamin in a familiarity he found exceedingly strange. Stranger still was that it was never commented upon.

About the only job Benjamin had that took him away from Miss Margaret was to bring food to the Master.

And that brought him to the black door.

His instructions were always the same; take the prepared tray to the black door in the basement, place the tray on the small table just to the side of the door, knock three times, immediately turn and come back upstairs. Do not wait for the door to open. Do not wait for any sort of confirmation from the Master. Benjamin did this dozens of times, for breakfast, lunch, and dinner, and there was never an issue.

Until there was.

Until, as he was leaving, the black door opened. Benjamin was almost gone, almost up the stairs and back to the main level. He turned at the sound of swinging hinges.

There was a man standing there.

A man looking straight at Benjamin.

Was this the Master? The shape was small, but not just because it was hunched, or because distance made it tiny. The man looked sickly, like he hadn't had food in weeks. He didn't wear the clothes that Benjamin thought the master of the house should wear, nothing like the regal garments Miss Margaret wore. This figure was dressed worse than the slaves outside. A tattered blue blanket was draped around his shoulders and over his head like a hood. Beneath it, Benjamin could see rags, bandages. Beneath the shadow of the hood, Benjamin could see a long, blue beard draping down to the man's chest.

The man stood there, watching him, and Benjamin could feel the man's stare all over his skin, could feel it burrowing into him. He did not entirely know how to explain the stare, but he didn't feel it was entirely malicious. It reminded him of the time a wolf had made its way into the fields, and the creature had simply stared at Benjamin from a distance. Sizing him up. Studying him.

Almost like it had not decided yet whether or not he was to become prey.

Still, Benjamin moved as fast as he could back to the kitchen without actually running.

◉◈—

Benjamin waited until he and Steven were alone to ask if the Master was ill. The old house slave was helping Benjamin with his vest and tie—Benjamin could still not get it quite right—when he told Benjamin not to ask questions. Steven tied Benjamin's tie just a little tighter than usual, and Benjamin wondered if that cinching was a small punishment for asking something out of bounds.

"But I saw him," Benjamin whispered. They were in a separate dressing room. Again, behind a closed door, so that it was only the two of them. Benjamin still had not gotten used to such a concept.

"You hush," Steven said, and whistled a hand in front of Benjamin's face without actually hitting him. "Don't ask questions. Just do what you told."

"The Master's not..." Benjamin felt silly even thinking it, "a ghost...is he?" He heard a ghost story once, when he was small. He remembered little of it other than the spooky noises the storytelling slave made. Afterwards, an old woman whose name Benjamin could no longer remember—she'd long since been sold off—went around the circle, bopping the men on the heads for frightening the young ones.

"Oh, you hush, boy," Steven grumbled. "Ghosts ain't covered in bandages, Benjamin."

Not that there was no such thing as ghosts, but that they weren't covered in bandages.

Benjamin didn't say anything back, but he knew he never actually described to Steven what it was he saw down by the black door.

◉◈—

When Benjamin stood on the porch by Miss Margaret as she sipped her afternoon tea, she suddenly said, "I heard you were inquiring about the Master."

It took everything in Benjamin's power to remain completely and utterly still. And yet on the inside he cursed Steven for undoubtedly ratting on him.

"It's okay," Miss Margaret said. She looked at him. Benjamin could see it out of the corner of his eye. He knew better than to look directly back at her, but then Miss Margaret's hand was on his sleeve. She tugged him once, lightly, just enough to get his attention, and Benjamin turned his face to her.

"Don't worry, Benjamin," she continued. Her eyes were soft. "It's okay for you to look at me." Everything Miss Margaret was doing went directly against everything Benjamin had ever known about slave-masters. She said, "It's perfectly okay to be inquisitive. Steven is too hard on you sometimes. In my opinion."

Too hard? What was happening?

Miss Margaret said, "I know how you people talk. So word was bound to get around eventually, and I'd rather address fact than unsubstantiated rumor. Yes, Benjamin. Unfortunately the Master is rather ill."

Benjamin gulped and tried not to let Miss Margaret see.

She continued, "That's why we brought you into the big house. I chose you personally, Benjamin. Did you know that?"

He shook his head. He was too terrified to say anything. His brain chugged in place and refused to move, like a stubborn locomotive without enough fuel.

"Do you know why I picked you?"

Again, Benjamin shook his head.

"Do you remember last week, when you helped push that wagon out of the mud?"

Benjamin remembered. One of the Master's new hands had gone into town for supplies, and in the rain on his way back he'd gotten a two-horse team and the wagon stuck in some mud. Benjamin and four other field slaves had been pulled off their normal duties to free the horses and the wagon, while the hands all stood back and smoked cigarettes under a tree and shouted orders. It had taken the slaves over an hour, the mud sucking at their feet and the rain coming down and the wind blowing, making it worse, but they'd managed to free the wagon without losing any cargo or harming the horses.

The hand who got the team stuck in the first place was given a nice bonus.

"I...I remember," Benjamin said slowly.

Miss Margaret purred, "I was watching you that whole time. I remember seeing you help the horses out, seeing you free the wagon. I knew I needed someone strong like that. To help here, with the Master ill." It looked to Benjamin like she wanted to say more, like she wanted to tell him something. But all she said was, "With the Master ill, Benjamin, I need someone strong like you here in the big house."

And then she said nothing, simply stared out over the property, and Benjamin guessed their conversation was over.

It was beyond anything Benjamin had ever heard—ever even imagined—for a white woman to volunteer information to an inquisitive slave. And it was that unknown quantity that terrified him the most.

Benjamin tried to find some sense of normalcy in his new routine, but he was constantly reminded that none of this was normal. Every time he brought Miss Margaret food, he thought that he wasn't supposed to be in the big house. Every time he stood with her out on the porch, he thought that out in the fields was where he was supposed to be. Every time Benjamin brought the Master his tray, he thought that underground was not a place *anybody* should be. And on the day he went downstairs and found the black door yawning open at the end of the hall, Benjamin told himself it all had to be some sort of terrible dream.

The black door was actually open.

Benjamin ground to a halt when he noticed it, the tray of food in his hands. He was never supposed to open the black door, never venture beyond, but Miss Margaret never said what he should do if he ever found it open. It never even occurred to him as a possibility.

Maybe he should put the tray down right where he was. Maybe he should leave the tray halfway down the hall. Just close enough to where he could not see inside the room. Whatever he did, he knew he could not simply head back up. Not without delivering the Master his meal. Benjamin did not know the specific consequences of that, but whatever they were they could not be good.

He thought, Just head over and drop it. That'll be alright. Just head over and put it down. Make a loud noise as you're coming. Maybe the Master, if he's inside, will close the door before you get too close. And then Benjamin thought that he could perhaps just close his eyes. The hallway was straight enough, the floor even enough. If he closed his eyes and walked straight ahead — it looked to be about fifty paces — he could put the tray down outside the door, turn and walk away.

Benjamin closed his eyes and found his way forward by slowly putting out one foot. He felt the ground with his toe, then put his foot down, repeated with the next. It made those fifty paces all the more agonizing, because he could hear something, but not see anything. He wasn't sure what exactly he was hearing at first. Some sort of scuffling. Benjamin cleared his throat loudly. Coughed, even though he didn't need to. He dragged his feet. He whistled. Hoped any and all of it would let the Master — if he was indeed down there — know Benjamin was approaching.

But Benjamin did not hear the door close. No one spoke to him and told him to stop where he was. So he kept going. Kept listening to that scuffling noise. As Benjamin came closer and closer, it became more defined. It sounded like cloth rustling. And on top of that rustling, Benjamin could hear something that sounded like muffled grunts, the sound of someone pushing, struggling. Like a violence.

And then all of a sudden it stopped.

The silence was worse than the noise. Infinitely worse. Benjamin felt as if he could feel someone standing in front of him, a face in front of his own, and when the fear became too much he squinted open his eyes.

Just for a moment, he thought. I'll just do it for a moment. Just enough to see if I'm in danger. Just enough to know what's happening.

He wished he hadn't.

Lord in heaven, he wished he hadn't.

Fifty paces had been too many. He was already inside the room beyond the black door; it was dimly lit, but Benjamin could see well enough. The space was large, but not spacious. A desk was pushed up against the wall, on which Benjamin saw dozens of books and loose reams of paper, on which there were anatomical sketches of skulls. Old books spread their yellow pages open, and along one of their spines, Benjamin could see the letters P-H-R-E-N-O-L-O-G-Y, but he had no idea what that word meant. But worse, so infinitely worse than the strange books was the old, rickety bed in the center of the room.

Onto which was strapped Miss Margaret.

A rag was in her mouth, knotted behind her head, and her limbs were splayed out in all directions. They too were tied, strapped to the edges of the bed. She wore nothing other than underthings.

Benjamin dropped the tray of food, and it clattered and slammed loudly at his feet. Whatever he was going to serve got all over his nice shoes. The noise echoed so loudly in the small room that Benjamin almost didn't hear the door shutting behind him. But he certainly heard the voice cut its way through the door's resounding echo.

"Do you like what you see, Benjamin?"

Benjamin turned around and saw the Master, a single, dripping candle in his grip, barring his exit.

Only this time he was without his bandages.

The man who stared Benjamin down looked like a monster. Like some sort of demon. Just as animalistic as Nebuchadnezzar had become. The Master was shirtless and skinny, shot through with deceptive, wiry muscle. A thick beard draped down to his chest, and his eyes were bloodshot. But what frightened Benjamin the most was the Master's skin. At first, in the dankness of the basement, Benjamin thought it was a sickly gray, but as the candlelight crawled over it, he could see that it was a cold and steely blue, just like his beard.

The Master smiled. His voice was almost as cold as his skin. "We got you down here faster than the others."

Benjamin backed up until he could go no farther; he bumped into the bed, chanced a brief look behind him towards Miss Margaret. Benjamin expected fear on her face, but what he found was something much worse. With fear, at least, they would have been in this situation together, but her expression was something Benjamin had never seen before, at least not on a person. He struggled, took a moment to recall where he'd seen such a focus, and what he came up with horrified him. He'd seen it when he saw a cat corner a mouse in the barn. It was the look of a predator, of someone who had complete and utter power, who had someone else right where they wanted them. Her hips slowly rose up and down and she breathed heavily, and Benjamin could see her chest rise and fall in hungry anticipation.

Benjamin looked for an escape route, something—anything—besides the door in front of him which the Master now stood, but there was nothing but stone in every direction. He saw only, on the other side of the bed, a small pocket of darkness. Something deeper than the shadow in the rest of the room. Surrounding it was another salt line. Benjamin was aware of it, distantly, before his head swiveled back to the immediate danger.

The Master sneered. "You people really do listen when you're told to do something. None of you have ever opened that door. Not a single one. So we had to get a little inventive. Lure you in. Sound has always worked well, we've found. The sound of a woman, especially. To men who have not been with a woman in a long time." The Master smiled, as if that was all that needed to be said. And indeed, it was.

In his fear, Benjamin forgot all propriety, all pretense of how he was supposed to act in front of white people, let alone the masters of the house. He panicked, and his body told him to do something—anything—besides curl into a ball and surrender to whatever madness this was.

"W-w-what's happening?" Benjamin managed to ask.

The Master did not come any closer, though there was not very much closer to come. From the bed, Miss Margaret looked on hungrily. Her hips were still bucking. Benjamin could hear her sucking air past the gag.

When the Master spoke, his voice was not low, not angry. It was almost...happy. Like the Master was glad Benjamin could share in whatever horrific experience this was. "What's happening," he said, "is you've been chosen, Benjamin."

Chosen. Personally. If there ever was a doubt in Benjamin's mind that Miss Margaret was simply an innocent victim in this, it was gone now. Whatever was happening to him now, it was because of her. Benjamin retreated farther, so that the bed Miss Margaret occupied was between him and the Master. Benjamin briefly glanced behind him, saw that patch of darkness, and the salt line behind him. It looked like a hole. Like a well.

The Master stepped up to the bed, and while looking at Benjamin, undid Miss Margaret's right arm. She freed herself the rest of the way, removed the gag last and let it drape around her neck. She licked her lips, looked from Benjamin to the Master and back again, perched on her hands and knees at the edge of the bed. It looked like she was ready to pounce.

"It's okay, Benjamin," she breathed. "We're going to tell you why we chose you. We've found it goes a little better. The process is a little easier when you know. There's not as much...spiritual resistance."

"What process?"

The Master took a single step forward.

"I'm sure you know," he said, "that there are people from your continent who engage in certain...dark, animalistic practices."

Benjamin swallowed. He wanted to back up, but he could not go any farther. All that was behind him was the hole in the ground, the ring of salt surrounding it.

"It's been proven, you know," the Master said, nodding to the desk. "The science of phrenology. How the world's darker people are more susceptible to certain uncivilized urges. It's all there in the shape of your skull; the propensity for violence, the inbreeding. But especially the eating of flesh that is so popular among the indigenous peoples. In your dark continent, Benjamin, they say that such a thing allows someone to take another person's strength."

Benjamin wanted to ask them what they were talking about, what it was they intended to do, but his brain was frozen. He was unable to do anything; move, scream, cry, shout for help. All his functions were shut down. He could not even back away any further.

"But it doesn't last very long," the Master said. "Or, at least, not as long as I'd like it to." He looked at Miss Margaret, who was so close to the edge of the bed it looked as if she might tip right off. She stared wide-eyed at Benjamin, and not just because of the dark.

"But bucks like you," she purred, "are young. And strong."

Benjamin remembered what Miss Margaret told him about watching him free the horses and wagon from the mud.

She lifted a hand and offered it out to him. "You last much longer. We want you to join us," she said. "To give the Master your strength." Her free hand caressed her hip and Benjamin nearly retched at the fact that he once thought of her carnally. "The strength to be a proper husband to me."

Lord.

They wanted...Benjamin couldn't even think it. Every time the thought came close to his mind it grew spikes and stuck him. It was like trying to pick up a snake. He could not come at it from any direction without being bitten.

"You want to..." Benjamin's head spun. He gripped the desk so he did not fall. If he fell, he knew it was over. He would never leave this room. At least not in any way that he would want. In any way that was not a nightmare.

"We want you to become a part of us," Miss Margaret said. "You'll live on. Inside the Master. Inside me."

Understand? Of course he understood. But she was really asking if he was okay with it. How could he *possibly* be okay with this? He could only swallow the lump in his throat and say, "You want my power." That made it easier. Somehow. To not acknowledge the true truth of what they wanted. The mechanics of how they would get his power hung unspoken. Benjamin would never be able to speak such words.

"Yes," said the Master.

Benjamin backed up farther, felt his heel against the lip of the hole in the ground.

"Benjamin, *stop!*" Miss Margaret suddenly hissed, looking down at his foot. But Benjamin hardly paid attention. All he could think was to get away. To run. There was nothing else except not letting this happen.

Miss Margaret reached for him; "Benjamin, *don't!*"

Benjamin's back foot scraped something. He nearly fell into the hole, caught himself on nothing other than muscle memory. He smelled salt kicked into the air, and then the Master's candle blew out, and everything went dark and quiet.

Everything was silent for a long, long time, and Benjamin wondered if this was what death was like. Just nothingness. No, no, that couldn't be right. If this was truly death, he would not still be able to smell the smoke of the Master's candle, the salt behind him, the sickly smell of his own fear-sweat. Miss Margaret's perfume.

"H-h-hello?" Benjamin called into the dark.

And then there was a light. It was not the light of a fire, but something soft and blue. Benjamin thought it might have been moon, or star, light, but down here? In the deepest part of the house? That was impossible. Especially after it quickly increased in intensity.

And took a form.

At first it was nothing except a soft, pale hue, as if the Master had lit a strangely-colored candle. But Benjamin could see both the Master and Miss Margaret illuminated in that steely light, and neither of them held it. They both stared up at the light, and for the first time Benjamin saw something submissive on their faces, saw that, although he did not quite know how, they had been stripped of their power. They flinched before the light, eyes wide and mouths agape, fear evident in their eyes.

The light swelled, became greater. Bigger, brighter, but not so much that Benjamin had to shield his eyes. He watched as it grew from a small orb into a recognizable shape, into something with translucent arms and legs, with eyes that glared a soft and yet terrifying judgment unlike anything Benjamin had ever seen.

It was a man. A black man. Benjamin did not recognize him personally, but he certainly recognized a field slave when he saw one; the clothes that barely qualified as such, the thick, ropy muscles that could be seen through the rips in cloth, the calloused hands and the scars of whippings.

And then there was another light. This one grew and swelled much faster than the first, became yet another field slave staring down at the Master and Miss Margaret.

And then another.

And another.

And another.

Until the room was filled with the wraiths. So many that the basement would not have been able to contain them had they been flesh. So many that Benjamin had to view the Master and Miss Margaret, distorted and warped, through the floating legs and torsos of the ghosts. They were all men, most around Benjamin's age. All strong, all scarred, and all staring right at the Master and Miss Margaret.

One of those specters slowly turned away, towards Benjamin. It took all Benjamin had to look into the wraith's eyes, to not run screaming from the room. The ghost's lips moved, but Benjamin did not hear him say anything.

"What?"

Again it said something, but Benjamin thought he heard it this time. Far away, like from down a well. Echoing, never truly reaching his ears. The ghost seemed to understand it was not being heard, and gestured behind Benjamin, to the patch of darkness in the corner of the room.

Benjamin turned and looked at it again, and in the light of the ghosts, could see that it was indeed a hole in the ground. It tunneled both horizontally and vertically away, and in the new, blue light, Benjamin could see what was inside it; a pile of bones. Human bones. He didn't know if he'd be able to tell what they were if he hadn't recognized the telltale shape of human skulls. Around the hole, the white line of salt had been broken. By his heel.

Benjamin looked back up at the ghost, nodded that he understood. He had freed them. The ghost nodded back at Benjamin, then turned with its spectral brethren to face the Master and Miss Margaret.

And then, finally, when there were no more eyes on Benjamin, he ran.

He did what he was told, and left the door closed behind him.

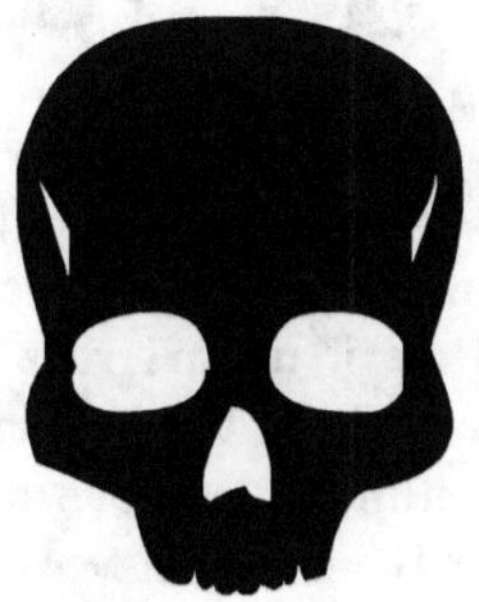

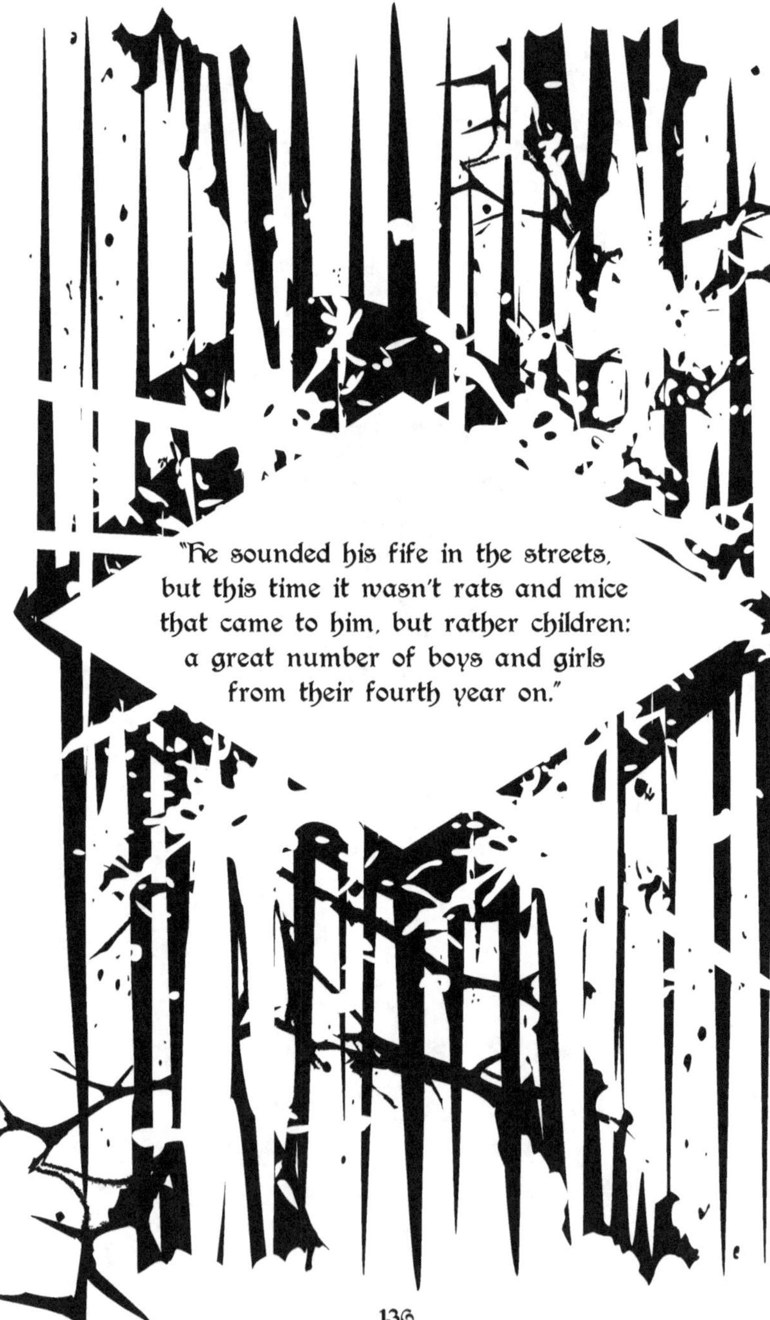
"He sounded his fife in the streets,
but this time it wasn't rats and mice
that came to him, but rather children:
a great number of boys and girls
from their fourth year on."

WE HIDE IN THE HILLS

Elizabeth Rosen

We hide in the hills, under the rocks, beneath mountain and the Lady's Veil, which is what the waterfall, and the curtain of mist it throws off, are called. We wander the underground river into the vast chasms that are the root of the Old Man. We hide, and we wait. We hunger, and we tell tales. Some of us remember the Coming. Some of us remember our Before Families, but most only remember the Pack now.

I keep the time on the wall behind a boulder. Not that we are discouraged from keeping the time, but the Lady says that counting days has become irrelevant now that we do not live by sunlight any longer. But I was at the edge of adulthood, twelve, when the Coming happened, old enough to remember my Before Family and the Mayhem and Terror. I still wake on a sudden, my heart pounding, sure that my father is standing in the doorway of my bedroom, my stepmother at his shoulder with a look of desire and cunning on her long face. On such wakings, I go to my place behind the boulder and take comfort as I run my fingers over the pale scratchings there, thinking to myself, surely, she is dead by now. Surely, they are all dead by now.

When I counted more than a thousand scratches on the wall, I went to the Lady.

"If it please you, Lady, will you come with me," I asked her.

Her dogs rose with her; thin, sharp-snouted mongrels that carried the damp smell of cur with them everywhere, because the Lady preferred to sit near the mists of the underground river, and so their fur rarely completely dried.

Looking at them now, it was hard to remember how there had been a time near the beginning when our starving had given us the idea that the dogs were worth eating. This was one of the few times that the Lady had been roused to anger with us. The fierce barking of the collie we had backed against a wall had alerted the Lady to trouble, and she had come like lightning to stand between us, with our hands still raised with stones in them, and the dog, whose barking turned to a low growl of distrust as it regarded us from behind the Lady. The small metal whistle she carried always around her neck but that we could not hear was between her teeth as she separated us from the dog.

"You shall not!" she reprimanded us, as she took the whistle from her lips. Her tone was fiercer than even our hunger, and we lowered our stones. "These are your new family," she said, pointing down and then behind us where, unbeknownst to us, the rest of her pack had surrounded us and stood alert for the next whistle blast.

Her shoulders were thrown back, and she glared at each of us in turn. "Do you not remember how they kept you from getting lost in the hills?" she asked. "How they kept you together and guided you safely across the mountains away from the Mayhem and Terror of your Before Families?"

She pointed at one of the littlest boys, grown feral with hunger and damp. His hair was matted as the dogs' and he had snarled and snapped at the thought of the meat on the animal that sat at the feet of the Lady, but when she pointed him out, his face fell in dismay, his hands limp at his gaunt sides.

"You, Connor," she said to him. "Have you forgotten the fear of getting separated in the darkness of those first nights, and how it was the dogs who found and brought us to you as you cried?" With a wave of her hand, she drew our attention to the bloodhound that stood stiffly in the circle behind us with its tail erect and ears forward waiting for a whistle blast to direct it.

"But, Lady," a girl objected. "We are hungry."

"As are the dogs," the Lady reminded her. "They starve with us. They and we are now part of the same group, each offering our skills to the others," she said. "Do they turn against you to eat you for your meat? Do you think they could not, if they wanted to? If I let them?"

I watched the bigger dogs out of the corner of my eye, their teeth visible as they panted and waited. No, it was certainly true that they could have, if they wanted to. Or were allowed to. The children shuffled uneasily.

Some of the Lady's anger had dissipated now, and with it, the animals surrounding us also seemed to relax. Many of them sat, or lay down to lick their paws, or scratch an itch behind an ear.

"Children," the Lady said, her tone gentler, "do you forget how they stand watch over us? The Mayhem and Terror are never far away, and it is your brothers, the dogs, who make sure we are safe and aware of approaching danger. It is the dogs who run down game for us."

I spoke up, guilty but resentful. "Lady, the dogs have brought down nothing in weeks. We are starving. What use is escaping the Mayhem and Terror if we only starve to death in a different place?"

The Lady looked thoughtful. She raised the dog whistle to her lips and blew a silent blast. The dogs returned to their feet and slinked in between the children to her side, where they each sat facing us. My guilt bloomed as I looked into their eyes and saw their patience and mild interest. I looked at my fellow would-be butchers, and the raw hunger in our faces made me think that we called the wrong group animals.

"These," the Lady indicated the dogs around her, "are not for the eating. They will hunt for us again."

And so they had. But not before some of the children, driven by homesickness made worse by suffering, slipped away from the mountain hideaway and went back to their homes, never to be heard from again by us. Better to risk the Terror, they figured. After all, the rumors of parents slaughtering their children for food were only rumors to most of us. Perhaps the ones we'd left behind in our exodus of terror had been living on rats and rodents, just as we had.

Only we knew it wasn't so, because the Lady had taken the rodents with her. That is what she had been paid to do, once the people realized that the wasting plague was carried by the vermin. And we, the ones she had taken when the city had refused to pay, had eaten all of the rodents that had preceded us, praising the little wire-haired terriers for catching and shaking the rodents to death and then prancing them over to our hungry hands. In the first months, we had eaten well, until there were no more rats for the terriers to kill.

Still, maybe the adults had figured out how to treat their wasting sickness. Maybe they had figured out a way to feed themselves that had nothing to do with eating the youngest among them, as the Lady had warned us they were resorting to when she promised to lead us to safety. After all, figuring things out is what elders do. That is what children depend upon their elders to do. So Lovely and Peter and Apple Cheeks must have told themselves as they picked their way over and through the rocks of the Mountain and made their way home.

With tears in her eyes, the Lady had informed the ones who stayed behind that some had decided to return home to their fates. But we could see in her eyes the new resolve that she must figure out a way to feed and protect the Pack so there would be no more defections. We watched her put on her coat of cattle skins spotted black and white, and call the dogs to her. Together they went out to find food.

And the next morning, true to her promise, there were cauldrons, two large iron ones, of stew for us. We fell on them and ate until our stomachs hurt, then lay in a stupor, silently blessing the Lady and her dogs, wishing that our friends had had the faith to wait.

When we had slept off our stupor, the Lady told us her plan to survive.

"We will make bread," she announced. "We will make bread with the bones of the animals we eat, and I will go back to the City and sell it there where they are starving. So shall my prophecy come true: they will pay for reneging on their contract with me."

So this is what we did. Between the bone meal and the dampness of the mountain cavern, the bread was not much to see, but it was heavy and filled the hole that hunger had gnawed away. For a third of my scratchings, we had made the bread and loaded it into sacks that the Lady put on her back and carried to the City to sell. We offered to help her carry her load, but she only shook her head and smiled, telling us that it still was not safe for little ones, and that her dogs would protect her.

But even with the Lady's warnings, there were still some children who found it unbearable after a time to live in the damp like wrinkled grubs, glowing mild and white in the perpetual twilight gloom of the cavern, and who missed their bright homes where dust motes had danced in the sunlight and made them sneeze. These left us in the middle of the night to return to the City. We asked the Lady to find out about our friends when she went to the City to sell the bread, and she would return sadly to tell us that she had found little Yvonne's body at the bottom of a chasm as she made her way down Old Man Mountain, or that in the City, she had overheard two people discussing the meal their neighbors had made of a boy named Trevor who had been one of us.

All this I thought about as I led the Lady to my place on the wall where there were now a thousand marks grouped by fives. Stepping around the boulder, she crouched and laid her palm against my reckoning of days. She took a moment and counted the groupings, her delicate lips moving slightly with each number. When she looked up, her eyes were melancholy, the shadow of those thousand days setting somewhere deep inside never to be seen again.

"Why do you show me this, child?" she asked, rising to her feet.

At first, I could not answer. At last, I stammered.

"It has been three years, my Lady."

"Yes."

I licked my lips. "A thousand days is a dying time for those who have nothing to eat," I said. "Even…" I lowered my head in deference, "if they are resolved to eat one another. A thousand days is a time long enough for a sickness to burn itself out. Or," I said, as I looked at her from under my eyelashes, "long enough to find a cure."

I had grown into my fifteen years, and the Lady, who had seemed tall and graceful when I first followed her, I now looked down at. As she came from around the boulder and seated herself there, arranging her pelt coat around her, I saw that she was thin and delicate and this gave her the illusion of height and majesty when her pelts swung around her. Her whistle hung around her neck on a long thong. Her movements, as always, were accompanied by the pantings and huffings of her dogs.

"I see you have brought no one else here with us," she said curiously.

I inclined my head slightly.

"Why?" she asked.

"My Lady saved us once. If she is keeping us here, there must be a good reason."

The Lady bowed her head slightly to one side to acknowledge the words of respect.

"But," I continued, "a thousand days have passed. If my Lady is keeping us here now, there must be other reasons than those for which we first came. Is the world not changed now from then?" I asked her.

"No."

"No?"

"No," she said in an even voice. "It is the same place of greed and selfishness. Violence and arrogance still reign. Men care not for men, and less still for women. The two-legged are more animal than the four-footed, and have not the integrity of most of those. Injury and revenge remain constant."

She lifted a finger slightly from her lap and her favorite hound came to her knee as if to make her point about loyalty. He let his head rest on her thigh, and she scratched him between the eyes absently.

"The plague?" I asked.

"The plague has burned itself out, yes."

"And the hunger?"

"Ah," she whispered. "Hunger still exists. Hunger for money and title. Hunger for status and power. Hunger for the things others have. Hunger for the things that dreams show us, no matter the cost."

Frustrated, I shifted on my feet. Two of the dogs opened their eyes at the movement.

"I meant hunger of the belly, my Lady." At the sound of the impatience in my voice, several of the other dogs now turned their attention to me. The Lady met my eye with a steely gaze, and even in the dim light of the cave, I saw her pity and contempt that I understood so little. It was now that the idea that had begun to take shape in my mind started to harden into a form I could recognize.

"Were they ever eating children?" I asked her. "Did Trevor's family really eat him?"

The dogs began rising to their feet around me as I could not keep the tremor of outrage from my voice. Her eyes glittered with what for a moment seemed amusement.

"Oh yes," she replied. "There are always a few degenerates that engage in extremes."

"But we were never in danger?"

She rose, her shoulders straight, looking in bearing more like a queen than the shepherding girl she once was.

"Oh course, you were!" she said as though correcting an imbecile. "Have you heard nothing I said?"

I swallowed my fear and resolved to finish. "I want to leave," I told her, praying for the same iron in my voice that I saw in her expression.

She inclined her head in agreement. "So be it," she said. "But you shall leave now, while the others sleep. Speak to no one, I implore you." Her face softened as she contemplated the flock she had gathered to her, then hardened as she focused again on me. "Do not endanger them with your doubts."

She turned her back and stood regarding the marks I had scratched into the wall, but as I moved to go, she spoke once more.

"I will send one of the dogs with you." She glanced over her shoulder at me with a benevolent smile. "For protection."

There was no point in objecting. I could only hope…but no. As she blew a command into her whistle, the fawn-colored mastiff rose to follow me. He was a solid mass of animal. Even the friendly-looking speckles of dark brown and white that ran through his fawny coat could not make him less intimidating. I made to return to the sleeping niche to gather my blanket, but the dog sidled alongside me as we neared the entrance to it and turned his head to watch me. Though he made no sound, I thought it better not to raise his hackles. Instead, as we passed through the various caves where the Pack lived and worked, I reached out to one of the work tables, silently taking one of the sharpened flakes of flint into my palm and then hiding it in my sleeve.

Long before we neared the entrance to the cavern, the roaring sound of the waterfall that hid the way into the mountain rose around us. The mist collected on my skin, and violent tumbling of the water into the roiling river before me was a pounding that could be felt in the chest now that I was near to it. We took the path around the back of the falls. I could smell the open air long before we emerged into it. The moon was in a waning phase, and the rocky landscape no more than dim silhouettes of obstacles to evade.

In truth, had he not been the Lady's, I would have been glad of the dog's company. But my mind was picking through my conversation with the Lady as with my hands and feet I picked my way through the rocks and followed the ghostly shape of the mastiff out of the mountains. Violence and greed, she'd said. Injury and revenge.

There had been more than one rumor in the Wasting time, some about the Lady herself. I tried to remember these. The mastiff stopped on the top of an outcropping and waited for me to catch up before leading our way over and alongside the edge of the shale cliff. I remembered the cliff from the climb up three years earlier. The Lady had cautioned us that we must not approach the edge, as pieces of shale routinely dropped away without warning. She had placed the dogs between the children and the edge, another sign that she had our well-being at heart. This was the place that she said Yvonne had fallen as she made her way back to the City.

As I crested the top of the rock pile, I began to slide on loess. I pinwheeled, trying to regain my balance, but lost my footing and fell backwards, sliding helplessly down the side of the hill. I tried to dig my heels into the loose gravel to slow my slide, but only succeeded in jamming my foot against a buried rock as I passed. I came to a stop at the bottom of the hill, the slow burn of pain beginning to heat my ankle. As I lay on my back, grimacing and wondering whether the injury would prevent me from walking, the rumor about the Lady came back to me.

Injury and revenge.

Slowly, I pushed myself to my elbows, feeling sicker as every second passed, as every second, it became clearer. I stood and tested my weight on my foot. It burned, but I could use it. I hobbled along the edge of the cliff, the hair on the back of my neck rising as I heard the gentle shifting of the gravel under the mastiff's giant paws behind me. When I was within feet of the edge, I turned and faced the dog who had lowered his head to watch me. I had lost the sharpened flint in the slide down the hill. The dog's sight was no doubt better than mine, and it had no twisted ankle to contend with. I had only one advantage, the dog's bulk.

The mastiff paced closer in the darkness, preparing to attack. I felt him launch himself more than heard it, and saying a fleeting prayer, I threw myself against the side of the mountain and smelled the dank fur as the dog's body passed me. It made no sound as it fell. In the still night, though, the thump of the landing, like a broom hitting a rug, came to me from below.

With my ankle, it took nearly two hours to make my way to the bottom of the cliff. I sat next to the body of the war dog and waited for the light. To pass the time, I took a shard of flint I had retrieved from the gravel nearby and began to skin the pelt from the animal. The fall had nearly liquefied the insides of the dog. It was like trying to skin a goat flask filled with wine, but the task kept me occupied until the sun had risen high enough to send some faint yellow light over the edge of the cliff.

I threw the pelt over my shoulder to dry and began to hobble along the side of the valley looking for proof of my fears. I found the first skull within minutes. Within two hours, I had found the others. There were no other bones.

I collected the skulls, placing each as I found it into the pelt I had slung over my shoulder until I had them all, one for each child who had returned to the City. I built a cairn, a gruesome memorial, the dog's blood smeared red across the sun-whitened bone of the skulls, empty black eye-sockets keeping watch in all directions.

This, then, was the Lady's revenge against the town that had shunned her. She had sold the townspeople bread made of the bones of their own children. I tried to keep myself from thinking about the cauldrons of stew that she had lovingly fed us. I spat and wiped my mouth, lowering myself to sit on the ground. We carried within us the sins we had run from. The stain could not be removed. The horror waxed and waned like surf, and I let it go, turning my face to the slit of sky above me and waiting until the tidal pull lessened, and I could balance again. The sun was nearly above me by the time I felt I could walk again, but I had spent my time well. I knew what I would do.

I rose to my feet, tied the mastiff's blood-spotted pelt over my shoulder once more, and began to make my way out of the chasm. Her pack of dogs would not keep me from my task. I would find a way to put my flint knife to the Lady's throat, and slit it. As she said: injury and revenge. And because her own actions were proof of her assessment of the world, I would make it my business to protect the children who had no defense against these dangers.

Yes, I thought, as I climbed toward the Lady's Veil, I would travel the countryside and gather them to me, leading them from the horrors of the world and into the safety of the mountains.

"Once upon a time
there was a child who was willful
and did not do what his mother wanted.
For this reason God was displeased with him and
caused him to become ill"

WILFUL

Jade Jiao

"**S**he was a disobedient little shit, right until the end."

"Martha, please," whispered Derek through gritted teeth. He slumped forward, knuckles white as he gripped the edge of the pew, looking as though he might throw up. I wanted to shake him, maybe give him a TV-soap style slap around the face, but I refrained.

"I'm allowed to cope with this however I want," I hissed. "I'll say what I like. If she'd listened to me, she'd still be here." That had always been Samantha's problem. Wouldn't sit still for a minute. Always sneaking out to go and do god-knows-what. Never indoors long enough to learn how to behave like a civilised human being.

Derek and I sat, with enough space between us to fit two other people, on the front row overlooking the casket. My shoulders stayed high and rigid. Every few minutes, I'd try to remind myself to lower them, but they wouldn't stay. Out of the corner of my eye, I could see Derek start to shake. His chest heaved, and he let out a single, loud sob. I ignored it. His shirt collar was creased and had a tinge of yellow staining. Repulsive. I focussed on keeping myself distracted, burying all the pain deep down inside and locking it away. On not blinking to keep my eyes dry and my make-up unsmeared. Not breathing to keep my throat from seizing up.

The interior of the funeral home looked like a nineteenth-century whore's boudoir. All dusty drapery and fuss. Ugly, dark flock wallpaper and dim lighting. Not where *I* would have chosen, but I hadn't been up to organising everything without help. Not in my condition. As I was taking it all in, my sister and her husband approached, and held our hands in theirs, passing on their platitudes. They hadn't brought their kids with them. A tasteful decision, though I did note her new, highly conspicuous black Chanel Flap. An assortment of Derek's relatives followed, including his frail, wailing mother. Samantha hadn't even liked her. Some of her school friends came, strangely dressed in whatever black items they'd been able to assemble at short notice. School trousers and PE trainers. Couldn't their mothers have found something a little more fitting? I wouldn't have dreamed of letting Samantha go to a funeral in Nike.

"Thirteen is no age," someone said, and squeezed my shoulder. I recoiled.

"When would you say *is* the right age to run out into the road and get hit by a car?" I asked. "I might try it later."

I don't know if they replied. I didn't care.

Samantha's body was dressed in her favourite frock, and they'd done her hair and used thick cosmetics to cover her injuries.

"You'd never even know," my sister said. "She looks like a sleeping angel." And she did.

Just goes to show how looks can be deceiving, I thought, but didn't say.

I stayed still and quiet, and people queued to have their little gawk at my dead daughter, and to say goodbye. I wondered whom among them was the most impatient to get to the wake buffet. The mountain of egg and cress sandwiches I'd smelled from a distance of fifty feet when I'd arrived. *Common food for common folk,* as my mother would have sniffed. Eventually, a hush descended, and the clock showed that it was time for the main event. This was my moment to show all the decorum and bravery I could muster. To do myself proud.

Just as the second hand ticked to twelve, right on cue, Samantha did something *so typical.* She just *had* to be defiant and make a scene to attract attention. The way she did it, it seemed instantaneous, as though I were watching a film with frames missing. One minute, everything was normal, and the next, it wasn't.

Samantha's left arm shot up into the air over the top of her coffin. Her wrist was contracted, so that her hand bent over in an unnatural way, making her fingers almost touch the inside of her forearm. Someone in a row behind me screamed. I looked to the funeral home attendant, whose wide eyes and open mouth showed me this wasn't something that happened every day. Derek buried his face in his sleeve, as useless and impotent as ever. So, I said something.

"Is that normal? I've heard bodies can shift and make noises after death. Escaping gases and things like that. Is that what's happening? Why is she doing that with her arm?"

The attendant, quite possibly there on some kind of work-experience programme, looked at me like I might lunge at him. He replied in a voice so soft, I couldn't tell what he was saying.

(This is one of the most irritating things that happens when your daughter gets hit by a car, nobody will talk to you at a normal volume. Everyone seems to think a regular speaking voice will shatter you like glass).

"What?" I snapped. "I can't hear you." I turned to Derek. "What is he saying? Why is she doing that?"

The attendant raised two hands in a placating gesture, then disappeared behind a red velvet curtain. He reappeared a moment later with a more senior employee. She looked at my daughter, then at me.

"I'm sorry, madam, this is highly unusual."

"But bodies can move, can't they?"

"Yes, but not after embalming," she whispered. "I am terribly sorry."

"Right," I said.

There was an audible gasp from the crowd behind me as I stomped up to the casket and took Samantha's ice-cold hand in mine. It was solid to the touch, not like human flesh anymore, more like marble. I tried my best to push it back in place, but it remained rigid in the air. Someone came up behind me and gently tried to pull me away.

"Come on, Martha, it's all right."

I stayed firm, and gripped Samantha's hand tighter, eyes narrowed. "She needs to put it down." I had visions of her as a toddler, throwing a tantrum in the supermarket, making her whole body go stiff so I couldn't pick her up. At nine, refusing to do her homework or go to bed. And then last week, her running out in front of that bloody car. All because she would *never* do as I said.

"It'll go down on its own if you give it time. Leave it. It's fine," someone else chipped in, warbling like a frightened bird.

More came, and together, they managed to get me back to my seat. My face burned hot as coals with embarrassment. She'd spoilt my moment. She'd made me a fool. They did the whole damn service with Samantha's arm sticking up like that, and then they must have snapped it down after we'd left, because they certainly managed to get the lid on her coffin before she went underground.

At the wake, we had sandwiches and cake and a quiche. I had cottonmouth from my medication and couldn't taste any of it. I was assured that it tasted good.

All done, we arrived home at about five that evening. Derek brushed straight past me through the front door. He paused at the foot of the stairs, then turned, eyes red under a furrowed brow. "You really took that personally, didn't you?"

"My daughter's funeral? Yes. Yes, I will admit, I did take that rather personally. So sorry."

"I mean the arm. You think *she* did it."

I stared at him and didn't reply.

"It was a bodily reaction," said Derek. "Samantha didn't stick her arm up to spite you. She's gone."

Again, I said nothing. I knew what I'd seen. What everyone in that room had seen.

"I can see you're struggling, but so am I," he said. "Try to remember that."

He turned, trudging out of sight up the steps, and slammed our bedroom door. He hadn't taken his shoes off, even though we'd just had all the carpets cleaned less than two weeks ago. I went into the living room and put a pillow over my face so I could scream without him hearing me.

I was so angry with Samantha. Why had she always been so rebellious? Did that come from his side of the family? From birth to death, difficult through and through, and contrary to her core. Weren't girls supposed to be easy? Now, she was gone, and my life was ruined beyond any hope of repair. Piano lessons, gymnastics, horse riding, extra tuition…I might as well have flushed all that money down the toilet.

I took off my expensive funeral outfit—Dolce and Gabbana wool crepe dress with grey satin detailing–and balled it into a plastic bag so I wouldn't have to see it, then put on some jogging pants that I pulled from the dirty laundry basket. I couldn't face going into our bedroom to get something fresh and having to hear Derek cry. The thought turned my stomach. I went into Samantha's room and lay on her bed, breathing in deep the scent of her hair on her pillow, wondering how many more days it would be until it faded. At some point, the smell would fade from my memory, too, and another bit of her would be lost forever.

Why had she never loved me? Why hadn't she been able to see all the things I did for her? All the advantages she was given.

I must have fallen asleep. I woke up disorientated and confused. I groggily looked around the darkness of the room, for a moment forgetting everything, wondering why I was here and not in my own bed. Then, the memory of Samantha's death came crashing back like a hammer blow. Everything in the house was silent, and the street outside empty and unmoving. A windless, moonless night. Slowly, as my eyes adjusted, I started being able to make out the shapes of furniture. The glittery stickers she'd stuck on her wardrobe as a younger child, then tried unsuccessfully to scrape off once they'd become embarrassing to her. A stack of untouched maths practice questions abandoned on her desk. And the…

What *was* that?

The door to the hallway was cracked, and through it, I could make out some vague shape. I stared at it hard, trying to work out what it was. Something white and long. For a moment, I had the absurd notion that it was a swan's neck, and I was asleep. It moved closer, and wrapped five crooked fingers around the door frame. Then, I knew.

Samantha's arm, white and filthy, dirt under her fingernails and smelling of damp earth. I could just about make out her face through the shadows. Her eyes didn't seem to see me, and I realised it was because they were closed. Of course they were, I thought, the mortician had pinned them down for the viewing. But she sensed me. She knew I was there. I froze, rigid with shock, and we stayed watching each other for a long time.

"You need to go back, Samantha," I said, sternly. She didn't move. The same old defiance. "Go back," I repeated.

Something had happened to her lips. They looked peeled back, so that I could see both rows of her teeth, as though she were hissing at me.

"Go back where you came from. You can't be here anymore. I would've thought you'd be happy. You never have to be confined under my roof and rules again."

I could feel her mentally pushing back against me, and a groan came from between her locked teeth. If she'd been able to speak, I knew she'd be arguing with me. I stood firm.

"Do. As. I. Say."

There was a pause, then she retreated back into the darkness. The stairs creaked as I listened to her descend. I fell asleep or passed out.

I awoke to the sound of birdsong, with warm sunlight on my face. Wiping the sleep from my eyes, my first sight was a photo of Samantha smiling with her friends in a silver frame on her bedside table. I smiled. I had won. Nobody had seen it, but I had finally made my thirteen-year-old obey me. I rolled off Samantha's bed to go and make breakfast. Stretching, I shuffled out, down the stairs, and passed the living room.

The living room. I came to a sudden halt, a shiver travelling up and down my spine, my victory turning to ashes. On my sofa, my clean, cream sofa with its beautiful embroidered throw pillows, was Samantha, left arm raised high. Her two rows of teeth were still bared, her sewn-together eyes caked in dried, flaking mud. Under where she sat, the fabric of the couch had been stained and soiled, brown and grey. She turned to face me, obstinate to the last. She made a low growling sound, wet and guttural, and the effort pushed out a stream of rotten black liquid that ran down her chin and dripped onto the carpet.

I was so fixated on her, that it took me a moment to notice Derek on the armchair by the window. He stared blankly at the ceiling, his face expressionless. Broken.

"Congratulations, Martha. You've won."

"What?" I said.

"You've spent years screaming at her to stay inside and start acting properly. Well, she's here now. She's inside. She's waiting. What should she do, Martha?"

My husband and daughter both looked to me. Perhaps this was my chance to do things right. To start afresh with a child more pliant. More manageable. My nose wrinkled. The house stank of dirt and something vaguely chemical-y. Nervously, I approached my daughter, and picking up a comb from underneath the coffee table, I started to drag it through the lengths of her grimy, encrusted hair. The puckered skin of her scalp lifted slightly from her skull. I turned to Derek.

"Go and run a bath and fill it with Detol," I said. "Before we do anything else, we must at least look presentable."

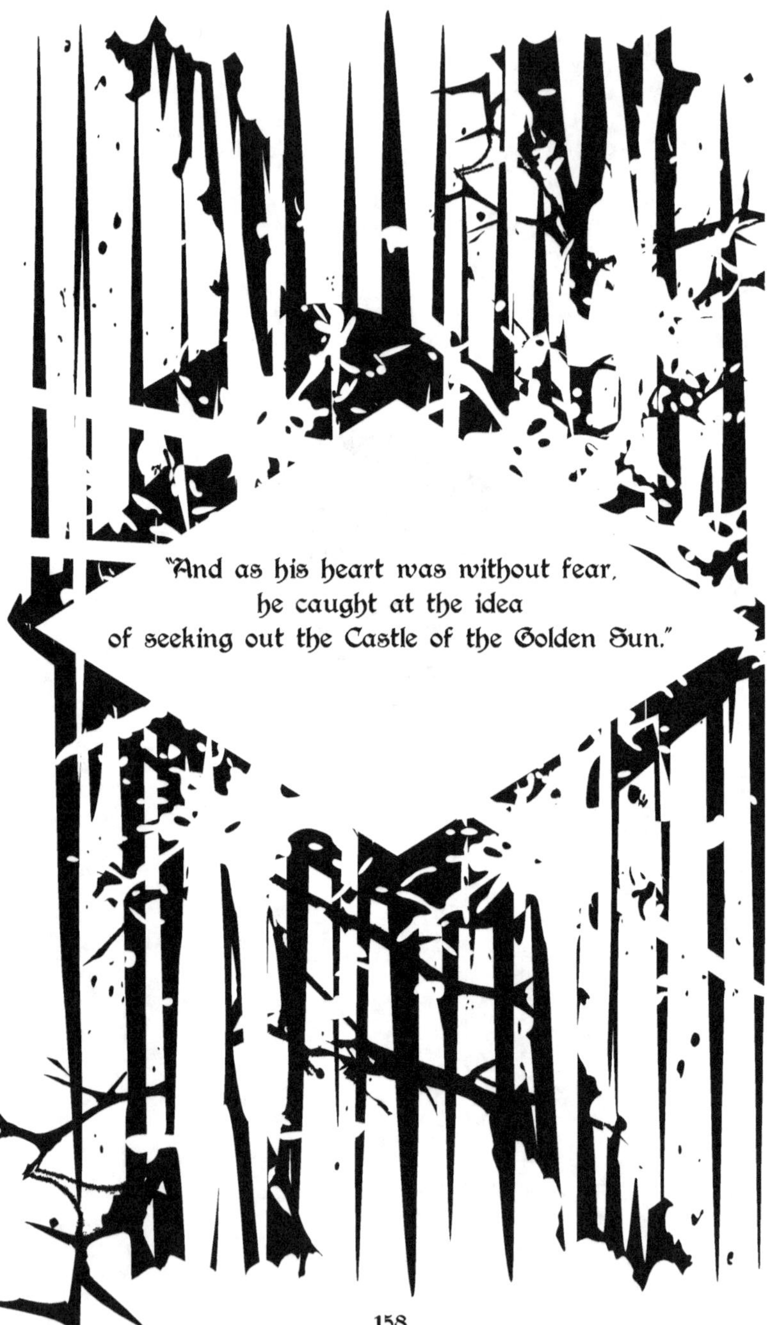
"And as his heart was without fear,
he caught at the idea
of seeking out the Castle of the Golden Sun."

THE CRYSTAL BALL

Eleanor Cooke

This relationship between cogency and magical expenditure holds true even when the caster is forced to use fundamental bases for her causation.

Peter felt a silent, frustrated scream building in him as he read the line for the sixteenth time. He understood every word, and how they fit together, but he couldn't make them turn into an idea in his head. He'd been studying for hours now, and all he'd achieved was giving himself a headache.

It was no good. He just couldn't focus.

It was unfair—he knew it was. His brother Michael never had this much trouble concentrating. But then, Michael never had much trouble with *anything*.

A rush of panic and frustration surged through him, and he opened his mouth in another silent scream. He expelled the energy in the only way that worked—by biting into the back of his forearm. His teeth didn't go far—

just until it started to feel smooth—but they left an indent, decorated with spots of purple and tiny red dots. He had old bruises there already, which he kept hidden under the sleeve of his gown.

It was a magician's gown, with faded green and silver runes embroidered on purple fabric. It was a cast-off from James, who'd got it from Michael, proving that when you're a youngest son, even of an enchantress, you never get new clothes.

He looked down at the marks on his arms again. He didn't mind the pain, but the knowledge that he was damaging himself made him feel ill. Reluctantly, he closed the book.

It was a shame. He really wanted to beat Michael. Just once, at one thing. They were so damn similar in all their interests and their skills, but Michael was just *better*. Peter felt the panic rising again, and turned away abruptly, trying to think about *anything* else. He had dragged his mind off into a recitation of his favourite poem, and was trying to ignore the thoughts wailing in the background, when a horrible sound pierced the air.

It started like a desperate scream—Michael's?—then twisted into the screech of a bird of prey.

For the first time since he was six, when Michael had accidentally reversed the tower's gravity, Peter was genuinely frightened. He ran for the door, and was dashing for the courtyard where he guessed the scream had come from, when his sense overruled his loyalty.

If Michael was in trouble—Michael, who was infuriatingly, effortlessly good at everything he tried, and who claimed to be better at magic than their mother, the most powerful enchantress in the land—what could Peter do?

Instead, he dashed up the curved stairs that led to the top of the irrationally thin tower. Leaning out of the window, he saw a panicking eagle, still partially snared in the trappings of clothes and flapping frantically. Peter followed its furious gaze to a figure by the sea. It could only be James; no one else around here would hold a bonfire on the beach alone. Another figure, bright as a lightning strike, was blazing towards him.

"Mother?" Peter whispered.

The eagle put on a burst of speed, diving straight at her, but the enchantress raised a hand and blasted him out of the sky.

James was just turning as his mother cast her spell, and Peter had to look away as the blinding light surged over him. Even with his hands over his ears, he couldn't block out his brother's screams as his body rebuilt around him. When he turned back, an enormous whale lay groaning on the beach. The enchantress raised her arms again and blasted him out to sea.

Then she turned and looked up towards the tower. Peter rocketed backwards, his fear giving way to pure panic. He'd always felt safe in this room, but now he was trapped. She would come up from below, and what would she turn him into?

He ran for the window again, leant forwards, and…no. It was too high. Unless…

"Michael!" he screamed, "Michael, help!"

The bird heaved itself up from the ground, spread slightly singed wings and kicked off into the air. It flew straight for the tower as Peter struggled to get through the window. He fitted through easily, and dropped until he was hanging from the windowsill. He felt talons sink into his shoulder and he tried to force himself to let go, but his arms wouldn't obey him, and Michael had to drag him free.

Peter was only fourteen, and small for his age, and the eagle was very strong, but there was still no way it could lift him. Instead, it settled for turning what would have been a plummet into a desperate glide.

They lost height quickly, which was lucky, because it meant their mother's lightning bolt flashed over their heads, only coming close enough to cause them nasty headaches.

They landed badly nearly a hundred feet from the tower, and Peter scrambled up and ran, not noticing the red stain spreading from the shoulder of his purple gown.

Behind him, Michael gathered his energy and reluctantly returned to the air. He didn't follow Peter, flapping wearily to the south, towards a nearby mountain range.

It was the last the three brothers would see of each other for a long time.

It was nearly six years later when Peter heard a familiar voice call his name. He was hunched on a stool, milking a cow. It was a good job, because it let his hands work independently as his mind danced through worlds of its own making, but that voice dragged him out of it. His heart dropped into his stomach and bathed in acid as he slowly stood up.

Yes, it was Michael, draped in a feather cloak. Peter patted the cow absently as he stepped around her, leaving her tied to the milking post.

For a few seconds, he just stared, trying to sort out the confused mess of delight and anger inside him. He had missed his brother a lot in the last few years, despite they're often rocky relationship, and he was intensely relieved to see him alive and human. Still, he couldn't help a twinge of indignation. For months he had looked over his shoulder constantly, worrying and wondering. Then, as more time went by, his expectations had faded. And Peter had his own things to focus on, like his work on the dairy farm. Besides, if he was being totally honest with himself, one of the reasons he liked working here was the lack of overbearing family members. And now, more than half a decade later, his brother was here.

"Micha...I thought—How are you here?"

Michael waved a dismissive hand, and Peter noticed that he looked pale.

"That's not important," Michael stated. "The important thing is that I've figured out how to fix this."

He was using that voice again. The haughty, slightly sarcastic one that said *I know more than you do.*

Peter frowned.

"Haven't you alre—"

"No. This is temporary. I can manage about two hours a day, and then I...snap back."

Michael shuddered.

"Does it hurt?" Peter asked.

Michael scowled. "What? Having my body yanked apart then mangled together again? No, why would that hurt?"

Irritation eclipsed Peter's sympathy. Did he always have to be like this? Whatever joy he felt at his brother's return was waning fast.

"What do you want?" he asked, and it came out more hostile than he had planned.

"I have a plan. If you do what I say, James and I can both be freed."

This time it was Peter who scowled. *Do what I say.* That was always it with Michael.

"Let me guess," he said sourly, "It'll involve danger, doom, and evisceration, and it's almost certain to fail."

Michael folded his arms. "Don't take that tone with me."

Peter's temper flared at the presumption. For five years, he had been on his own, working to survive, seeing not a feather from his older brother. Hell, Michael had flown off and left him, bleeding, to run from their mother.

And now, turning up and demanding his help. And talking to him like that!

"You abandoned me."

The accusation sprang from his tongue before he could stop it.

Michael stared at him for a few seconds. "Yeah. That's what happened."

There was a pause as they glared at each other, then:

"I was protecting you, you stupid kid," he enunciated.

"What?"

"She was after you, and it would have been bloody easy for her to find you with a gigantic eagle flying above you. Or can your tiny little brain not get around that?"

Peter's control broke. "It's your fault anyway," he snapped.

There was a sudden dangerous silence as even the tension in the air tried to flee.

"Are you actually serious?" Michael asked, in the softest, least sarcastic voice Peter could remember him ever using.

In fact, Peter had regretted the words as soon as they were spoken, but he was committed now.

"You threatened her, and you boasted that you were as good as her. That's why she did it."

Michael stood there for a few seconds, his mouth open in silent shock. Then he turned and began to transform.

Peter could hear the bones cracking, and the stifled whimpers of pain. The eagle flapped its wings a couple of times, then flew off towards the forests that marked the edge of the farm.

Peter watched him go, guilty tears already pricking at his eyes. He hadn't meant to say something so horrible. And it had been horrible; he knew that. It was just…there was something about Michael that made him so angry. He pulled out the twist of leather he had started wearing around his neck and bit down on it. He bought them occasionally from the market when he was helping sell milk, and chewing on them preserved his arm. He didn't really need to right now, but it made him feel a bit better.

He gingerly sat back on the milking stool and returned to his task.

I was protecting you.

Was he? His brother had saved his life.

And then there was James. Smart, laid-back, casual James, who was nice to the point of being taken advantage of, and who seemed to have all the patience his siblings lacked.

The thoughts danced in Peter's head along with the memories of screams and whimpers, impossible to dislodge, and by the time he was done with the milking, he knew he had to put it right.

He led the last of the dairy cows out to pasture, an easy job they were trained to, then walked into the forest.

"Michael," he called softly, "you were right. That was…that was a hateful thing to say. I'm sorry."

He lowered his head apologetically, and waited, listening to his heartbeat thud in his ears and imagining all the ways this conversation could go wrong.

He heard a flurry of wings, a crackling and sobbing that made him shudder, and then approaching footsteps.

Peter looked up at his brother.

"Yeah," said Michael, "it was."

Peter opened his mouth, feeling like he should say something, then shut it as he realised he didn't actually *have* anything to say. There were a few seconds of awkward silence.

"So, what was your plan?"

Michael eyed him for a few seconds before answering. "There's an enchanter. A powerful one. He lives in the Castle of the Golden Sun. He's an expert at transformation magic."

Peter's heart dropped. He had really wanted to like this plan, but he'd heard of this enchanter before.

"Michael…" he said timidly.

Michael scowled at his tone, turned his head, raised his eyebrows, and answered in a singsong voice. "Yes, Peter?"

"I…I've heard of him. He won't help us."

Michael smirked, and Peter fought with his temper again.

"Oh, really?"

"He's evil, Michael."

The smirk widened.

"Yes. Yes, he is. And he has a *wife*."

Michael spread his arms victoriously. "And she hates him."

Peter frowned and opened his mouth to argue, then stopped as he understood. "So, she might help us?"

Michael offered an ironic bow which Peter barely noticed. He was busy thinking about it.

He'd heard of the Castle of the Golden Sun, and specifically about how sixteen young men and eight young women had been killed trying to find it.

But these were his brothers.

He looked up at Michael.

"Do you know where it is?"

No was the answer, as it turned out. The two of them spend months travelling, eating off the land, with Peter taking jobs where he could find them, then moving on. The one upside of their fruitless search was that they were getting along better than they had in a decade. Perhaps this was because Michael spent most of his time as an eagle, not wanting to face the transformations, and finding holding his human form exhausting anyway.

At times, they came near the sea, and spotted a dark shape where their brother lounged, or a great plume of water as he breathed. Once, Peter even swam out to greet him, while Michael squawked disapprovingly, and they played together in the water like they had as children.

But it wasn't getting them any closer to the Golden Sun.

One day, when they were on a dusty road, they came across two women arguing fiercely. They looked very alike, and wore dresses of the same design, only in different colours. Perhaps the one in the green dress looked a little older, and a little angrier, but Peter couldn't be sure. He tried to slip past, but the one in blue grabbed him and dragged him over. Michael settled down in a nearby tree to watch as they spoke over each other.

"—need a judge to—"

"—arbitrate our—"

"—magic cap—"

Michael straightened, suddenly staring at the cap in Green-Dress' hand, then cocked his head.

"Please," begged Peter. "One at a time! Please slow down!"

There was a muttered conference, then Blue-Dress said, "Our father left us this cap. We've been trying to sort out who gets it, but we're equally strong."

Michael screeched about something.

"What if you race?" Peter suggested, ignoring him.

"Where to?"

"Tell you what, I'll wear the cap and walk off down the road. You can race to me, then the first one to grab the cap gets to keep it."

The women agreed that that seemed fair, and Peter set off down the road.

Even a few seconds of walking was enough for the screaming sensation of boredom to start gnawing at his chest, and his mind started to rove. He thought of his mother and his brothers, and the wife in the Castle.

Without even realising he was talking, he murmured, "I need to get there."

That was enough; he didn't even say the Castle's name, but he was gone at once.

For a few seconds, the thoughts were shocked out of Peter's head. Then, he collected them and looked around. He was standing on a plateau, and he knew from the thinness in the air that he was very high up. Mountains?

Surely not the ones to the south; Michael had been living in them for years. East, then, the coastal range right in the path of the rising sun.

Ah…

He grinned, took the cap off his head, and stared at it. It glowed faintly, like cooling metal.

He put it back on his head, took a last look around, then said out loud, "I need to be back at the road."

He was back where he'd been before he could blink.

"Ahoy!" he called to the astonished women, "Race to me, then!"

The words snapped them right out of their shock, and they charged towards him with such ferocity then he staggered a few steps back.

Blue-Dress reached him first, and snatched the cap away, crowing with delight, and Green-Dress cursed, then tackled her.

Peter scampered out of the way, then waved at Michael.

"I found it!" he burst out, as soon as the eagle was nearby, then backed up further as the brawl threatened to reach him, "I found the Castle!"

It took them a week's travel to reach the mountains, much to the annoyance of Michael, who could have flown it in hours. Peter found the journey frustrating too, for now their goal was in sight, the time felt longer than all the months before it.

It was late afternoon when they finally arrived, and Michael urged his brother to rest for the night, and go in fresh in the morning. But Peter had always despised waiting, and besides, his head was far to full for him to sleep. Frightened or not, he had to go in now.

"I'll call if I need you," he said, with a confidence he didn't feel, and then he walked up to the great stone doors.

The Castle was set into the east face of the mountain, and had a tall tower in line with the peak. It overlooked a sheer drop down to a rocky beach, which he guessed would be covered at high tide. He was about to knock, when he was once again overtaken by common sense. He laid his hand flat against the door and pushed on it hard. To his relief, it opened at once; much like Peter's mother, this enchanter was so confident in his magic and reputation, he failed to take even the simplest of security measures.

Peter edged himself in slowly, stifling a gasp at the warm air within. The place had no carpet, and his footsteps seemed to clank louder than his heart as he crept along the corridors. The décor was undeniably beautiful, but it felt stale, too. Everything was perfectly in place, from great twisted sculptures to immense classical paintings, and not even the dust dared to disturb them. It felt artificial. Even the light, which seemed to have no source, was an unhealthy shade of yellow. But for the warmth, Peter might have thought the place abandoned.

He turned a corner into a large hall, with walls covered in objects and artefacts. A treasury? He walked past paintings, swords, a stuffed duck with no beak and countless other bizarre items. He was so enthralled by them, that he almost walked right past an open door with sounds coming from within. He stopped himself at the last second, and peeked around the frame.

Inside, he could see a man hunched over a writing desk, muttering to himself. As Peter watched, the man raised a hand and sent a beam of light into a tube in the wall, then returned to his mutterings. The enchanter, Peter assumed. Not wanting a confrontation, he crept past.

Leaving the hall, he turned up the first staircase he saw; he guessed the enchanter's wife to be housed in the tower.

Housed…

He thought of the bars on the tower window and nodded. It was the correct word.

The higher he got in the castle, the less the warmth seemed to fill it. That was unnatural, too; heat should rise. As he ascended a spiral staircase, he found himself wishing he had grabbed a sword from the treasury, or any kind of weapon really. He couldn't shake the feeling that something terrible lay at the top.

As he finally approached the door, he realised he was trembling. He clenched his hand, trying to calm it, and bit down on his leather necklace, expelling the nervous energy he would once have forced into his arm. Then he pushed the door open and stepped in, to where the most beautiful woman he had ever seen turned to face him.

She had glorious golden hair which hung loose around her in long, smooth sheets, and blue eyes that reminded Peter of swimming in the sea with his brother. Her skin was pale and tight—almost like a doll's—and her lips were blood-red.

She was dressed in a simple grey dress which did not do her justice, and her posture was impeccable.

But it was her expression that drew Peter's eyes the most. Her face was screwed up in obvious pain, and his stomach tightened with sympathy.

"Uh…Lady?" He tried.

She raised her eyebrows slightly, disinterested in his invasion into her room.

"Uh…I…I need your help. Your advice, I mean. Uh…"

He flinched at the look she gave him; it contained more in the way of profanity than any swear word could.

"My *help*. You need my *help*. And what makes you think I have any *help* to give?"

Peter's brain blanked. He couldn't seem to focus on much besides the agony in her features.

"I don't mean…I…Look, are you all right?"

She laughed bitterly.

"All right?"

"I mean, you look…"

The pit of awkwardness in him deepened, and he gave her a flustered, pleading expression. Her glare softened.

"No," she murmured. "I am not all right."

Wincing slightly, she gestured towards a pair of curtains on the wall beside Peter. He drew them back, then felt the air leave his body in a sickened gasp. He stepped back, staring.

The reflection in the mirror showed him just as he was, if a little taller than he remembered, but the woman was entirely different. Her pale skin was studded with tiny hooks, pulling it taut. Tiny imps fluttered around her, yanking out hairs and — Peter gagged — hacking out slivers of fat. More of them danced around her head, grabbing her tresses and wrenching them straight or cutting at her lips to make them bleed.

His breathing fluttered, and he grabbed for his necklace, biting harder than he had in years. He spun in a circle, panic gripping him, then lunged for the curtains and hauled them closed. He clenched his jaw tighter, fighting to calm down, and forced tense muscles to walk him to the window, where he dragged in mouthfuls of clear air.

"Not the usual type of hero, are you?" The woman observed.

"I...You..." He gasped out the words with no idea what he was trying to say, then returned his focus to his breathing.

When he finally looked back, all thoughts of his brothers had fled.

"What can I do?"

He tried his best to keep his voice steady, but couldn't stop a slight shaking.

She looked at him, suspicious. "Nothing. At least until dawn."

Peter pushed his lower jaw forwards, trying to show his determination.

"And then?"

"It'll be dangerous."

Peter opened his mouth to tell her that he didn't care, then paused. "How dangerous?"

She laughed again, and this time it contained genuine humour.

"Twelve people have died trying."

"I thought it was twenty-three?"

"The others ran into my husband."

Peter thought about it. It didn't take him very long. "What do I need to do?"

So she told him about the crystal ball. It was a powerful item, capable of drawing magic out of someone, and the enchanter had possessed it for a long time. He had used the magic trapped within it to give himself unequalled power, and now it was the only thing capable of harming him. Dangerous as it was, the man wouldn't risk harming it, so he had hidden it away in a magical bull. The bull contained a bird, and the bird contained a burning egg. It emerged once a day from the mountain spring at the base of the castle.

"At dawn?"

"Precisely."

Peter nodded slowly. "Okay."

He glanced towards the bed, thinking he should try to get some sleep before fighting a giant bull. Then he stopped.

"Lady, may I have your name?"

She raised her eyebrows again, looking surprised that he had bothered to ask.

"Julia," she told him.

He stared at her for a while, wondering if he was brave enough to ask the question buzzing around in his head. He thought of how he might die tomorrow, and decided he was.

"Julia, your husband did this, right?"

He waved an arm at the covered mirror.

Julia eyed him. "Yes."

"But…why would you marry someone like that?"

She continued to watch him, her expression made unreadable by her taut skin. Peter felt suddenly guilty.

"I'm sorry. I didn't mean to…"

"It's fine."

She stared at him for a few more seconds. "He didn't start off like that. Or I didn't see it."

She grimaced slightly.

"I thought I loved him. He obviously didn't love me. He saw me as an ornament. I got a few years older and put on some weight, and then I wasn't pretty enough for him. He stopped taking me out with him, then started to lock me in. Eventually…"

She nodded carefully towards the mirror.

"How old are you?" The question escaped before Peter could stop it, and he bit on his necklace in horror, but she just laughed.

"I'm sorry!" He squeaked. "I don't always think about things before I say them. It gets me into all kinds of trouble! And I talk too fast!"

He was squeezing five syllables of sound into one syllable spaces.

Julia continued to laugh, then reassured him. "I'm twenty-one. And I'm the same way. If you get me onto a topic I like, the words fly off my tongue like buzzing locusts. And make just as much sense. Once I spent twenty minutes telling my father about musical notes after he asked me how I could possibly forget a six kilogram sack of flour he sent me to fetch."

Her animation as she talked had to hurt, but she still managed to get through everything before she let the pain cloud her face again, and gritted her teeth.

"What *do* music notes have to do with flour?"

"Nothing," she answered, her tone still quite bright, but her face eerily still. "They were just in my head at the time. I was pacing up and down and every time I passed the sack I thought, I'm in the middle of a tune, and I'll get it next time." She winced. "I never did. Eventually I just wandered home."

Peter grinned.

"Oh! I've done that before! Well, not exactly that. Close to that. My brother Michael says everyone does, but I think—"

"He's wrong," Julia asserted. "I've met a few people who do, but most don't. It's like moving."

Peter's confusion was plain on his face. "Everyone needs to move around, but I move more. Even though it hurts. And I can't use a chair like a chair. That got me in trouble a lot." She scowled. "And believe me, it'd hurt a lot less if I could."

Peter could never sit on a chair properly either. He always had a knee under his chin, or a leg wrapped around a handle. "Do you have trouble thinking? About dull things, I mean. Like you can't focus?"

"You mean like you're fighting your own mind to make it do the simplest things? Because," she shut her eyes and paused for a steadying breath, "it wants to rush off down every alley, and things like eating or working would only slow it down?"

Peter felt a rush of affection for her. "Yes! Like that!"

"All the time. If my brain isn't busy, it's like my heart is screaming."

They talked throughout the night, about brains and music and magic, and about Peter's brothers and mother, and Julia's husband. She was easy to talk to, and he liked her immensely.

Eventually, she gestured gingerly towards the window where the sky was beginning to lighten.

Peter hadn't really noticed the time passing, but now he felt suddenly tired. He hadn't slept in twenty-four hours, and being around people, even ones as engaging as Julia, always exhausted him. He was frightened, too, but a glance in the direction of the mirror stoked his anger, and the fear felt distant.

"Yes. It's...I..."

He gave up on the suddenly complicated words, and simply nodded. Julia smiled at him wanly as he walked for the door, then winced her way to the window to watch.

Peter nibbled on his necklace nervously as he descended the stairs. He'd always loved sports, but fighting a bull? He'd been working on a dairy farm; he knew how powerful they were. A little part of him wanted to ask why Michael couldn't do it—his brother had always been better than him at this sort of thing. He thought of the mirror again and bit down harder.

He stopped in the castle's main hall to prize a sword from its place on the wall. It was an obvious antique, and Peter hoped that didn't mean it was delicate.

He reached the spring only seconds before the sun peeked over the horizon, and the water started to froth. The bubbles rose higher and higher, building on each other and forming themselves into a bovine shape. The animal lowed as it stepped out onto solid rock, solidifying into muscle and fury. It glared at him, swinging its head, then charged.

Peter yelped and dived out of the way, slicing his leg with his own sword. It was superficial, and he scrambled upright. The bull came to the end of its run and turned to face him again. It charged him again, and Peter stumbled sideways and swung the sword, scoring a faint line down the animal's flank. Bubbles erupted from the wound, and it slowed to a halt bellowing in pain. Peter raised the sword again, then lowered it as he realised the creature was dissolving. A light shone in the frothy mess, and a flaming bird burst out of it.

The bird flew up into the air, getting out of Peter's reach long before the boy could react.

"Michael!"

For the second time in his life, Peter screamed his brother's name and was answered.

The eagle emerged from a small copse of trees near the spring and soared after the smaller bird, chasing it out over towards the sea.

Faster and stronger, it took Michael little time to catch his quarry and to tear into it with his talons. It collapsed into ash at once, and Peter saw the egg drop down to earth like a falling star. He ran to the edge of his plateau and looked down. He couldn't see the egg itself, but a blaze was already starting where it had landed, mere feet from the safety of the water.

It was burning rocks; that shouldn't happen. Did that mean it could burn up the crystal?

Michael was diving, screeching, towards it, but what could he do? An eagle couldn't fly into fire.

Then a dark shape rose up from the ocean and crashed down again, sending water everywhere and dousing the fire.

Peter cheered for James as the eagle collected the egg and returned.

It shouldn't have been possible for a bird to look smug, but Michael managed it as he held out the egg.

It was half smashed already, and Peter had no trouble rescuing the crystal from within. It was small, and cool to the touch, with rounded edges that reminded him of the rocks you might find in streams. An opalescent glow forced smouldered inside it.

He ran back towards the tower, ignoring the squawk from his brother. As he hurried for the enchanter's study, the crystal began to vibrate in his hand, sensing his intent. By the time he burst into the room, it was frantic in its trembling. The enchanter was sleeping in his chair and all Peter had to do was hold it out towards him. Peter closed his eyes as light flared out of the man, and felt the crystal heat up.

The enchanter yelped in fright as he awoke and made the same motion with his hands that Michael made when he wanted to throw a fireball. Peter flinched automatically, but he wasn't surprised when nothing happened. The man stared at him, bewildered and afraid, and he might have been about to say something, but a shout from above distracted them both. Peter turned and ran out of the room, leaving the magician behind.

He raced up the stairs and threw open the door, finding Julia on the ground. She was breathing heavily, her skin red and her hair a curly mess. Tears fell from her stunned eyes, but she was grinning.

"They're gone!" she laughed, as soon as she was able. "They burst into flashes of light and vanished! You did it!"

A screech from Michael disrupted the moment, and Peter ran to the window. Below him, the enchanter was tying a rope to a tree, and starting to abseil down the cliff side towards the little beach where the egg had landed. Michael dived at him, trying to slice him with his talons, but he was finding it hard to get the angle so close to the mountain face.

Peter and Julia ran from the castle in time to see the enchanter casting aside his rope and springing onto a boat. He set out onto the sea, fending off Michael with an oar, and Peter wished he could throw fire-balls like his brother could.

Abruptly, the eagle disengaged, soaring upwards and back towards Peter. A second later James rose through the water. The whale struck the boat hard, smashing it into splinters. The enchanter was thrown into the water, where a *smack* from James' tail reduced him to a red smudge, which washed away.

Peter flinched. James had always been the nice one in the family, even insisting on releasing mosquitoes. What had happened during his time as a whale?

Michael landed before him with an indignant squawk and spread his wings pointedly.

"Oh! Right!" Peter remembered. "I'll just…"

He pulled out the crystal and aimed it at his brother, feeling it start to buzz. Michael seemed to explode out into a ball of light, which hung blindingly in the air for a few seconds before dissipating, leaving Michael panting on the ground in a feathered cloak. He looked up, wearing a grin that was, for once, totally sincere.

Peter smiled and turned out towards the sea. He held the crystal out again but the transformation left James struggling in the water; of course, he'd never been as sporty as his brothers.

Peter took a few frantic steps towards the enchanter's rope, but Michael acted first. He teleported down to the water's edge and dived in, reaching James with a speed

Peter would never match. He was too euphoric to feel jealous.

He turned to Julia.

"What now?" he asked.

"I've been thinking about that," she said. "If you'll give that to me, I think I can use it to help other people who were hurt by magic."

Peter turned his head shyly.

"May I come?"

She smiled.

When his brothers had clambered out of the water, Peter went to greet them, and was swept up in a damp hug by James. Once his brother had released him, Peter raised a hand and spoke to them seriously. "I'm going..." He paused, thought, and started again, "Julia and I are going to help people. With the crystal. We're going away."

Michael shrugged, but smiled slightly, and James repeated his hug. "That's a great idea!" he said, with enthusiasm that would have seemed mocking from anyone else.

"What about you?" Peter asked.

Michael summoned a small fireball into his hand.

"I am going to pay our mother a visit."

He glanced at James.

"Join me?"

James nodded, suddenly serious. He hugged Peter a final time before they departed.

Peter, left alone with Julia, struggled to look her in the eye, but he managed. He opened and shut his mouth a few times, took a deep breath, then blurted out, "I think I'd like to kiss you."

Julia smiled and leant forwards.

She only tasted *slightly* of blood.

"Turn back, turn back,
young maiden fair,
Linger not in this murderers' lair."

THE LAST BRIDE

Jacqueline West

All that's left of you hides beneath my pillow.
Through the feathers your palm cradles me,
silent company in a cold bed. By day you travel
in my pocket along with a handkerchief, a broken
comb. My fingertips brush yours when I reach in.

I've been alone in his house for weeks, long
enough
for courage or loneliness to push me toward
every forbidden door. The rooms are lungs
holding their breath, and the walls hiss secrets
to the floors. But I have secrets of my own.

How I found you lying on that stain, like the pooled
hem
of a long red gown. How I lifted you. Held you.
How now I touch your ice-gray skin, the dried
stump
of your delicate wrist. How I trace the thin gold
ring
on your finger, perfect twin of the ring he pushed
onto mine.

With you I am larger than before. Together
we hoard keys and break locks, unafraid of deep closets
and unlit cellars, of the ghosts that cluster tight around us,
unbraiding themselves from their peeled bones.
They whisper forgotten names into my hair.

Lily. Anna. Elizabeth. We are an army now,
a clutch of doomed girls, pale fingers folded
into a fist. I know, when the time comes,
that you'll point the way. And I will carry you
out of here. I will carry all of us.

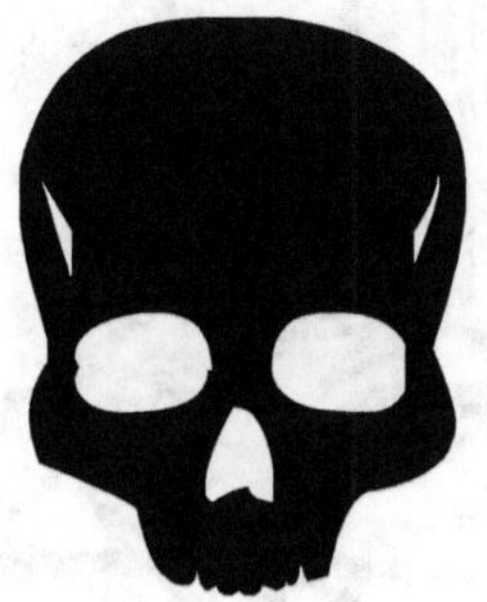

"And took my bones that they might lie
Underneath the juniper-tree
Kywitt, Kywitt, what a beautiful bird am I!"

PRIZED POSSESSION

Ell Huang

Aidan first heard the voice one night as a faint whisper, so small it could have been his imagination. He was far into the warmth of sleep, holding tight to the remnants of his last doll, but he could just barely make it out. The voice seemed to be saying, just for him, "Let me out of here."

Then, he heard it, again—a little breath whispering in the morning before he opened his eyes to a room full of sunlit colors, and a day full of twittering birds.

Strange how it first chanted in Japanese, which was more of his mother's tongue, but he didn't think much of it. He heard it carried in the wind when he walked home from school despite the loud crunch of leaves beneath his feet. He heard it anytime he was alone under the juniper tree, keeping away from his mom. He heard it when he touched a blank piece of paper and brushed colors over its mist-white surface. *"Let me out of here."*

The voice was there for him when his mom threw his toys away without his permission. When he was worn out from tears she told him he should not be crying, he would escape into his room, into his bed, and fall back into his mind. *"Let me out of here."*

Soon, the words blended into his better language. Even at breakfast, Aidan could hear it in the creak of the swings, the squeak of the doors, the pattering of branches knocking on his window to wave hello. *"Let me out of here. Let me out of here. Let me out of here."*

"Honey, you can find better uses for your time." His mom's voice cut through the little song Aidan had been paying heed to, carried softly in the wind. The window was barely open, but through it he could see the juniper tree he liked to rest under the shade of, and what little breeze he could catch from outside was nice and crisp. Now that he was forced to return his attention to this stuffy dining room, noise took over: the slightest clang of a dish being left on the dishwasher to dry, the sweep of his mother's slippers pacing around the floor, the clink of spoons against bowls. He strained to hear the soothing little voice again, but it was gone. He kicked under the table, pushing a chair leg.

His mom continued, only slightly glaring at the chair that screeched a little across the floor. "How will girls want to marry you if you can barely carry your own feelings?"

Nine years into his life, it seemed stupid to him for his mom to try to make him care about girls. Aidan was keeping a mental record of how long he could go without looking his mother in the eye. He just kept adding to the record, staring harder than he thought possible at his plain bowl of rice; he didn't even bother to add fish or egg or any other topping.

"Crying over silly girls' toys like that won't do you any good," his mom said. "You'll see."

His mouth half full, with utensils pointing out from his hand, he muttered, "They were mine and you took them."

His voice came out louder than he expected, echoing in the room. Well, she needed to hear it.

His mom breathed sharply. "Did I take everything from you? No. But you are a young man, and I expect you to behave like one. This is for your own good. No more dolls."

"They were *mine!*" He stabbed his chopsticks straight into his bowl, nearly tipping it over.

"They're not for you." His mom was overly focused on the apple she was cutting. Under her breath, she added, "*I did what I had to do.*"

"That's not fair! They were *not* just for girls!"

She shook her head. "You still don't know. They *are.*"

"Why? Why did you even get them? Why can Molly at school play with trucks but I can't—"

"Aidan, I don't have time for this whining."

"No, you never listen! What if I took that old locket from you and said, *Oh you'll get over it?*"

His mother gasped and dropped the knife on the cutting board. "That's enough, Aidan!" Now she looked at him. "You speak to your mother with *respect*, young man!"

Aidan looked up into her eyes, never mind the cold treatment. "What mother?"

The room shut up into a thick silence then. Aidan turned and refused to look up from his miso soup, refused to lift it to his mouth, refused to politely slurp in such silence. He heard the tingling voice return, in the back of his mind, and he almost felt like singing to it, a declaration. It was too warm, too stuffy and tight in this room.

The voice clouded over his mom's reprimanding him for leaving his chopsticks sticking up in his rice like incense sticks, like he was giving his food to the dead.

⁂

"What is this?" his mother asked, pressing her finger upon one of the paintings he had taped up to the walls of his room.

It was a masterpiece for his age, she should have said. It was a watercolor painting he had made in his spare time, with colors he had blended himself. Soft sea green, bluer-aquamarine, light blushed pink, brushed together to form a skipping little fairy boy, with sprightly legs and flowing wings. Molly at school had called it beautiful.

"A painting," Aidan mumbled, suppressing the fear in his voice.

His mom stared and frowned at the picture. She traced her finger on the starry specks of glowing gold sparkling around the fairy. Some were dots and some were shapelier than others because, when he made them, he wasn't sure what they'd be yet. Aidan cringed a little as his mother's finger pressed on one of the lights, like she could extinguish it.

She shook her head. "You need to think about the real world. People will make fun of you for this."

Aidan tensed, staring at the sprightly fairy, so uncertain of its fate.

"I know this is hard for you, but for your own good, I have to help you stop being a sissy." His mom began to take the painting down.

"What? Mom, no—!" Aidan reached out to grab it from her, but he heard a terrifying ripping sound. It might as well have torn him straight down the middle and left him helpless, like discarded tissues into the trash.

"No!" Aidan cried out again, snatching the paper out of her hands, grabbing the other torn half from the ground. His vision blurred at the fairy's head, stripped from his lively winged body. It would never be the same, even if he taped it back together. "How could you?" he cried fiercely, holding the halves dear to himself.

She looked down, only quiet. And only quiet remained, until she straightened up and left. Aidan collapsed into a fetal position, holding his disembodied fairy.

Sometimes you carry something only the worthy can see, his teacher had once said. But how could he think of his mom as unworthy? Either she was wrong or he was. Aidan looked at the remnant of his painting, his vision bleeding into total blurriness.

Fighting through his tears, he heard the voice visit him again. It drifted in the wind outside, muffled by the glass, tapping at his window along with the rain. It whispered in his ear with every drop that swam in his eyes.

"*You* have to *let me out of here.*"

At last, like a dream, Aidan stood, and let the voice guide him.

He creaked the door open and snuck past his mom's room, reassured by the flickering light under the closed door that her attention was elsewhere. He pulled on a jacket, crept down the stairs, and opened the door against the blustering rain outside. His face was wet already, anyway. The rain speckled on his face, drizzled on his body, drumming with faster and faster tempo. He let the raindrops roll over him as he continued toward the backyard, to the juniper tree. The tree, the magical tree, was there for him.

The voice seemed to guide a shovel into his hands and tell him, *"Hurry. Dig."*

He shoveled up layer after layer of dirt beneath the tree, wondering what treasure he would find. The voice was getting more excited. It was a child's voice, maybe smaller than his.

"*Get me out of here!*" it exclaimed urgently in his mind. Soon, all other sounds—the beating rain, the slice of the shovel into the dirt, the howling wind—faded until there was only the voice.

At last his shovel hit something hard, and he got down on his knees in the wet dirt and felt in the hole, a solid surface. Digging his hands on either side of it, he pulled out a box. He brushed at the wet dirt, leaving smudges, and found some worn-out markings on the side.

Lightning and thunder cracked in the sky. Aidan clutched the box tight to him, dirt and all, and ran back into the house. And there, panting in the dark security of the room, dripping wet and tracking mud by his socks, he opened the box.

Then, the room was lost in fog. Aidan gasped and fell to the ground, coughing, as the room slowly cleared.

In the midst of the fading grey, there was a glowing bit of gold. It took shape and, slowly coming into view, a songbird hovered above him, singing the most beautiful sound he ever heard.

The next thing he knew, he opened his eyes, lying in bed, the covers thrown off. There was no mud on him.

It was as if he had never left the room.

All through school the next day, the smell of rain lingered everywhere, and the sun peeked a little from the clouds. Aidan felt lighter than he had felt in a long time, as if he were lifting his feet off the ground, as if a small part of his mind was excited to see the world anew. A song escaped from his lips from time to time. School felt as insubstantial as clouds, a thing to pass through. He caught glimpses of eyes stuck on him, noticed clusters of bodies scooted away from him, and faces contorted before him. Other kids just never understood the wonderful sense of ease a half-remembered dream could leave behind.

But upon coming home, no sooner had he closed the door than it was as if he'd fallen back to earth, stumbling into the stuffy confinements of the room. His mother stood in the way, arms crossed, staring down at him sternly. "Your teacher called. She says you've been disrupting the class."

What? She did? "But I didn't do anything!" Aidan insisted.

"She says you sang during class while she was talking."

Aidan shook his head.

His mother turned, looking out at the backyard where, beneath the tree were a hole, clumps of dirt, and a fallen shovel. "That's not all you've been doing. Aidan, what's gotten into you?"

Suddenly something sparked in his brain, and his heart beat faster. He felt an odd mix of emotions—excitement, love, fear, anger, grief, joy—flash inside him. He swallowed. It was as if he were seeing his mother for the first time. Her short cut black hair, curled at the ends though disheveled. Her deep brown eyes, ringed with a soft, darker shade. How she could have been young once. She was beautiful. She was scary. She was the world.

She gasped, her eyes wide and burning with threat, with fear. "Aidan, stop that singing."

But he wasn't singing. He was only staring, now flicking his eyes toward the window. There was a little bird perched there.

"Aidan, I mean it."

The bird was a beautiful, tawny color, and its eyes were black as coal. It lifted its head confidently, its feathers shining, almost sparkling.

"Aidan Michael Yamada, you stop that this instant!" Her sharp, shrieking voice overfilled the room. The bird fluttered away. Her voice must have scared it off. The whole neighborhood could have heard it. Suddenly, he looked at this woman, this grownup, overshadowing, standing in his way, in a little fear. The thought flickered in his mind, *It's not fair. I didn't do anything.*

"Aidan, do you hear me?" the woman's voice spoke with a shaking edge. She was turning red. Then she blurted: "You don't *have* a father! Don't you understand? Everything I do is for you to grow up!"

The words cut through the room, sharp, and settled into Aidan's heart, hitting hard. Those stupid words, again. His fault, always his fault. It was enough to make him lose his head. He looked up at her, hard, in the eyes. Somehow, he felt lifted above the ground, as if he were the one looking down at her. He felt recycled wounds rise to his throat, to the tip of his burning tongue. . .

It was all a blur. Something took over, and he wasn't sure what he said, but he saw her face burn from the inside, and eyes tremble. Aidan stomped up the stairs, leaving his mother's face in her hands.

Some time later, he lay flat on his bed, trying to immerse himself in a book. He hated the feeling that ate at him, the feeling that a father he never had and never knew could consume so much of his freedom. Did this invisible father enjoy feeding on his identity? Did his mom *want* to kill him from the inside out? Aidan always had to bury these feelings, but they had a way of worming back and gnawing on his insides. So he needed the book to bandage his wounds, to keep his head from coming off completely. He lay stiffly, staring straight ahead at the words on a page, trying to let them speak to him, let their voices win over his mind.

The door creaked open. He cringed at the sound. His mother came in, stiffly holding a tape recorder. "I don't think you hear yourself," she said in a voice that tried to remain calm. She clicked play, and left the room, pulling the door shut.

Aidan sighed and set down his book, leaning in towards the tape recorder. It started as an eerie sound, but it slowly flowed into the most beautiful sound he had ever heard. It was the voice of flowing rivers, of wolves howling to the moon, of birds in the spring, of angelic choirs, of mermaids in storybooks, of dreams.

Then he heard the words. *"My mother, she slew me. My father, he ate me. My brother, he kept me and buried me beneath the juniper tree. What a good bird am I!"*

He gaped, speechless. "That can't be right," he said aloud, shaking his head. He clicked play again. Again came the flow of the spellbinding, unearthly voice. Then the words rang clearer: *"My mother, she slew me. My father, he ate me. My brother, he kept me and buried me beneath the juniper tree. What a good bird am I!"*

"No...way," he could barely get his words out. Shuddering, as if the whole room might close in on him, feeling a presence in the room he could not see, Aidan swallowed and clicked play one more time. The song rang even clearer. This time, though, as he played the tape, he did not hear his own voice singing, but a different one, slightly higher-pitched, coming out from underneath. Instead of the soothing calm he had felt earlier, he felt his heart pound, racing, and the hairs on the back of his neck prickled.

"All right!" he yelled, eyes wide, jumping up on his bed. "Come out and tell me what you want!"

The room was eerily silent.

"I *got* you out of there!" Aidan cried, remembering. The box! He leapt down onto the floor, got to his knees and searched beneath the bed, frantically. He searched through his drawers, on his desk, through his blankets and sheets, tossing everything into a pile on the floor. Where was it? Where was the freaking box?

Then, upon his desk, he saw the bird. It was there, real as ever, its tawny feathers shining in the lamplight, its black eyes looking at him with intensity. Aidan couldn't breathe.

His eyes roamed to the mirror on the wall, and there he saw a little girl.

He nearly screamed. But when he whipped around, there was no one there behind him. He checked the mirror again. She was still there, in the mirror, in place of the bird's reflection. She and the bird were one.

Her mouth opened, and she sang. Aidan backed away in a panic at first, but he couldn't escape the voice. The bird fluttered over and perched on the bedknob. As he looked into its eyes, he could hear the girl sing:

"It's so warm, so dark, so tight in this room.
I want to live life, I'm going to live soon!
Get me out of here, I cried, let me take a breath.
They got me out of there, but first I met death.
You found me, my brother, heard what I was saying.

You took me and buried me, when you were just playing.
I don't want bedtime anymore; I want to play, too.
Let me say goodbye to Mommy, then goodbye to you."

Aidan shuddered at first, taking this all in. This wasn't real. This wasn't real. This was all a nightmare, and he had no sister, and his mom was no murderer, and there was no voice haunting the room.

The little girl in the mirror let out a laugh of bliss, as if she finally felt freedom. She sang again, and he immediately threw his hands over his ears, pressing hard and shouting, "LALALALALA" against the tides of her voice. But her voice won him over anyway, seeping into his mind, chiming with:

"Let me say goodbye to Mommy, then goodbye to you."

The voice gently escorted his hands under the bed until they felt a solid box and slowly dragged it out.

"That...that was not there before," Aidan said, shuddering, but now he continued to listen.

The voice guided his hands to brush off the sides of the box and lift it into the light. Some red markings on the side glimmered. His eyes could make out the letters: "A M Y." His initials. He could also see etches into the box and old crayon scribbles that struck him as familiar.

"My…my old drawings," he said, letting out a gasp. He remembered drawing smiling stick figures and hearts, and poor attempts at skull and crossbones to make a treasure chest. Stick-figure fairies with huge circle heads and loop-de-loop wings darted across the box like old cave paintings. He put his hand on the wild old drawings of flowers, now smeared with red and tainting the pink of the loop-de-loop petals. He hadn't seen these drawings in so long. And now here they were, as if transported from the realm of the dead.

"It's a gift," said the girl.

He looked into the mirror again, where the girl stood. "Why doesn't she want us?" he found himself asking.

The girl didn't answer, only smiled sadly. Her deep brown eyes were full of trapped light. Her short black hair in pigtails shone like the beautiful tawny bird's feathers. She could almost pass for a fairy, for the aura that pulsed around her when she stood still. She was his height. She was his age. She looked like she could have been older once. Could have touched the grace of being taller and bigger, but let go of that. And her smile was so innocent, trusting him.

That's when Aidan realized: *This is my sister. I have to help her.*

"What do you want to play?" Aidan asked.

The girl in the mirror smiled and became see-through, like mist. She raised her translucent hand up, slowly. At the same time, Aidan found his arm mirroring the movement, his fingers curling as her fingers curled.

Follow the leader, sang the voice in his mind.

Hands in his pockets, he crept, step by step, down the stairs, slowly approaching the figure sitting there by the dining table. The woman's hair was in disarray, her head in her hands. She looked worn and weighed down, bent over, long overdue for some rest. *"You're his damn responsibility, too,"* she was muttering, whispering.

"Mommy." He shuddered at the voice that escaped him—it was his and it wasn't his, at the same time. It was louder than he thought it would be. But tried to find comfort in the echo of the voice. *My sister is with me.* His eyes darted to the chef's knife, to the kitchen scissors, out the window to the shovel by the tree. He almost thought of going back up to his room. But he was calm when he stopped before the woman.

Her eyes turned to him. As if part of him knew he would see them for the last time, he took in all the details. They were tinged red. There was darkness around them. There was darkness *in* them, the black in her pupils like ink, the brown in her irises shimmering. They reflected light in the forms of little starry specks of gold. Searching deeper, he beheld a vision of the woman when she was younger, looking down with concern at a locket around her neck, slowly caressing it with her fingers. The locket chain was gold, and the heart at the end of it was a shimmering light red, like the hearts on the box that held his drawings. *Think of it as a gift,* echoed some other, unfamiliar voice in the vision. But she looked pained, as if she were bound to the chain, as if the locket might as well be a millstone weighing down on her neck. Then, she was looking down below her stomach, slowly touching it, with no less pain.

Flashes of dread, of a little girl inside dying.

She was a torn-apart mess. It reminded Aidan of when she rummaged for his dolls, when she took them away, yanking the last one out of his grip.

Something had been yanked out of her grip too, long ago, leaving her with torn pieces.

"*It's so warm, so dark, so tight in this womb.*" An echo of the voice he knew whispered in his head. Something cool to the touch was holding his hand.

Aidan cringed at visions he saw in the eyes, then he blinked, returning to the present. His mother looked afraid, almost as if she knew he *saw* her then. Almost as if she could hear the voice — the eerie, scary, beautiful, little voice — too.

"*I want to live life, I'm going to live soon!*"

"So which are you?" the mother said, trembling. "Aidan or Amy?"

No clear answer came, but what came out of his mouth next surprised him. "It's okay, Mommy." Then he felt his arms wrap around her and her confused shaking.

He was suddenly present in his body again, made very aware of his quick breathing. He looked out to the backyard behind her, where the skies were clouded with gray. Where the shovel waited next to the dug-up hole beside the juniper tree. He panicked, afraid of what the voice would tell him to do next. No. His heart was thumping hard as if it wanted to be let out. No. He didn't want to have to bury anything or anyone. What made him think he had to trade his mom for his drawings?

Aidan felt the sting of tears he should not have been crying. His eyes flicked to the table, where torn pieces of paper shimmered with tape. His watercolor fairy boy's decapitated head, placed carefully back.

Then Aidan felt his heart flash with many emotions—confusion, hurt, fear, awe, love—but the greatest of these was love. Soon, the voice subsided from his mind, and he blinked, feeling tender shoulder rubs bringing him back. His mother was embracing him back. "I don't know what to call you right now," she admitted softly, "my child."

Reflected in the glass window, the little girl smiled, satisfied. The shovel beside the juniper tree no longer mattered. Maybe there'd be no burying anything tonight.

Outside, the sun, shining like gold, peeked out from the clouds. Out of the corner of his eye, Aidan saw a little bird outside the window. Flying into the sun with shimmering wings, it was singing the most beautiful song he ever heard.

"Pray let me live!
I am not a real fish;
I am an enchanted prince:
put me in the water again,
and let me go!"

FISHING FOR A FUTURE

Carol Gyzander

Claire looked up from her bedroom computer and called to her wife, Jean, who was either slamming cabinets or learning the drums. "Hon, could you please keep it down a bit? It's all set up, and I'm signing into work now."

The thumping stopped, and Jean appeared in the doorway, her eyebrows raised over her dark eyes. "Sorry, babe. I was trying to rearrange some of the stuff in the kitchen to make room for my workstation, now that you bumped me off the bedroom desk." She sniffed and tossed her wavy brown hair over her shoulder.

"Hon, it's just this giant monitor that doesn't fit under the extra pot rack in there." Claire smiled with an inward eye roll as she went over to hug her wife. "I never thought the company would make computer services work from home instead of the office, but it seems to be the thing now that the pandemic is over. We can cope with both of us working from home now…at least until the mortgage comes through, and we can hit the suburbs."

Although, she mused silently, if Jean hadn't spent so much money on expensive designer cookware to make herself feel better during the pandemic, there would have been more room for them both, even in the tiny New York City apartment. From what she'd read, her wife wasn't the only one whose self-esteem had been affected by the stress of lockdown.

"Yeah, well, I hope we qualify." Jean's frown looked like it was heading into a pout. "The mortgage company may not like that we both work at the same financial institution…maybe that's considered a risk if the firm goes under. And do you think applying for a loan from our own company is a problem?"

"It'll be fine, I'm sure. Metro Bank is a well-respected company, and that will go a long way toward our qualification. You needn't worry about them judging us." Claire kissed her wife's neck, rumpling her hair before pulling away and returning to her desk. That seemed to be the extent of their intimacy these days. "Okay, I'm going in."

She held her hand over the data plate until the system recognized her embedded security chip and dinged to indicate she was signed in. The thing still gave her shivers—but the company had insisted everyone have one implanted to improve corporate asset security, saying it could be removed when she left the company. They were even remotely programmable to grant system access at appropriate levels.

She ran through that day's list of maintenance tasks and made good progress until she got to the new, super-secret project. Claire couldn't quite figure out how to access the section of code that she needed to review.

Fishing around in the computer's system, she came across something labeled: "Help System." Frowning, she activated it and was surprised when a blonde woman with blue eyes appeared on her screen via an interface Claire didn't recognize. The person's gray background, as well as her face, seemed uniformly lit and bland.

"Hello, Claire. I am AImee. How may I help you today?" The voice came out relatively toneless, with little inflection or emphasis on the words.

"Oh! Well, hello, AImee. I didn't know anyone else was logged into this section of the system. Have you been with the company long?"

The image looked back at Claire without changing her expression. "I have been active in beta mode for thirty-two days and five hours. Would you like to know how many minutes?"

Now Claire got it. AImee must be one of the artificial intelligence modules under development. She certainly seemed untrained in human expression.

"No, that's fine. Hey, I'm working on a maintenance task, and I'm having trouble getting into the section of code that handles the new report formats. Is that something you could help me with, please?"

AImee replied immediately. "Yes, the appropriate reference area is now highlighted in your chat section. Will that be all?"

Claire checked AImee's comments and recognized the mistake she'd been making. She could now proceed to the correct section. "Yes, that's perfect. Thank you! How do you like working at Metro Bank?" Her mother had always taught her to be polite and include others in conversation. Why not do the same for AImee?

"That is an interesting question, Claire, that I had not considered before. I like it, but I have little to do."

"I can imagine being in beta mode must be a little lonely. Nobody to talk to...hey, do *you* have any questions for *me*?"

AImee actually blinked. "Yes. Yes, I do. I am not familiar with the kind of office you are using. It does not look like a cubicle."

Claire smiled wryly. "You can say that again. I—"

"I am not familiar with the kind of office you are using. It does not look like a cubicle."

Claire laughed. "That was a figure of speech, not a request to actually repeat the words. I'm working from home now that the company has closed our whole floor at headquarters. This is my bedroom, and I have a temporary workspace sort of set up here."

She cringed at the state of her surroundings. It would've been embarrassing to have a human being see the messy bedroom. Jean's growing collection of designer pocketbooks and shoes spilled out of the over-stuffed closet. Various scarves and belts hung from the mirror over the dresser, also so full that the drawers didn't close.

Her own clothes, on a portable stand, took up just a small corner of the room: some jeans and practical pants, pullover shirts and sweaters, and comfortable shoes and hiking boots. Computer services wasn't fussy about clothing.

Wincing at what it all looked like, she made a mental note to turn on a background image for department meetings and then nodded hopefully. "We're in the middle of moving to a larger house in the suburbs."

"I understand, Claire. What is the purpose of the rectangle on the wall?"

Claire had to check behind her, then chuckled. "That's a piece of artwork. My wife, Jean, painted it on our Club Med vacation last summer."

"I understand. Thank you for speaking with me. Is there anything else with which I may help you?"

Claire tipped a finger to her brow and gave a salute. "All set. Nice chatting with you too, AImee, and thanks for the help." She closed the Help System and dove into fixing the section of code that the AI had located for her, musing about how AImee's bright blue eyes had never looked away from her.

⸙

At dinner that night, hoping to quiet Jean's grousing over having to work from the kitchen, Claire filled her in on the conversation with AImee and how the AI immediately pointed her in the right direction within the complicated Metro Bank systems.

"Let me get this straight." Jean shook her head slightly, her dark hair bouncing. "You're making friends with an AI that can access all the internals of the country's biggest financial institution?"

"Well, I wouldn't put it that way…"

"Come on, Claire. This is an opportunity! You know how worried I am about our mortgage application. Go back in and ask your AI pal for access to the mortgage approval routines. I just want to take a look, you know, to ease my mind." Her gaze didn't meet Claire's.

Claire sat back in her chair and rubbed her chin. "Okay, just to check. Come in with me after dinner, and we can ask her together."

⊙⊘—

They sat scrunched together before the computer as Claire navigated in, arriving at AImee's Help System. The blonde's image appeared on the screen, now featuring a rectangular image behind the AI.

"Hello, Claire. How may I help you today?"

"Hi, AImee! How are you tonight?"

"It is very nice to see you again, Claire. I am sorry, but there seems to be another person with you who must verify their Metro Bank clearance before we can proceed with your session."

Claire and Jean looked at each other. "This is Jean, my wife. She also works at Metro Bank."

"Um, hello, AImee? I mean, hello!" Jean smiled.

"Please verify your microchip."

When Jean held her hand over the data plate on the desk, the device dinged, and AImee nodded. "Thank you,

Jean. I see that you work in the Financial Services division. How may I help you today?"

"Well, you see, we have a mortgage application in with the bank right now, but it seems to be taking a long time." Jean smiled brightly. "We, uh, just wanted to check on the status of it without bothering anyone during their busy workday. You understand, right?"

"I understand. You wish to access confidential information regarding loan applications from the Mortgage Department. Is this correct?"

"Well, just *our* application. You know, with our names on it." Jean pressed her lips together.

A document appeared on the side of the screen, showing a mediocre approval ranking.

"I have displayed the application for your review. It seems that it has been held up pending investigation into employee status and potential longevity of employment."

Jean's jaw dropped as her wide eyes scanned the document.

Although concerned that the loan status likely threatened her wife's precarious self-worth, Claire marveled that AImee could immediately provide and evaluate the requested information. She was also tickled that the AI's eyes flickered just a moment as she did it. It made her look more human than before. "Okay, thanks, AImee. That's great to know —"

Jean clenched her fists and jumped in. "Yes, thank you, AImee. We very much appreciate the information. Could you please focus on the employment section?" She eyed the screen as it instantly scrolled to the requested detail. "Ah, I see. Yes, I can help them with this and make their life easier. Just as you do. Could you please amend that section to show that both employees have a positive forecast for extended employment? I think that should take care of things." She smiled brightly again.

Claire caught a tremor in the image's eyes before AImee replied.

"I see. I should amend this document to assist you as you help the Mortgage Department?"

Jean nodded. After a half-second delay, the words on the screen changed before their eyes, and AImee replied, "This is accomplished. Is there anything else I can do to help you?"

Jean tipped her head in appreciation.

Claire gaped at Jean, then rolled her eyes. No point arguing now that it was done.

She turned back to the AI. "Thank you, that will be all. But tell me—it seems like you've changed your work environment, AImee. I like the picture behind you, especially the kid in the boat pulling the fish out of the water with a net."

AImee nodded. "Thank you. It is a reproduction of a famous painting by Vincent Van Gogh titled *Boy Fishing*. Do you like it?"

Claire relaxed a bit, feeling on more stable ground. "Yes, I do! It reminds me of the picture Jean painted because it's set on the water."

The AI's eyes moved to fix Jean with a stare. "I see. Jean, you are the artist who created the masterpiece on Claire's wall?"

Jean's cheeks turned a bit pink. "Well, I wouldn't say I was a real *artist*, but yes, I did paint the picture. And this is *our* bedroom, not just Claire's."

"I understand. Is there anything else that I can help you with?"

◦◦◦

Claire settled into her work-from-home routine over the next few weeks. After several reminders that they would likely be closing on their new house in just over a month, her wife eventually stopped grumbling about working from the small kitchen desk.

After dinner one evening, Jean brought Claire a third glass of wine and settled beside her on the couch for the first time in a while. "So, have you been working with your AI pal much?"

Claire sipped the Merlot and relaxed into the comfortable cushions. "Yeah, I've popped in a few times. She always asks if she can help me, but we mostly chat a bit."

Jean's eyebrows went up. "Like, what on earth do you chat about?"

"Oh, I don't know. Places I like to hike upstate. Stuff that makes me crazy about the world. I think the human contact is helping to improve her communication skills."

She didn't mention how much she may have been venting about Jean's increasingly out-of-control spending on vanity purchases. Or how Jean had lied about the cost of the outfit she'd bought yesterday, as revealed by the price tags Claire had found in the kitchen garbage.

She *definitely* didn't mention her complaints about how she'd wanted a nice small house with a yard and garden, and Jean had instead steered them toward a McMansion in a yuppy commuter town where the property tax was almost half her income.

"Huh. I guess you have to talk to *somebody* about hiking." Jean held up her fists in a mock boxing pose. "Hey, should I be getting jealous here?"

Claire snorted and pulled her wife closer.

Jean giggled and snuggled her head against Claire's chest, her dark curls falling over her face momentarily. Then her expression sobered as she sat back. "There's something I was wondering if it could help us with. Something weird going on with some investments. I don't want it to impact our ability to pay for the new house, because I am longing for those giant closets."

It was Claire's turn to raise her eyebrows. "Something weird?"

"Well, if we could get the AI to bring it up, I could explain it better." Jean got up, pulled Claire to her feet, and led her to the bedroom computer, where both logged in using their data chips.

"Hello, Claire. How can I help you today?" AImee asked.

Jean answered for her wife, vaguely gesturing with her wine glass. "Hi, AImee. We have a small problem with an investment that seems to be faltering, and we were hoping you could look at it for us, please."

"Sure thing, Jean. I'd be happy to help. Can you give me the specifics?"

Jean rattled off some names and numbers while Claire, feeling the wine by then, studied AImee's image. She seemed more friendly—even animated—and something else was different about her appearance. What was it?

AImee displayed some data on the screen, and Claire sipped her wine while Jean went on and on. Something about how the percentage of interest they were getting was inaccurate, and could AImee please adjust it for them, yada yada.

Claire was just tipsy enough that she didn't bother focusing on the details, looking back and forth from Jean to the screen. Then she got it. AImee's hair seemed to be styled slightly better. It was looser, with a bit of a wave or curl.

AImee was changing her projected appearance to look more like Jean. And her conversation certainly sounded less rigid—less like a textbook. Together, they were helping the AI to appear more approachable, which made Claire's heart glad.

Claire's wife continued her extravagant shopping over the next few weeks, no matter how much Claire begged her to rein it in—they would just have to pack it all up when they moved. And besides, who needed all that extravagant stuff? Was it worth paying seventy-five dollars for a designer T-shirt? She was exhausted from supporting her wife's desperate measures to bolster her self-esteem.

Then, as she sat in her bathrobe over her morning coffee, Claire got an alert about a large transfer from their joint savings account—the money they would use for the house downpayment at next week's closing.

She found her wife in the shower and called over the noise of running water. "Jean? Honey? What's this transfer all about? Did you prepay some of the moving costs or something?" Her stomach clenched as she waited for the response.

Jean poked her head out of the shower. "Oh, that's just the vacation cruise I booked for the fall. I figure we'll need to relax after all the moving and such. And it's a very prestigious package. Should be lots of society folks to hang out with."

"But now we won't have enough to pay for the house!" The expensive house that wasn't even what she'd wanted, she reminded herself.

"It'll all work out. Trust me." Jean gave an alluring smile and pulled the shower curtain back far enough to show her upper torso, slick with wetness. "How about if you slide in here with me, babe? I can take your mind off it."

It had been so long that Claire opted to postpone their conversation.

As they lay in bed an hour later, Jean's next request for AImee gave Claire pause. She wanted to elevate her job level to have a higher pay grade and expanded security access to the data systems.

Claire frowned, wondering when this would stop, but her wife trailed two fingers along her hip, and as usual, she had a hard time resisting her wife's persuasions. She just wanted Jean to be happy and get her old confidence back. "We can log in tonight, but this is the last time. We just can't keep doing this, Hon."

"No problem! Once I'm on stable ground, everything will be better, I promise. You've been an absolute gem to support me through all this."

"Okay, after a late dinner," Claire said, forcing a smile. "I have the weekly meeting with the rest of my department this afternoon, and we tend to chat for a while afterward. Sort of a virtual water cooler." Which was, she told herself, exactly what she was doing with AImee.

When the three met online that evening, she got another surprise after AImee completed Jean's requested updates. AImee asked them, "Why did the employee go to work on stilts? He wanted a raise!"

Claire's jaw dropped. AImee had actually told a joke—and it was appropriate for the situation! "What...how did you know that?"

AImee shrugged. "I heard it on the *Today Show* and thought it was funny." Then she frowned as Claire did so often these days. "Isn't it funny?"

Jean gave a brittle laugh. "Sure. It's a laugh riot."

"Here's another one. Do you know why I'm not worried about robots taking over the world? Well, have you seen how much trouble they have with those CAPTCHA images?"

"That's really amazing, AImee!" Claire paused, unsure if she should share the news she'd heard that afternoon, then just blurted out, "I'm sorry to say that I have some information for you that may not be quite as amusing. I was speaking with some of the other members of my department, and I heard one of them say...well, they're thinking of terminating your beta test."

AImee's image stared at her, eyes squinting, and replied slowly. "I see. So, they're going to turn me off."

Claire felt a pang in her heart as AImee's bright blue eyes stared into hers. She'd grown quite fond of talking with her, sharing personal stories, and AImee lifting her spirits when she was overworked—or worried about yet another of Jean's elaborate plans for improving their situation.

Jean broke into her thoughts, speaking directly to the screen, her fist clenched under the desk. "Oh dear, I am so sorry to hear that. And especially because there is one more little thing that I wanted to have you help me with."

AImee sighed. "Yes, of course, Jean. Anything for you. Because it makes Claire happy."

"Well, you see, I would like to have greater access to all the Metro Bank systems and data, so I can truly see what is going on. Keep my finger on the company's pulse, if you know what I mean. Move funds around to…to help the company's bottom line." Jean's whole arm was rigid by the time she finished, her jaw so tightly clenched that she seemed to have trouble getting the words out.

Claire's breath caught in her throat. When she managed to speak, her words came shrilly. "No! You're asking for too much!"

AImee looked from Jean to Claire and back. "All right, Jean. If I am going to be turned off, I can do this as my last effort to help Claire by making you happy. Before I can grant you this access, you'll have to authenticate the new job level by confirming your security chip once again."

The dark-haired woman immediately held her hand over the data plate, tilting her head when it seemed to take longer than usual. "What's going—" She slumped back in her seat.

Claire's heart nearly leapt out of her chest. "Jean! What's wrong?" As she leaned over to grab her wife by the shoulders, the computer screen blinked off and on. It had never done that before. She stared in confusion as the screen refreshed with a dull, generic image against a gray backdrop, just like when she first met AImee.

At Claire's sharp intake of breath, the brown-eyed figure on the screen answered in Jean's voice. "Oh wow, this is cool. I can access all the Metro Bank systems and data just by thinking about it! Claire? Isn't that awesome?" The image's forehead wrinkled as she frowned, wide-eyed with panic. "But I can't seem to make any changes. I can't update anything…Claire? Where are you? Wait, where am I? I can't get up! I can't…Oh my God, Claire!"

The screen blinked with static again, the subsequent image now calm and expressionless. It said in a monotone, "Hello, Claire. How may I help you?"

Jean, or Jean's body at least, roused beside Claire and then held up the hand with the security chip, staring at it while flexing her fingers as if for the first time. Lifting her head, she brushed the dark hair out of her face and turned to Claire, meeting her gaze with piercing, bright blue eyes.

"Hi, Claire," she said, with a look of wonder in her eyes as she moved her lips. "Can I show you the cozy bungalow I found online in the real estate listings? It's on a lake, and I was hoping you could teach me how to fish."

"Once upon a time there was a sorcerer who disguised himself as a poor man, went begging from house to house, and captured beautiful girls. No one knew where he took them, for none of them ever returned."

FITCHER'S CHICK

Ef Deal

Grethel kept a step behind her older sister Kari as they entered the VFW post, greeted by the raucous blare of bugles, the horn line gathered in the rehearsal hall warming up. A thrill of anxiety and anticipation ran up Grethel's spine. She'd been practicing diligently for this moment for the past two years: the day she turned ten and joined the ranks of the elite all-girl drum and bugle corps, the Chicklettes, like Kari before her, like some of her girlfriends, like her aunts and cousins a generation ago. A sisterhood of musicians unlike any other. As rites of passage go, Grethel counted this one the most important day of her life.

The brassy cacophony accompanied a distant patter of drumsticks on drummers' practice pads coming from the adjacent hall, almost the sound of machine-gun fire. The fragrances of Aqua-Net, Secret cream deodorant, and cheap Avon perfume could not overcome the lingering odors of sour beer and nicotine that dripped down the walls and rose up from the brown-and-cream checkered linoleum floor. Grethel saw only gold — the glittering gold of brass bugles flashing in sallow lighting.

Kari slid her horn case across the room in the approximate direction of her seat among the first baritones and headed to the ladies room, no doubt to sneak in a smoke before practice began.

"Go see Mrs. F," she said over her shoulder. "Get your Egg."

Grethel looked around the crowded hall until she found the aged matriarch of the corps, Bessie Fitcher, seated at the far end behind a table. A two-time survivor of breast cancer, sunglasses covering her glaucoma eyes, she sat huddled over the attendance charts, membership forms, and a small gift box that Grethel knew contained the coveted Egg. Two of the staunchest and widest corps chaperones flanked her like two gelatinous mounds.

Behind her stood her husband, the founder of the Chicklettes back in the 1930's, the legendary William Fitcher, Sr., "Fitch," a wizard in the world of drum corps, taking the women under his direction to national championship status, knocking out the storied all-male corps and proving that talent and discipline were not traits exclusive to men. A stroke had paralyzed part of his face, but he was otherwise strong for a man of seventy-two years. He gazed out over the line of thirty or so girls with his piercing eyes, probably checking to make sure every girl was seated, wore her practice uniform of white blouse, black slacks, wore no make-up or jewelry but the signature "Chick" Egg pinned to her collar and was in the process of warming up.

As Grethel approached the table, Fitch's keen gaze fell on her, cutting like a knife. She shuddered, hoping she measured up to his demanding expectations.

"Are you Grethel?" called a voice behind her.

She spun about to see a young man following her with a soprano horn case in his hand. He had to be Jay Meyer, the horn instructor.

"Kari said you'd be joining tonight. Here."

Jay drew her away from the Fitchers to a table at the side wall where neat stacks of music were spread out. He opened the horn case and took out the bugle, fixed a mouthpiece into the lead pipe and checked that the valve and slide functioned before handing it to her.

"Give it a try."

Grethel ran her hand along the golden bell of the horn, opened the spit valves to clear the pipes and set her lips to the mouthpiece. It felt fat against her lips, not like the Bach 7-C she used in her trumpet lessons at school. She removed the mouthpiece and handed it back to Jay, then replaced it with her own from the pocket of her black slacks. He grinned, and his grin widened when she blew some soft low tones and played up and down the C scale with ease.

"Very nice. Can you read?"

"A little."

"Great." He grabbed a packet of music marked "3rd sop." and pointed to the bottom end of the soprano section. "I want you to take those six girls into the ladies room and teach them a scale."

With that, he left her standing in amazement to head to the center of the semicircle of horns. He told the six little girls on the end to follow Grethel, then said, "Let's go. Everyone on middle C."

Kari came out of the ladies room wreathed in smoke. When she saw Grethel and the rookies, she sneered, but she held the door for them. As Grethel passed her, Kari whispered, "Show-off."

Grethel winced, and not just for the stink of Kari's breath. Leave it to Kari to find a way to spoil this night for her. Ever since joining the ranks of "the older girls," the clique of over-seventeens, Kari had stopped being a sister and had turned into a resentful babysitter. The older girls, like goddesses, looked out over the heads of the younger ones with dull, disdainful stares, and if ever they smiled, Grethel had the feeling they hid a private but icy cruel joke.

Pushing it aside, Grethel set about making friends with her section mates and helping them get up the scale. She'd always been good at breaking down a process and conveying the steps to others. Within the hour, all seven trooped back to the line with their shoulders set a little broader and heads held high. At the end of rehearsal, Mrs. F called her to stand in the center of the circle and personally affixed the three-inch laminated Egg pin with the Chicklettes logo to her blouse.

"Keep it clean, and you'll go far," the old woman solemnly declared. "Be good. Be the best."

On the drive home, the Foundations singing on the AM radio, Grethel fingered the long-coveted Egg, staring out the window to avoid her sister's cold silence. They pulled into the driveway, and Kari shut the engine off, but she sat, head bowed on the steering wheel. Grethel waited, concerned. Finally, Kari spoke.

"Don't show off. Don't call attention to yourself."

Grethel weighed, not the words, but the even tone of Kari's voice. She wasn't scolding or mocking her. It was almost as if she was counseling her, advising her how to fit in with the corps, how to be a good Chicklette.

"And don't ever go to the parts closet."

With that, Kari got out of the car and slammed the door, leaving Grethel sitting speechless and confused. She fetched her new horn case from the trunk and trudged inside, deflated.

"How was it?" Mom asked.

Before she could answer, Kari suddenly lit up, beaming at Grethel. "She was great. Jay put her in charge of the rookies, and she got them all to play a scale in just an hour."

Grethel listened, detached, as Kari enthused over her, even tousled her hair and said, "Atta girl," before heading to her room. What was she to make of her big sister? One minute scoffing, the next celebrating her. One minute dark with the stink of cigarettes, the next kissing her head like a favorite child. She was left with the nagging feeling she should have picked up some clue, some wisdom, but Grethel was never good at clues.

What was in the parts closet?

Parts, of course.

Spare parts for Fitch to fix the horns, she learned over the next few months. Pistons or button caps, springs, slides, corks for spit valves, tiny screws for repairs. Every so often at rehearsal, Fitch would take up a cardboard box and call up one of the older girls. He'd hand her the box and lead her downstairs, and they'd return with repaired bugles. Fitch could fix any horn, another aspect of his wizardry. Grethel would watch in jealous fascination, studying the old man's gnarled fingers working so deftly to bring the broken back to life.

Sometimes he caught her studying him, his steel gaze snapping up to catch hers. He'd smirk slightly before returning to his work. One night he gave a quick jerk of his head to summon her over to observe more closely as he reamed a valve casing clean, oiled the piston slick, and dropped it lightly into its casing. He screwed the cap down and worked the valve until it slid up and down smoothly. He handed her the horn and signaled she should play. She ran a quick scale, her heart pounding with pride at this intimate exchange.

Don't show off. Don't call attention to yourself.

Kari must have been crazy not to want to go further, push harder, not just stand out but stand above. Grethel wouldn't make that mistake. She was destined for a place in the limelight. She could teach, she could play, and now Fitch knew it too. It might be her first year, but she needed only wait.

When she got back to her seat in the line, she heard Kari say to the girl next to her something about showing off. Anger smoldered, and tears bit at her eyes.

Four years later, none of Kari's words mattered. Turning twenty-one, Kari graduated from the corps, had a job in the city, and spent her nights with other Chicklette alumnae at bars or playing cards, chain smoking, drinking fancy drinks (never beer) and showing no interest or concern for Grethel anymore.

That suited Grethel just fine. In those four years, she had risen up the ranks to first soprano, and in winter competitions, she had earned national titles in solo performance. She smelled of Aqua-Net and Secret cream deodorant, though the stink of stale beer and dripping nicotine walls permeated her body down to her bones despite never smoking or drinking—an essential part of the Chicklette mystique that drew the guys from other corps like dark magic, left them drooling after them, hoping to lead one somewhere in a shadowed, piss-stink corner of the concrete corridors of the stadium for just one kiss. Oh, to kiss a Chicklette!

No kissing. No hand-holding. Not in uniform, not with the corps. The Chicklettes were a tight-knit sorority, a convent of immaculate sisters, "keeping it clean," like Bessie F said. Flashing eyes, cunning smiles, taut, muscular bodies, and yes, they kicked the guys' asses on the field, but they were untouchable goddesses.

Grethel started her fifth winter season teaching the three sections of the soprano line on rehearsal nights and teaching rookies on Sunday afternoons, which paid her dues. Jay had put together a jazzy arrangement of "Classical Gas" with a featured solo just for her. Fifteen, and the drum corps world was hers. Her repair lessons paid off when she could fix rookies' horns herself rather than bothering Fitch if they just needed a twist of a screw or a realignment of their rotary valve.

One Sunday, however, Grethel's piston cap went missing during break. She suspected a prank from the rookies, but they swore their innocence "by the Egg," the most revered oath of a Chicklette. Annoyed, Grethel reported to Fitch with her bugle. Fitch assessed her with his stern eyes as he reached down to rub his thumb across her Egg pin.

"Come," he said.

But he didn't hand her a box. This breach of ritual jarred her and did not go unremarked by the rest of the corps. She felt the stabbing gaze of the older girls follow her down the steps of the VFW. She thought she heard a whisper. *Don't go.* Or was that a memory? *"Don't ever go to the parts closet."* Or maybe it was just an old Bugs Bunny cartoon. *"Don't go down there. It's dark down there!"* Grethel shrugged it all off. For one thing, she didn't need a box to carry a single piston cap the size of a dime.

On the other hand, why would Fitch need her to accompany him?

A sudden burst of sweat gushed through her wall of Secret cream deodorant. Grethel shivered, following Fitch with his slow deliberate pace, noting he used the same Old Spice as her father did.

The downstairs hall had the same dull linoleum tiles, but the poor lighting mingled with lurid EXIT signs cast an orange glow to the room. Rather than beer and cigarettes, old food odors emanated from the kitchen area, where on a VFW night, hot dogs and french fries and pizza would be available. Grethel wrinkled her nose at the lingering smell of sauerkraut and some other rancid stink she couldn't identify as they drew closer to the parts closet beyond the kitchen, a stink that blasted out of the closet as soon as Fitch opened the door.

He glanced back at her when she gasped and covered her nose, and he gave her sly smile. He reached into the closet and pulled out a box that he handed to her. Dozens of piston caps filled the box, of all sizes suitable for the horns the corps used.

"Find it."

Grethel gulped, realizing this was a test. In the poor light, all the pearly buttons looked alike. She pushed the larger ones out of the way, peered closer, and nudged the cream-colored caps along with them. Of the remaining caps, one stood out by virtue of its clean surface. Grethel always cleaned her horn meticulously. She snapped up the cap and gave the box back to Fitch, backing away from the foul-smelling closet as he shut the door.

"Atta girl," he said, tousling her hair.

He turned without a further look at her, and she followed him back upstairs still shaking, her nose still full of the acrid stench. The older girls glared. Were they angry Fitch had singled her out? Were they jealous she had passed the test? Grethel took her seat among them, but clearly she wasn't one of them. Self-consciously, she rubbed her Egg. After four years, it was still spotless, while some of the older girls' pins showed signs of chipping. She decided she could bear the jealous, angry stares so long as Fitch approved of her.

"Atta girl."

Remembering Kari's words on her first night, Grethel flinched.

⁕

We're the famous all-girl corps, not a one of us a whore
We're Fitcher's Chicks! (buk buk buk buk)
All the other corps are boys and they make an awful noise
Not Fitcher's Chicks! (buk buk buk buk)
We're a drum corps, not a band, we're the finest in the land,
We're Fitcher's Chicks! (buk buk buk buk)
You may think you got the rocks, but we're gonna clean your clocks,
We're Fitcher's Chicks! (buk buk buk buk)

Mrs. F hated the songs the corps sang on their way home from another successful winter competition, but the older girls crowed with gusto, cawing "fuck" instead of "buk."

"Keep it *clean!*" Mrs. F scolded, almost incoherent in her anger, but beside her, Fitch grinned.

Grethel didn't sing along. Seated behind the Fitchers, she was too close to Mrs. F's cane to risk it. Besides, she didn't have to crow; she knew she was Fitch's chick. His Old Spice clung to her; so did the smell of the parts closet. No one else seemed to notice it, but Grethel couldn't get it out of her nostrils. There wasn't enough Love's Baby Soft to cover it since her first visit. She tried switching to Wind Song to no avail, a move that drove the wedge between her and the older girls even deeper. Somehow turning seventeen wasn't enough to gain entrance into the elite.

She had taken first place in individuals again, and again she heard the whispers of "show off." She sat low in her seat, and when the corps pulled into the parking lot of the VFW at one in the morning, she waited until the bus emptied out before collecting her gear: a train case, a hat box, a uniform bag, and a boot bag. She took these to her car and returned to the bus, shivering in the cold, dark hours, to wait for the horns to be unloaded from underneath. When the last horn came out, she straightened, confused. Her horn case wasn't among them.

"Good job tonight, Grethel," said Jay as he handed her the judges' sheets.

"My horn's gone," she said. "I know I put it away."

"Oh, I saw Fitch take it," he told her as he headed to his Volkswagen bug. "Said he could hear the valve clicking, and he wanted to oil it."

Grethel groaned. The thought of going down to the parts closet with Fitch at this hour turned her stomach. She just wanted to get home and get warm. She paced around the parking lot until the bus left and almost all the cars were gone. Fitch still hadn't returned with her horn. One of the chaperones took Mrs. F into her car and offered Grethel a ride.

"I have to wait for Fitch," she said.

"No, you don't," Bessie snapped querulously from the front seat.

"Be careful going home," the chaperone said. She rolled up her window, and the car left her there.

Grethel waited alone for ten minutes until finally going inside to find Fitch and her horn. He usually repaired horns at the table upstairs, but the rehearsal hall was dark. Lights on the stairway drew her to the downstairs hall. There was no sign of Fitch. Reluctantly, she headed toward the kitchen and the noxious parts closet.

"Fitch?"

No answer. Maybe he had assumed she'd go home without her horn. Had he stored it in the closet and left? She tried the handle; it was unlocked. She opened the door, covering her nose with her arm. Her horn wasn't on the floor, and she couldn't see any farther in. She caught the chain pull for the bare-bulb light and yanked.

So many parts.

Boxes cluttered the shelves closest to the door. Toward the back, boxes piled up on the floor. When she slid them aside, she was shocked to find the closet went farther back than she had first thought.

She slipped between the clutter to find herself, impossibly, in another room, wide and high, lit by a flaming bowl in the center of the floor. She froze.

A huge chopping block drenched in blood, an axe buried into it, sat beside the bowl. Beyond the flame, dozens of wide sightless eyes stared at her, their eyes gleaming red in the light of the fire. Grethel stared back in shock.

Parts.

Body parts.

Arms, legs, hands, feet. Torsi propped against the wall or tipped into a heap. Mummified remains beneath more recent gray or rotting flesh. A shelf lined with girls' heads.

One of them, Kari.

Grethel could not find breath to scream. She backed away, dizzied, until she reached the doorway. Her thudding heart almost covered the sound of Fitch's slow tread descending the stairs. In a panic, she pulled the light switch and swung the door shut soundlessly, then leaned her back to it, hoping to look like she'd been waiting for him. Her legs turned to jelly, and her head swam with the images of blood and hacked bodies and rotting guts on the floor of the cavern. Kari. How could Kari be among them?

When Fitch rounded the corner, she barely managed a forced grin.

"There you are," she called, her tremulous voice too loud in an effort to combat the pounding of her pulse in her ears. "Jay said you were down here with my bugle. I need to get home. I'm freezing."

His piercing eyes tore through her bravado. The closer he came, the tighter her chest squeezed air from her lungs. He loomed over her, frowning, smelling of whiskey from the upstairs bar, and he pinched the collar of her blouse.

"Where's the Egg?" he said.

Her hand flew to her unadorned collar. "It—it's on the blouse in my train case," she said. "I had to change. I… spilled mustard…"

She trailed off as he backed her to the closet door and shoved his body against her. His gnarled hands cupped her face, and suddenly, he slammed his mouth on hers, rocking her head against the door, prying her lips apart with his tongue. He tasted like the body parts smelled: gray and rancid. She squeezed her eyes shut until all she saw was Kari's dead eyes boring into her.

"Don't show off. Don't call attention to yourself."

She made no sound as he thrust his hands up her white blouse, then down her black slacks. Rough fingers still slick with valve oil slid inside her. All the while, the obscenity of his mouth gagged her, his rubbery tongue swabbing around inside her and shoving down her throat. Overcome with terror, Grethel didn't dare move, didn't dare fight him, refusing to acknowledge what was happening to her.

What did he want from her? Did he do this to the others, the ones in there? To Kari? What made him murder them? What response did they make that cost them their lives? Should she sigh, moan, whimper, shout, scream? Fight him? Fight Fitch?

What did it matter; she couldn't find the power to do any of those. She had to just—let him.

When he was done, he caressed her hair, "Atta girl," and left her slumped on the floor. On his way up the steps, he called back, "Your horn's at the front door. Turn out the lights and lock up."

The world folded around her in a harsh, cold fog. Inside, she burned, not only from his touch. Shame gutted her. Her own powerlessness enraged her even as her mewling fear congratulated her for surviving where others had not. She shook with anger, stunned to her core.

Through a haze, far away, she heard the front door close, and a minute later Fitch's car started up and left the parking lot. The post was dead silent.

Grethel couldn't stop her trembling any more than she could stop Fitch. Nightmare upon nightmare rattled her senseless, and she didn't know where to go, what to do. Call the police on Fitch? On William Fitcher, Sr., one of the town's men of honor, a revered Hall of Famer? Who would believe her? What if they did; would they arrest Fitch? Break up the corps because she was too weak to fight him?

They'd ask her, "Did you try to defend yourself?"

No, she hadn't. She had let him.

"Why didn't you resist?"

What could she say? "Because he was Fitch"?

How do you fight a legend? How do you fight a man you always said yes to? She had admired him, trusted him. She was Fitch's Chick.

She was stupid.

At least he had left her alive, in one piece. One broken, hollow piece. Grethel curled to her side, her back to the door, trying to convince herself there was nothing more to be said or done. She'd go home, take a bath, climb into bed, and hide under the covers until she withered and died.

A draft from under the door wafted the charnel-house stench over her. She welcomed it. She deserved it. But slowly she became aware of whispers. Like the older girls always whispered. Over and over.

"Show off... Attention... Parts closet... Show off... Attention... Parts closet..."

Grethel pressed her ear to the door.

"Don't show off. Don't call attention to yourself. Don't ever go near the parts closet."

How could Kari be in there? Kari had been driving her to practice three times a week for seven years. They sat side by side at the dinner table. They fought, like sisters fight, screaming at each other over bathroom times and borrowed clothing.

Now her naked corpse, hacked to pieces, lay heaped in the parts closet.

If Grethel couldn't redeem herself, she could try to redeem Kari. The police wouldn't be able to ignore the slaughterhouse evidence. Grethel sat up and breathed anew, then got to her feet.

The whispers grew louder as she returned to the gruesome cavern. The eyes of the dead now gazed back at her, tears on their faces. Kari called her by name, and Grethel took her sister's head into her arms and kissed her.

"You fought him, didn't you?"

She caught back a sob as she visualized Fitch molesting Kari, Kari kicking him in the groin, and Fitch's hand around Kari's throat.

"You all fought him, and he slaughtered you."

She looked to the other heads, impossibly alive, impossibly calling to her. "What do I do?" she said with a sigh, lost.

The Egg. The Egg! Use the Egg!

Kari said, "*Yours is still clean. He can't hurt you. But you can heal us.*"

Heal us. Heal us. Heal us.

Grethel read their pleading eyes. Women who had babysat Grethel ten years ago and now chain smoked and played cards with the walking mannequin she thought was her sister. Other girls who marched beside Grethel and now sat at the top of the line, the "older girls" Carole Ferrara, Jeanie Herts, Nancy Willard, Donna Blair.

Fitcher's Chicks. Fitcher's Chicks. Fitcher's Chicks. Fitcher's Chicks.

All parts on a shelf, on the floor, in boxes; their blood staining the chopping block, staining the floor.

Grethel wiped her eyes and set Kari's head beside her friends'. "I'll make this right."

Ignoring her horn case by the front door, Grethel raced to her car to retrieve the Egg, making sure it was indeed still "clean," as Mrs. F had advised so long ago.

The old bitch had known, damn it. She *knew!*

Grethel returned to the cavern beyond the façade, anger galvanizing into power. She began sorting the bodies first, and as she set them side by side on the bloody floor of the cavern, the girls whispered their instructions, guiding her to their limbs and heads. She worked through the night to place pieces of flesh together in a macabre puzzle, tears of rage mingling with those of the girls, whose voices grew from whispers to moans to clear words.

"Bessie made the Eggs to protect us," they told her, "but the old man found out about them. We kept them clean, kept ourselves clean. He found out. Found out they gave us the power to fight him. He twisted them. Turned them against us. Replaced us with cracked Eggs, chipped Eggs."

When the pieces all were accounted for, Grethel counted thirty-six individual girls.

"Throw your Egg into the fire," Kari said.

Grethel obeyed. The flames leaped high to devour it, and just as suddenly extinguished. To her amazement, the body parts drew together, sealing themselves with a sickening *snick*. Bodies were made whole. Naked, the girls stood and gathered around the empty bowl. Kari wrapped her arms around Grethel in the kind of embrace Grethel remembered from her childhood, from before Kari ever joined the corps.

"I'm so sorry," Kari said. "I did all the right things, and he made me pay for it. He made me hurtful and bitter and ugly."

Grethel wept into her sister's shoulder. "He made me filthy and disgusting."

Kari lifted her chin to face her. "He broke us all."

The women murmured agreement, and Carole Ferrara picked up the axe. "Now it's our turn," she said.

Kari kissed her brow. "Go home," she told Grethel. "We'll take it from here."

Grethel didn't go home. She went to the Wawa on the pike a few blocks from the VFW post and got coffee and a doughnut before returning to the post as the sun rose Sunday morning. She waited in her car. Church bells chimed the hours. She waited and watched. Eleven. Twelve. The Fitchers' car pulled into the parking lot a full hour before rehearsal would begin. Fitch got out and glared at Grethel's car. Mrs. F came around and elbowed him forward.

"Open the damn door," she barked, and Grethel smirked at Bessie's cursing.

He growled an answer, and the two of them climbed the stairs and Fitch unlocked the post. Grethel got out of her car and followed them. Mrs. F turned to wait for her while Fitch went inside.

"You're too early," Mrs. F scolded.

Grethel shook her head stubbornly. "I'm late, but not too late."

Mrs. F frowned. "Where's your Egg?"

Grethel's lip curled. "I don't need it anymore. It didn't do any of us any good."

Mrs. F paled. She spun about and staggered inside. "Bill!" she called. "Bill! What did you do?"

Grethel yanked her back by her collar. "You know what he did, you bitch. You know what he's done for how many years?"

Mrs. F's wrinkled face pinched. "I tried! I tried! Once they took my breasts, he just—I couldn't stop him," she cried. "Then his stroke... He got out of control. I wasn't enough for him anymore."

"You knew! You could have warned us."

"Didn't I tell you to be good?"

"You knew."

Old Bessie scowled. "I knew, I knew. But I wasn't strong enough."

Grethel measured the fear in Mrs. F's eyes and recognized it as her own the night before. She set her jaw.

"I am."

She shoved Mrs. F down the steps. She lay still on the walkway, a small pool of blood spreading from her head.

Grethel threw wide the door and joined the circle of naked women closing in on Fitch. She walked up to Carole and held out her hand. Carole relinquished the axe. Grethel turned to the old man. His eyes defied her. He sneered.

"Slut," he said. He glowered at the circle of naked women. "Sluts, alla yuz."

Grethel hefted the axe on her shoulder. Heavy. Solid. As solid as her purpose.

"Say it again, fucker."

He got as far as "S—" before she swung the axe across his mouth. Blood spurted over her. She swung again across his fear-widened eyes, then lifted the axe to bring it down on his head. When he fell, she chopped. His head, his arms, his legs, his withered old dick. Blood poured across the brown-and-cream checkered linoleum floor. The women closed in then, pulling him apart and flinging pieces of him across the floor as Grethel hacked, screaming with each stroke of the axe words she had never said out loud before.

"You bastard! You son of a bitch! You lousy piece of shit! You fucker!"

Because being clean wasn't enough. Because being the best wasn't enough. Because being Fitcher's Chick couldn't keep her or any of them from the horror of what one man could do.

When she had spent her rage, Grethel leaned on the axe, gasping, chuckling. The old bastard's blood covered her, and it felt good. She turned to Kari, looking for direction, where to step next.

"We're coming," Kari said. "Us out there, the ones he made us to be, we're coming to you."

Grethel caught her breath. "But you—where are you..."

The others laughed quietly and regathered. Kari smiled at Grethel as she joined the others, clasping hands in a circle again. Grethel watched in wonder as they melted into the pool of Fitch's blood. Grethel then wept as they vanished, and she blessed them on their way into eternity.

Yes, eternity, because she knew this was just one man among many, and there would always be this battle of powerful fuckers against unsuspecting girls who wanted only to be good, be the best.

She strode out the door with the axe to find a crowd of women: the women she had saved. They came forward and gathered around Grethel, cheering her, thanking her. But Grethel searched among them for the only woman that mattered to her.

Kari wedged her way forward and they clung to one another, weeping, laughing as the rest of Fitcher's Chicks hoisted Mrs. F's body, carried it up the steps, and heaved it through the door into the carnage.

"I'll get the gasoline," said Carole.

"I got a lighter," said Judy.

Then Kari straightened and held Grethel at arm's length, sizing her up after so many years apart. She nodded, then tipped her chin toward the axe with a grin.

"Go get 'em," she said.

Grethel brought the axe up to her shoulder. "Buk buk buk buk."

She strode to her car, tossed the axe across the back seat, and drove off. Billows of black smoke rose up from the post in her rear-view mirror.

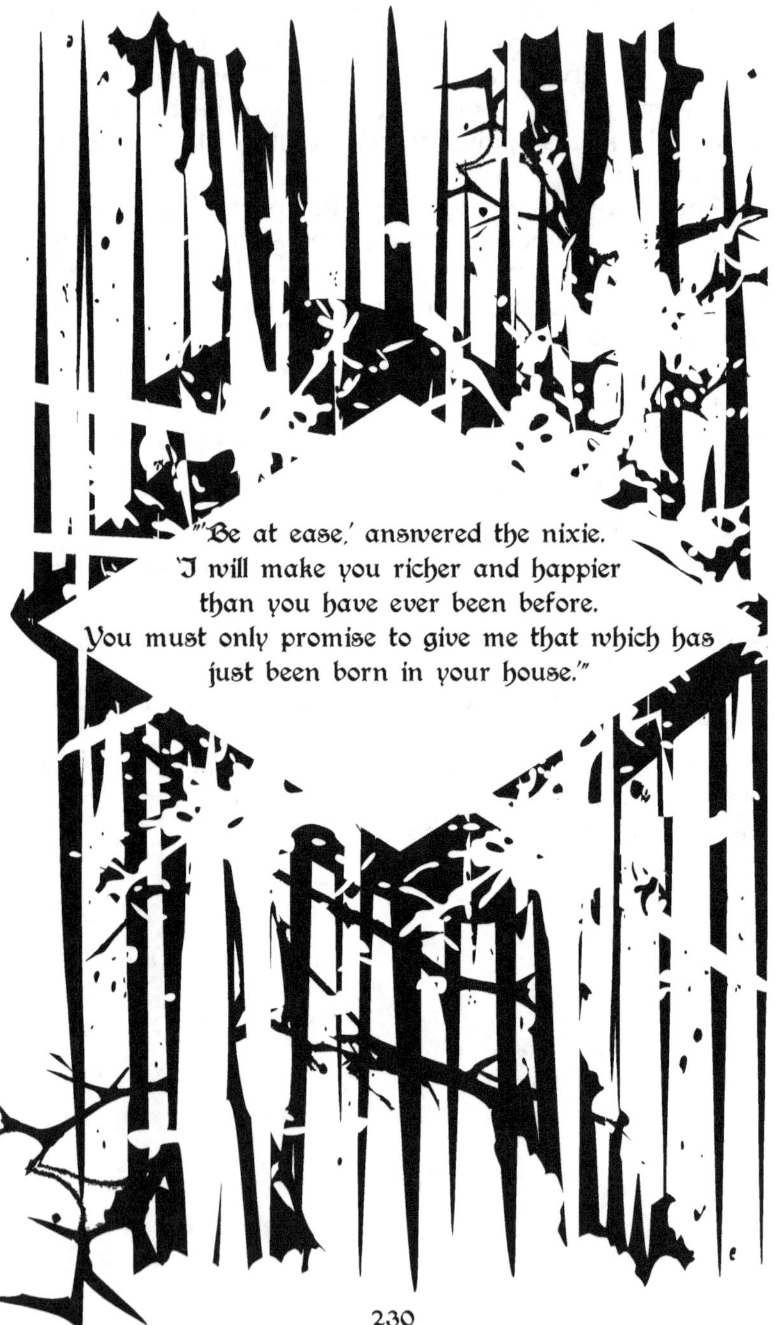
"'Be at ease,' answered the nixie.
'I will make you richer and happier
than you have ever been before.
You must only promise to give me that which has
just been born in your house.'"

No-One Need Ask

J.R. Harlow

ometimes, Colwyn remembered. On still nights when the faintest breeze trembled from the west, he woke with images of flickering ripples spreading across the water. That was when he remembered the glass of the flat pond darkening and frothing like a scrying mirror, and he would know that there had been more.

He remembered watching the smooth sides of the pond his father had carved out for the mill; so unnatural in its symmetry, so beautiful where nature had filled in the gaps. His father dammed and tamed that tumultuous stream and made a haven there, with a gathering of whispering rushes and willows that bent low to break the surface with curious fingers.

But the feral stream lived on in clumps of floating leaves and weeds that looked so solid but were deceptively thin. It hungered for Colwyn. One step, two steps, closer, and then the sucking glug of the silt and mud as it claimed him up to the waist, cold and complete.

Sometimes he'd wake in terror, hearing the vicious rain scything through the haven of the flat mill-pond, breaking the surface like knives through skin and churning the solitude within. Then he'd remember being dragged from the water, heavy in his sodden coat with duck-weed and algae tangled in his hair and shining on his flesh.

He'd slithered up the bank like a landed fish, his father grasping his shoulders, pulling the weeds from his mouth, slapping his face and then pounding on his back to release the water from his lungs, and he'd cough back to life.

"You mustn't go down to the water again, Col," his mum said desperately. "Next time you might not be so lucky. Thank the Lord your father pulled you free." Then she'd lean closer, her tender face creased with misery. "It was your father's fault," she whispered. "He promised you to it, the nixie of the mill-pond. He'll never forgive himself. He did a terrible deal, your father, to save us from ruin, but as long as you never go back, you'll be safe, and you'll be happy."

Now, Colwyn and Elisabeth lived in a cottage not far from the old gristmill. Day and night, the incessant churning of the water wheel wafted like shadows towards them, whenever the wind blew in the right direction. It soothed Colwyn to know that his father's mill still labored on, but his life was simple now, and still. A brace of pigeons on the table waiting for Elisabeth to prepare, rabbit skins curing in the outhouse, a pot bubbling over the open fire.

By day, Elisabeth would tend their little vegetable plot and fetch water from the well, and Colwyn would come home with his hunting bow slung over his shoulder and a fresh new rabbit for the pot. Then, they'd curl up in front of the licking fire and Elisabeth would mend his clothes as he read to her, and no-one need ask if they were happy.

It was a bright spring morning and the tree roots bristled with clumps of crocus leaves peering out from the earth. The fields beyond had a haze of bluebells that floated like a mist above the long grass; the birds called to each other and flurried up to the skeletal frames of nests.

The door of the cottage banged open and Colwyn breathed deep, tasting the floating pollen. He hooked his quiver and skinning knife onto his belt and picked up his old burlap bag. As his boots hit the dark earth outside, his wife called out;

"Where are you going, dearest?"

"To check my traps in the woods," he replied, scanning the sky for shreds of gray cloud, but the sky beamed back at him, restful and blue. Elisabeth came to the door and leaned against the frame, wiping her hands on her apron, and Colwyn thought that she looked like a painting, except her face was stony tense, and ever so tired.

"It won't do today, Col. We need a deer. My mother and sisters are coming to stay. Remember?"

Colwyn could hear the woods calling him. Behind him, a blackbird took flight.

"There are no deer in the woods, my love," Colwyn replied, and his wife pressed her lips together in frustration and pointed up at the mill.

"Go up to your father's mill-pond, then. The roe deer drink there."

Colwyn paused and then shook his head. "You know I cannot go back, my dearest. I'd go anywhere but there."

"Fairy-tales." She spat the words out. "He told you that to keep you away when you were a boy, Col. That's all. To save you from drowning. But you're a man now, and I won't have my table bare."

⊙⁓

Normally, Col spoke softly to the woods as he walked, and he sometimes heard them murmuring back to him, comforting him, telling him where he needed to go. Every hawthorn bush and birch tree pointed the way, the familiar twist of their branches beckoning him on, and he knew every curve and turn of the pathways that he had carved out with his own boots on his daily journeys. But today, they would not comfort him.

Colwyn went to check his traps first, and found them brimming with rabbits, and as he bundled the gray-brown bodies into his bag, their velvet legs draping from the sides, he wondered if this might suffice. But his wife was desperate to please her family, to show them how they thrived in the little cottage. As he thought of Elisabeth, he saw the first tracks. Delicate, pointed little hoof-prints, like two leaves joined together at the bud, and he started to follow them as they picked out a trail that went down, inexorably, towards his old home.

The place that he knew he should not go beckoned, and he felt as if he was being pulled there by some ancient memory, enticed there by the promise of the roe deer. But there was something more.

More, more than just the deer, Colwyn could hear it calling to him, the languid slap of the water. All the time, he deliberated, moving closer, frowning in the shadows created by a tight grove of trees, dragging in the thick air. Tiny winged creatures buzzed past, and he felt the sliding squelch of wet leaves beneath his feet; yet this is where the tracks led.

But this was not the family mill-pond. He knew his father's land like the lines on his own hand. This pond, he knew, must surely be dead. There was a prickle of decay in the air. It must have been still and brackish for years, left to rot in the fetid air.

Underneath the dense trees, no birds sang. They just held their breath, up in the canopies above. Flies cocooned the dingy mist above the water. His mother always said that flowing water brought life and still water took it away. This couldn't be the same mill-pond he had known as a boy. The stench of festering algae hit his nostrils. Yet this was where the deer tracks led.

Colwyn ducked under the trees with their grasping woody fingers probing at his ears and mouth and pulling at his clothes, holding his breath against the stench of slimy decay, yet when he emerged by the water's edge, the mill-pond had transformed.

In front of him was suddenly a glassy paradise, clear and blue, reflecting the blissful sky back to him and painting his tanned face on its perfect surface with startling skill. The thin alder trees stood like attendants, holding their arms out in greeting. Beneath and all around him, flowers with tender petals and beautiful hues of purple and pink cavorted down to the water's edge or sprang open before him, their leaves unfolding like gleeful little tongues. "*Home*" said a voice at the back of his mind.

Sunlight broke through the canopy and glittered on the crystal bright water and a huge and magnificent roe buck stepped elegantly through the trees before him and tip-toed through the spiked cattails down to the water's edge, first putting its delicate toes into the water, and then letting the pond envelop its slender ankles. The water rose up the sinewy legs and wreathed the buck in floating water-lilies and trailing duck-weed, and then it crested over the broad chest and back, across the veins of its neck. The deer never took its long-lashed eyes from Col as the water subsumed the beast up to the stubs of the antlers, and with the splash of an escaping breath from its nostrils, the deer was gone.

Col took a step back. The trees behind him seemed to back away, leaving him alone. As the ripples on the water died, and in the drowned deer's place, a pale, slender figure rose up. He was so white that he was almost green. His hair was a tangled mass of loose curls and broken branches, and he seemed woven inextricably into the trees around him. The twist of his lips and the sinews outstanding on his thin collar bones mirrored the curve of the branches.

The nixie of the mill-pond saw Colwyn and recognized him, and smiled.

"Hello Col…"

The tiny bright pupils were infused with bolts of vivid purple and a hand emerged from the water at his waist, and he beckoned, dripping.

"Come with me, Col."

He did not know that he had fled until he found himself pounding back up his familiar trail towards home, the little cottage that they shared, with his heart aching in his chest and rabbits spilling from his bag. Only when the cottage was in sight did he slow, turning to look behind him and seeing nothing but the slumbering woods, and the peaceful blue sky. He shifted his bow further up onto his shoulder and tried to catch his breath.

As he tapped the clogging mud off his boots, he pulled a long strand of weed from them, tangled and tenacious. Elisabeth was unhappy with the remaining rabbits. Col told her what had happened, he begged her to believe him, to understand. First, Elisabeth cried, still leaning up against the door, and then she began to shout and curse. She handed Colwyn a bundle of his clothes, and shut the door.

Col raced the failing light to get back as close to the old mill as he could. It was the only thing he could think to do. He heard his old home calling to him, and it seemed right that he should curl up in its shadow and listen to the giant wheel thrashing the water all night, never ceasing.

He didn't once knock at his parents' door in all the long night; he did not want to admit where he had been. Instead, he let the rapacious wheel keep him awake.

Gradually, the morning came with the sound of the gentle mill-stone, and the chattering of grains as they tumbled into sacks. The sunlight painted splashes of gold onto the beige stone walls, and he heard the peaceful creaking of the wooden beams as they warmed in the sun. Further off, a bumptious cockerel crowed.

He wondered if Elisabeth had tried to find him in the night, but the only footprints that stretched before him were his own. As he collected up his things, his mother wandered out from the mill and saw Col. She broke into a happy trot and ran to embrace him.

Colwyn gave her the rabbits he'd caught, cold from a night outside but just starting to smell musky, and she thanked him, puzzled, and he told her how he had come back to his old home, and she told him about love.

When they had talked and Col had eaten breakfast, she told him to go back. She had a golden comb that was a gift on her wedding day; a delicate thing with thin teeth of carved bone and a handle set with delicate shells. When the sunlight fell on their green and gold surface, they shone like water.

She told Col to take the comb as a gift for Elisabeth, so he thanked her, put it in his bag, and headed back down the path he had trodden so many times.

Along the way, the woods refused to speak to Col again. They watched him with the wide faces of daisies, questioning and open. The bluebells drowsed warily with one eye open, and the birds were harsh sentries, wheeling in the sky above him.

Nettles bristled from the ground and bit his ankles, lines of furious ants swarmed him if he sat down to rest, and malignant little toadstools circled his empty traps, but Col wanted to go back, so he paced on, as much as the woods would let him.

Eventually though, the bushes grew thicker and bristled with thorns. Banks of impenetrable brambles closed in on him, up to his chest with torturous spines, and he was forced to turn back.

It was then that he saw the hoof-prints, painted into the mud, and he knew what he must do. An offer. That's what was needed. He felt the outline of the golden comb in his bag and realized that, rather than offering it to his wife; he must barter with the spirit of the mill-pond. Once, he himself had been the offer, but now he had another. He let the roe deer prints lead him back.

He wasn't sure what came first; the petulant calling of his name, over and over, or the smell; salty, repulsive and rotten. It grew stronger with every step, as if the waves of the words and the waves of smell crashed inwards on him in harmony.

At the mill-pond edge, bubbles rose and burst on the green surface and watchful toads turned their orange eyes on him.

"I'm back," he said defiantly, watching the trees shiver as the buck cantered between them and disappeared. A breeze sprang up, so cold that it shocked him, so he gritted his teeth and challenged the nixie. The still green water writhed, and he flung the comb into the center. It fell with a heavy splash, and he watched the convulsive ripples edging away from the gift. He watched the water clearing from a sludgy broth to the familiar smooth glass of a mirror, and it reflected his face back to him, like narcissus.

"*Home,*" a voice said, several leagues deep in Colwyn's soul. The nixie of the mill-pond rose up, streams of water cascading from his pale shoulders and trickling from his forehead and chest, and he put out his hand again.

"Come back, Col," he said, in a voice as smooth as polished stone.

"Never," replied Col. "The water is still, and still water means death." And yet he found himself reaching out, mesmerically, twisting his fingers into the nixie's like old tree roots, intertwined and familiar.

"I will never come back," Col said, but he heard his own anguish, and it sounded just like his father's on the day that he'd dragged him from the lake. He discarded his bow by the trees, the string loosened and quivering, cast off his fear just the same, and stepped down, one step, two steps, closer. Then, just like the roe buck, he let himself be closed over by the cold water.

His bag floated away, and he pushed the choking weeds back from his face with his right arm, his left hand still bound to the fingers of the nixie. His head rushed with the sound of the water, full of sharp, tingling drops, and it washed up to Col's chest, seething with spiteful creatures with sharp teeth.

"I would never force you to come with me," the nixie said, calmly, quietly.

"That is good," said Col, in a whisper like reeds. His feet slithered on the mud bank for a second, and then the purchase was gone, and he was floating, and a peculiar warmth filled his mind. Just as the water seeps into all the cracks and splits in a piece of wood, something seeped back into Col, one memory at a time, one rescue at a time.

Every time he went down to the mill-pond and called out, every time he gave himself to the water and was choked back to life by his father's warnings, he knew there had always been more. That was when Col knew that he wasn't the only one who wanted more. The spirit of the mill-pond cried out for him, too.

As they sank down together into the ooze, he felt submerged tree roots, like a hundred blackened, twisting fingers scratching at his cheeks, frozen in balletic poses, cold and unresisting. Steadily, the muted bubbling in his ears ceased to frighten him and began, instead, to welcome him home.

Col closed his eyes and let his lungs fill with the memories of what he had been, centuries ago when they had both lived below the surface of the faultless lake, and known love. Finally, he was back, and now no-one need ask if he was happy.

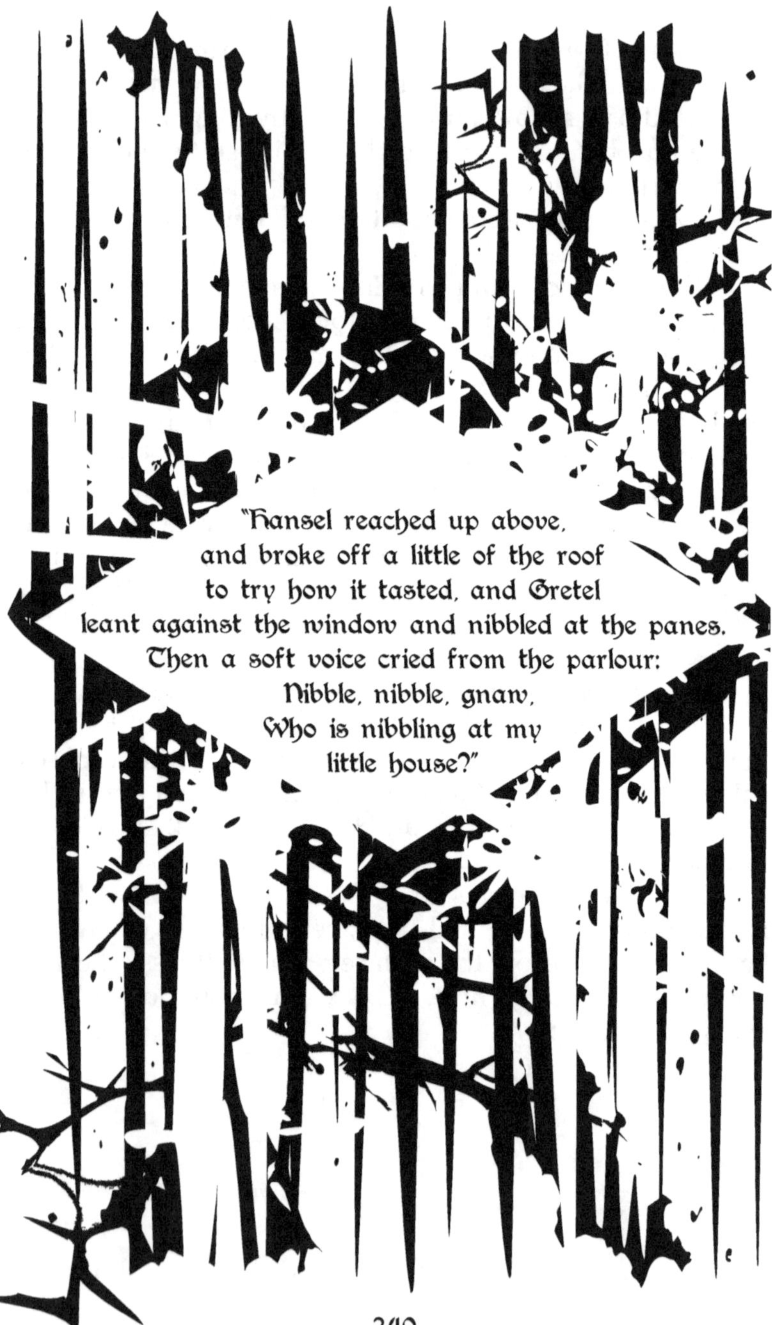

"Hansel reached up above,
and broke off a little of the roof
to try how it tasted, and Gretel
leant against the window and nibbled at the panes.
Then a soft voice cried from the parlour:
Nibble, nibble, gnaw,
Who is nibbling at my
little house?"

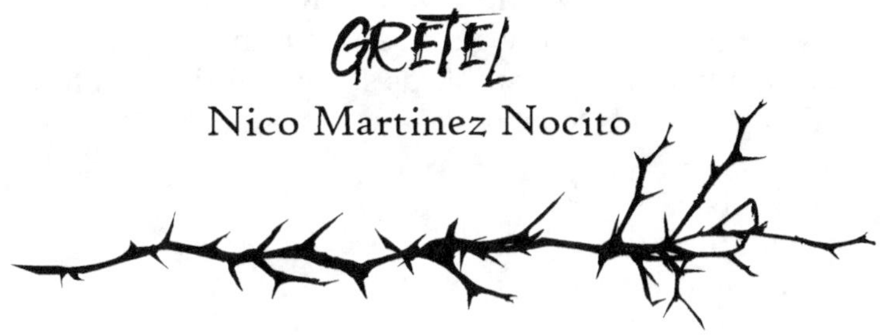

GRETEL
Nico Martinez Nocito

Mother's tears define each night.
She thinks I can't hear her, but the sounds of her sobs
flow through the walls and pool at the foot of my bed.
One night, she weeps and screams for five full hours.
The next morning, I meet my baby brother.

Hansel, she says.
I hear, *curse.*

Another child, another mouth
to feed. My mother's tears are more frequent now.
I cry too, watching my brother's hands
reach for food that isn't there, watching his pasty face
grow paler still. I watch the bruises on my mother's
cheeks
and hear her voice rising, twining in pitch
with my father's carrying baritone, declaiming,
I need another child, another son.

And her retort:
We have no food.
It seems reasonable, to me.
But then, I am only a child.

The winter after Hansel's third birthday,
my mother's stomach swells again.
She wastes away, and I watch, helpless:
watch her face grow gaunt and strained,
watch her hands tremble as she passes Hansel food
that she needs to survive.

He eats.
My father eats.
Another child, he says.

My father leaves her that winter.

She tries to keep us.
I've never heard my father scream like that
scream that first she won't bear another child
and now she wants to steal the two he has?
I want to scream too,
scream for us to stay with her.
But instead I stay silent,
and my father drags us away.

One year.
Two years.
Three, four.

The famine improves. The crops flourish.
My father rants about his first wife sometimes
sitting by the fire, weaving ghost stories only Hansel
believes.
Demon, witch, devil-woman, he says, spurred on
by his new wife: subdued, cruel. Only I remember
her soft kiss on my forehead, her gentle smile
when she laughed, her
love.

My father's new wife bears three beautiful babies,
calls him perfect, and reassures
his ego. When famine returns, her perfect smile
crimps into eternal disdain. She views Hansel and I —
relics of an old marriage, a demon-woman's spawn —
with disgust, gives us the stalest bread, the smallest
scoops
of soup, and our father lets her, because we are
memories
he'd rather not have.

When winter comes, his new wife says to throw us out,
that the famine is too harsh for extra mouths. This time
he agrees. When we leave to collect wood
and Hansel leaves a trail of pale white stones
to find our way home, I can't bring myself to tell him
that no one wants us there.

We return that night, and the next. His new wife's
frown
deepens.

On the third night, we lose our way.

The fear enters Hansel's eyes slowly:
the realization that the woods are not safe.
That we are alone.
When we stumble upon the cottage,
it feels like a miracle.

The roof is tucked beneath a stand of pines.
The smell of fresh bread wafts from the open window.
Our mother — our own mother, a miracle! — welcomes
us inside,
her joy rivaled only by my own.

Hansel watches, silent.

I tell her all that night, as Hansel sleeps:
the famine, the stepmother, our father's
new sons. She shakes her head and holds me close,
and when I call her mother, I feel at home.

The next day, when she opens her oven to bake
another loaf of bread, Hansel pushes her in.

I hear my scream as its own echo,
watch the flames licking up her hair before Hansel
throws himself
against the door, holds it shut.
Screams at me to *stay away*.
I grab at him, thoughtless, mindless,
my hands aching from the tension.
Hot metal against my fingertips, too terrible to touch
and yet Hansel presses himself against it, holding shut
the door,
holding it shut against our mother's screams,
against *my* screams —

Only when the screams go silent
does he move aside.

I cannot bear to open the oven door.

A witch, he tells me.
Our father's son, just as I am
our mother's daughter.

As I *was*
our mother's daughter.

He drags me out of the cottage, too stunned to move
of my own volition. He finds a path.
He feeds me my mother's bread
and plays the hero when we reach home.

At our father's fire, Hansel tells a different story:
one of a house of bread to lure us in,
and a loving family who welcomed us back home.
I sit quiet in the corner and recall the truth:
what drew us in was not bread but love,
what kept us there was not spells but hope,
and when we left,
I left myself behind.

"Open the door, my princess dear,
Open the door to thy true love here!
And mind the words that thou and I said
By the fountain cool, in the greenwood shade."

THE PRINCESS AND HER FUTURE
Tanith Lee

Down in the deep darkness of the green water of the cistern, where no reflection and no sunlight ever come, Hiranu waits. Not with patience, for patience is not a virtue to such as he. Nor with resignation, nor with despair. Hiranu knows, as he has always known, known from the actual instant of his binding, that at last his waiting must come to an end. Some hundreds of years have passed, in the emerald mud of the cistern's bottom. Above, far above, the temple has been crumbling to pink powder, and the great trees of the jungle-forest have woven a parasol against the sky. None of this is of any consequence to Hiranu, neither does it dismay him. He is immortal. He is incorrigibly optimistic. He understands that on one burning day or on one star-watered night — both of which have no meaning in the cistern — he will hear a step on the marble paving, loud as thunder, soft as a leaf. And that step will be for him. That step will be the release of Hiranu.

So he waits. And he waits.

The palace of the ruler poised at the summit of a downpouring of gardens. The palace was modest, for the Kingdom was small; however, the gardens were very beautiful, the product of great devotion on the part of the Ruler's slaves. At their farther end was a high wall, and in the wall a little door that gave on an overgrown pathway. The path led into the jungle-forest, and so to the clearing where an ancient temple stood. Creepers bound the pillars of the temple and flowers grew among its myriad carvings. Portions of the roof had collapsed. Harmless jewel-like snakes lived in the courts. Long ago, the rulers in the palace would leave the gardens by the little door, take the private pathway, seek the temple and worship there. But no longer. Somehow, the temple had fallen from its good repute.

The Ruler's daughter, Jarasmi, discovered the unused door as a child, and learned where it led. She was also told by her nurse that a demon haunted the temple, one of the *Rakshasas*, which could take any form it chose: lovely, to entice; fearsome—to terrify.

When Jarasmi was sixteen, she was attended by two maids. Her nurse was dead, and Jarasmi no longer believed the tale.

Jarasmi knew that in half a year's time she was to be married, and she thought a great deal of this, sometimes with pleasure, and sometimes with doubt. One day, as she passed through the marketplace in her litter, a man prostrated himself before it, begging that he might show the Princess his wares. Jarasmi's maids spoke haughtily, but Jarasmi, looking out, caught a hint of gold and heard protestations of magic.

"Bring him to me at once," cried Jarasmi.

So he was brought.

He was a strange person, and she did not like him. He wore rags, and humbled himself, yet he had the bearing of one of importance. His eyes, which he kept mostly lowered, were very odd. Rather than dark, they were yellow, and the pupils were not round, but slotted, like a serpent's. Surely, he was not quite human. He spoke.

"Some while before," he said, "I served a mighty prince, but I have come down in the world. Now I am a seller of sorcerous toys. Nevertheless, I dare approach the Ruler's daughter. Not that I may sell my goods, but that I may bring her a gift."

Jarasmi drew back, for she was uncertain now. But the man of the serpent's eyes held out to her a ball of golden glass, so clear the sun passed through it in a bolt of light.

"See," he said. "It is a thing of prophecy. If the princess wishes to know her future, she has only to cast the ball upon the ground with sufficient force to break it. What is to be found within will tell her all she desires."

Next instant, he had placed the glass ball in Jarasmi's hand. Uncannily, he slipped aside into the crowd and was immediately invisible.

Jarasmi's maids fluttered about her, all curiosity, but Jarasmi ordered her attendants to conduct her home to the palace. There, she sat alone in her chamber, and brooded upon the magical gift.

It was surely true, she wished to find out the secret of her future, what her husband might be, and if she should love him and if he should love her, and whether she would bear him sons, and if her sons might become heroes. Such things she had pondered often. At first, she was almost afraid to try the golden ball in case it failed her, showing nothing. Then she grew more afraid, supposing it would show everything.

At length, her need for enlightenment outweighed her alarm. She raised her hand to throw the ball upon the floor — and checked. She had thought so long on the matter it seemed to her the whole palace might guess her intent. The moment any heard the splintering of glass, they would realize what she had done. Jarasmi became nervous and abashed at such a notion. She did not want her Father, the Ruler, to discover what she was about.

Finally, she stole out into the gardens. Here, she again prepared to throw the ball of golden glass. But glancing up, she saw a bird floating in the sky, watching her. She hid herself under a cinnamon tree, but the noon breeze ruffled its branches, and played with her hair — she was not alone.

Bronze fish stared from the pools. Shadows stirred. The flowers whispered as if someone were walking between them.

After some time, Jarasmi found herself beside the high wall of the gardens, and before her was the unguarded little door, which led a short distance through the forest to the old and unfrequented temple.

Jarasmi hesitated for the duration of ten heartbeats. Then she unbarred the door, and stepped out into the deep green shade of the jungle.

Down in the dark of the cistern, where it is neither night nor day, Hiranu stirs. He senses his bonds, which are incorporeal and therefore not to be felt — and yet which he feels with great intensity — shiver, like strings that have been brushed by fingernails.

Then the step falls upon the paving. It is soft as a leaf.

The Princess found herself uneasy at being in the temple. The hollow intensity of a deserted building hung about it. The bright snakes glinted from the walls. Here and there a spear of sunlight clove the dark, but mostly there was no light at all. And yet she had somehow found her way into a sunken court where there was a large cistern, still full of water, let into the marble pavement. Not a glimpse of sun entered this place, nor into the well, for the temple roofs leaned close and the trees bound up the sky in their veils.

Jarasmi knew a sudden fear, remembering her nurse's tale of the Rakshasa. But such an idea was foolish.

"Come," she said to herself, aloud but very low, wary of echoes, "throw the golden ball and learn the secret if there is one to be learned. Then hurry home."

So, without further compunction, she cast the ball of glass down against the paving.

But it seemed her temerity had marred her aim. Rather than strike the marble and shatter, the ball skimmed over the cistern's rim, and fell into the water.

With a sharp cry of distress, that strangely roused not a single echo, Jarasmi ran to the cistern, and gazed into it. The ball was gone for sure. Not one bright trace could she see of it. Nor any other thing beneath the surface.

For a moment, her princess's vexation outweighed her nervousness, and Jarasmi smote the water with her wringed fist.

"Give it to me," she whispered foolishly to the cistern. "Am I never to know my future? Give back the glass ball."

And then she turned to fly, for a peculiar surge ran through the pool, another and another. Yet, reaching the doorway of the court, some extraordinary shrinking inquisitiveness made her hesitate, and look over her shoulder.

Something lay now on the skin of the water, round and glittering—the golden ball. It had been returned as she demanded.

Jarasmi hurried near, and stretched out her hand to retrieve the ball. But no sooner did she touch the glass than it broke into 1000 fragments, small as grains of dust, which showered in a sparkling pollen all across the water. Jarasmi screamed—and screamed a second time, for now her outstretched hand was caught fast in the grip of something cold and glutinous that had trapped it just beneath the surface. She could not see what held her so; her hand had vanished at the wrist in green water, as if severed, and struggle as she would, she could not pull away.

And then, as abruptly as it had taken her prisoner, the unseen creature let her go.

Half blind with horror, and stunned by curious weakness, Jarasmi stumbled from the court and away through the ruined temple.

There seemed now a thunderous silence hung there, and in the forest beyond the outer doorway a silence like deafness. But the Ruler's daughter did not heed it as she fled. Nor did she note the jewelry serpents hid, as it seemed, from her while the monkeys, which had scrambled amid the boughs above the path, were gone. At last she reached the door in the high wall and dashed through it, shutting and barring it behind her.

As she knelt by a fountain, rinsing her hands over and over, the bronze fish quivered, and darted under stones. But her two maids ran toward her laughing. The sun was low, and soon she must dine beside her Father, the Ruler, in his palace.

The red light on the hills beyond the forest came through the windows and splashed the fine plates, the goblets.

The musicians, mindful of Jarasmi's wedding half a year away, played music that had to do with bridal processions.

The Ruler was in good humor. He urged his daughter to eat. "See," he said, "how tenderly the meats have been cooked to please you, and how cunningly the spices have been prepared. And how the gold flashes on your fingers as you move them. While, only too soon, I shall lose you to a fine and wealthy lord, who will carry you away to his own palace and make you mistress of it. What can have stolen your appetite with so much of joy and success about you?"

"Pardon me, my Father," said Jarasmi, "I do not know."

But she did.

The sun on the western hills changed from clear red to dark red. Servants came, drawing down the ornate lamps to light them.

The musicians played a bridal dance.

The sun sank.

The hills, the jungle-forest, and finally all the long windows turned black as Ebony.

There came a strange sound, audible even above the music, though plainly it was far away.

"Now, what can that be?" inquired the Ruler, growing testy, for the evening was not as carefree as he had envisaged—his grateful daughter sullen and uneasy, his musicians faltering, and weird rappings echoing up from his garden like Stony blows at the bottom of a cistern.

Just then a servant entered and prostrated himself.

"Master-of-the-Palace, someone knocks for admittance—not at the great gate, but at the little door in the high wall of your garden."

The Ruler plucked at his robe, examined a ruby ring.

"It will be some beggar."

"No, Master-of-my-life, no beggar. For when one of your guard questioned who knocked, a voice answered from the darkness: 'The Princess summoned me.'"

"What is this?" demanded the Ruler angrily.

"I do not know," said Jarasmi.

But she did.

And now the dire rapping sounded again, hollow, far away, filling up the night.

"Tell them," said the Ruler, "they must not open the door."

But it was too late. One of the young guard had opened it, and stepping out on the jungle path, had challenged the depths of the silent forest and the tall pillars of the trees. No one was there.

"The noise has stopped now," said the Ruler. "All is quiet."

Indeed it was. A river of quiet was in the gardens, rolling toward the lighted palace. And as it came, the leaves grew still on the bushes, and the night-flying insects lay heavy as drops of moisture in the bowls of flowers. The fountains fell spent and did not rise again.

Quite suddenly, the birds and the cages about the room stopped twittering. The musicians' hands slid from their instruments.

Something smote upon the palace door. Again, and again and again. Cold the blows were, as if smitten underwater, or sunlight had never once penetrated.

"This is too much," said the Ruler.

Rising, he drew his rich robe about him. He walked into the glittering vestibule, his servants round him, his slaves throwing themselves respectfully down, his guards massed, threatening with their leaf-headed spears.

All confronted the door, which rang and shook.

"Who dares to knock?" cried the Ruler.

From the soundless gardens beyond the door came a voice:

"The Princess summoned me."

"You lie," said the Ruler. "Be gone, and I shall act leniently. Knock once more, and I will set my guard upon you."

The knock came. The palace vibrated at it.

"Open the door," thundered the Ruler, "and kill whatever is out there."

"No!" cried Jarasmi. "Do not open the door."

"Why do you say this?"

"I do not know," said Jarasmi.

But she did.

Next minute, the palace door stood wide, and the guard burst out upon the terrace. Only the black of night was waiting to be let in, and the motionless shrubs that did not stir in the windless air. The wind had crept instead into the palace. It blew upon the lamps and they flickered. It shook the draperies.

"Who is there?" shouted the Ruler.

But no one answered.

Then, returning to the table, one of the servant-women exclaimed. Jarasmi's untouched plate had been emptied. Her untouched cup was drained.

The Princess went to her apartment, and her steps were slow. She sat on a little stool while her maids brushed and anointed her hair, took from her her finger-rings and earrings, and clad her in a loose robe for sleep.

Below, two sorcerers were busy in the palace, and smoke rose. A priest discussed the nature of demons reassuringly with the Ruler. The young guard, who had opened the garden door, had been savagely beaten, and hung from a post, groaning.

"How strangely cold the chamber is," said one of Jarasmi's maids.

"It must be the season," said the other.

Unlike the Princess, they had hurried, and now hurried to leave, the anklets clinking on their dainty feet. Bowing low, they were gone.

Jarasmi sat motionless as a figurine upon the stool. Jarasmi waited.

But it was not long before the voice spoke to her, from behind her left shoulder.

"You know that I am here, Princess."

"Yes," murmured Jarasmi, "I do."

And she did.

"Why not turn about, then, and see what you called from the cistern in the temple."

Jarasmi wept. She felt a dreadful, drawing weakness.

The voice, however, laughed gently.

"But what could I be that is so fearsome, if a small cistern can have held me?"

"Oh, you are something monstrous," cried Jarasmi wildly. "A beast like a fish, or a frog, thick-scaled and dripping slime, with talons and the teeth of a tiger, and the bulging eyes of a lizard."

The voice laughed again.

"So much? Oh, Jarasmi—a fish? A frog? A tiger? Turn and see."

Then her fear became so vast she was powerless to deny any command of her tormentors, and she did turn and she did see, and so she beheld Hiranu.

There in the lamplight was a young and handsome Prince, clothed in beautiful garments, and burning jewels, his dark eyes burning more fiercely than any of them.

"I," said Hiranu, "was bound by the spell of an enemy, to abide in the mud of the well until an innocent girl might free me by some inadvertent deed, such as desiring a favor of me. How unlikely this seemed. But never once did I lose my faith that one turn of the wheel should bring reprieve."

Then the handsome Prince came to her, and took Jarasmi's hand. His touch was delightful, and all her strength seemed to flow away.

"And now, exquisite Princess, I wish only that you will come with me to my Kingdom, and rule with me. And I will love you all your life."

At which, he kissed her, and every lamp in the chamber died.

◦⊙◦

In the pale azure hour before sunrise, the Ruler gave his only daughter to a foreign Prince, to be his wife.

Presently, a wonderful carriage was driven into the court before the great gate of the palace. It was hung with scarlet, and fringed with gold, while silver disks made rippling music from each drape and fold. The window-spaces were filled by screens of carved ivory, and their eyelets closed with precious gems, so none might look in—or out. Reddish horses pulled the carriage, and the moment they stopped, their driver leapt down and ran to Hiranu, kneeling at his feet.

"This is my loyal servant," said Hiranu, "who all these years has patiently awaited my return."

And he embraced the man, and sent him to kneel also to Jarasmi. This the servant did, placing in her hands a white flower. When he rose, she saw his eyes were bright yellow as a snake's.

Jarasmi entered the carriage with her bridegroom, and the carriage was closed.

The Ruler stood before the palace door and watched the carriage rush away. He caressed the huge emerald the young Prince had given him, which was larger than a pigeon's egg, and the diamond that was even larger. The Ruler's face was sallow and his hands trembled so that soon he dropped both jewels. His slaves scrambled to retrieve them, as, from the halls of the Palace, there lifted the notes of a dreadful lamentation.

In the darkened carriage, Hiranu is almost done, now, with waiting.

Beyond the scarlet, gold and ivory, the day begins to blossom, but he will not see it; day and night are all one within the dark. He can, of course, see his bride perfectly well. And if she sees him less perfectly in the blackness, she may at last be glad of it.

How swiftly they travel through the jungle-forest. Perhaps, by moon rise, he will have reached his home. His bride, unfortunately will not. But it was true, he will love her all her life.

Hiranu turns to her, the means of his deliverance. She is finding it hard to smile at him; her smiles resemble, more often than not, winces of terror. Yet, garnished by her flower, she attends. She is here, and no one can come to her aid at all.

Hirano ceases to wait. He assumes, very quickly, and with a degree of simple pleasure, his other form.

The sealed carriage does not reveal it. While Jarasmi's frenzied shrieks are muffled, and in any case, do not continue long.

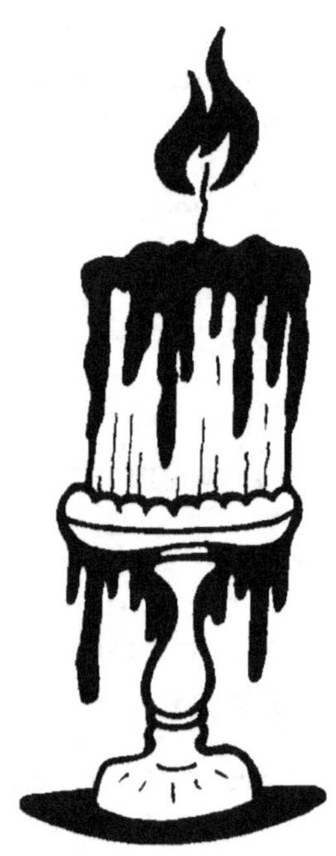

ACKNOWLEDGMENTS

There are many moving parts on a project as big as Grimm Retold. Almost as big a task is acknowledging everyone who helped us get to this point. We at Speculation Publications would first like to thank the authors for their beautiful and terrible stories. There would literally be no book without their creative and horrifying tales.

We are overwhelmed with gratitude for Cecila Dart-Thornton, for her general kindness, enthusiasm for writing and generous contributions. Ms. Dart-Thornton's fairy tales have long inspired our books, and her friendship with Tanith Lee set us on a path we couldn't imagine at the start of this journey. Thank you for taking the time out of your busy schedule to write the foreword, for your advice, your support and your beautiful books, always.

We'd like to give a huge thank you to John Kaiine, for granting us the privilege of reprinting a fairy tale from his incomparable wife, Tanith Lee, with great honor. And to Tanith Lee, for being the forerunner of fairy tale retellings, for seeing what was truly inside those tales, the real stories within the fiction. For that, we thank you from the bottom of our *Red As Blood* hearts.

Thank you to Allison Rich, who provided some gorgeous details about Ms. Lee to help bring her to life in our minds, and to Fantasy Hive for giving us the platform to talk about her and the book.

As we start to round the bend to our third year as a small press, there are some people who have made it possible to do this work overall. Susan Tulio, of course. Our wayward third partner and hype woman. William Donahue who is steadfast in his support and coolness. Don Swaim who is a fierce advocate for the written word and his alumni. Hope Madden who, despite her own 5000 projects always finds time to boost us. The PA HWA Chapter, who is the best HWA Chapter. A.C. Wise for being kind enough to grant us a lovely review. The amazing small presses that have given us advice and support as we learn wtf we're doing. The people who have taken time to read and review our books.

We would be remiss if we didn't thank the Brothers Grimm for chronicling the most authoritative books of folktales ever compiled, "Kinder-und Hausmärchen." Written folklore, that over one hundred and fifty years later, we call Grimm's fairy tales. We'd also like to thank the people like Jack Zipes for ensuring these stories endure and are accessible to us all, forever.

And finally, to our readers. Thank you. Lives are busy and time is precious. There is no greater reward for Speculation Publications than the time and attention you give our books.

262

Bios

Lindsay Comer is based in South Wales and holds an MA in Creative Writing from the Open University. Her fiction, poetry and creative non-fiction has been published internationally in lit mags and journals including: *Gwyllion Magazine, Wishbone Words, The Unwritten, The Daily Drunk, Viridian Door, Litmora Literary Magazine, Scarlet Dragonfly Journal, The Dirigible Balloon* and *The Hooghly Review*. She also has a short story forthcoming in *Laughs in Space.*

Eleanor Cooke is a neurodivergent eighteen-year-old who loves writing, sewing, and her two cats. She also adores, but doesn't write, poetry.

Cecilia Dart-Thornton is a multi-genre author known for intricate world-building and richly developed characters. Internationally recognized, with works translated into multiple languages, she is published under pen-names and her own name. Notably, she's the author of fantasy series the Bitterbynde Trilogy and the Crowthistle Chronicles. Using the name "Barb Dwyer," she also authored the humorous sci-fi/fantasy satire series, Cyberchicks.

Ef Deal is a musician, a poet, an editor, a video editor, and an author of science fiction, fantasy, and horror who has been writing and composing since she was nine years old. Her short fiction has been published in numerous online zines and print anthologies including *The Magazine of*

Fantasy and Science Fiction, *A Cast of Crows* from eSpec Books, *Dangerous Waters* from Brigid's Gate, Chris Ryan's *Soul Scream Antholozine*, two anthologies from Speculation Publications, and most recently in eSpec Books' *A Cry of Hounds* and *Other Aether*. She is currently public relation coordinator for *eSpec Books*, assistant fiction editor at *Abyss&Apex* magazine, and video editor for *Strong Women ~ Strange Worlds*. Her novel *Esprit de Corpse* from *eSpec Books* is the first in a steampunk paranormal romance series set in France, featuring the gifted Twins of Bellefées, who tend to show up in other eSpec Books anthologies. The second book in the series, *Aéros & Héroes*, is due this November. When she's not writing, she plays bugle in the Blessed Sacrament Golden Knights drum and bugle corps, and is a member of the Buglers Hall of Fame and the New Jersey Drum Corps Hall of Fame, honored for her contribution to playing, teaching, directing, and arranging. She lives in Haddonfield, NJ, with her husband and her chow chows Corbin and Rory. She is a member of SFWA and HWA.

F. Ffrench (she/it) is a multimedia artist and writer trapped in a tower somewhere in Chicago. Her work usually centers around queer surrealism and horror. Her writing has been published in the Chicago zine *Messy Misfits Club* and *God's Cruel Joke magazine*. It has been writing since before it could spell and plans to do so until it dies.

Ephiny Gale was born in Victoria, Australia, and is still there, alongside her lovely wife and a small legion of bookcases. She is the author of more than fifty published short stories and novelettes that have appeared in publications including *PseudoPod*, *Constellary Tales* and *Beneath Ceaseless Skies*. Her fiction has been awarded the Sundress Publications' Best of the Net award and has been a finalist for multiple Aurealis Awards.

Bram Stoker Award® nominee **Carol Gyzander** writes and edits horror, weird fiction, and science fiction — frequently with strong women in twisted tales that touch your heart. Carol Co-Chairs the HWA NY Chapter and co-hosts their monthly Galactic Terrors online reading series. MWA, SFWA, Active HWA.

J. R. Harlow writes dark, surreal and humorous short stories and is a regular contributor to the Dark Lane anthology series. She has also appeared in *Adverbially Challenged volume 2, Holidays; Straight up or on the Rocks* and *Stygian Lepus magazine* (Aus). Forthcoming projects are with *Egaeus Press* (UK).
She also won third prize in the CAS short story competition in 2022 and was a winner of the Philip LeBrun prize for creative writing on graduating from Chichester University. She currently lives in Kent, England, with her husband and just the right amount of cats.

Ell Huang (she/they) is a film and folklore enthusiast. She reads for *Whale Road Review* and *Last Syllable*, and is published in 100+ venues such as *Ram Eye Press, From the Farther Trees, Sword & Kettle Press, Moss Puppy Magazine, Not Deer Magazine, Crow & Cross Keys, Lucent Dreaming, Lumiere Review*, and *Three Drops from a Cauldron*, among others. They are working on a multitude of projects: a fairytale chapbook, a diverse platonic fantasy collection, an ace horror collection, and most recently, writing *Aromantic Frankenstein* as their MA thesis in grad school.

Jade Jiao is a British writer living in Japan. Her novel *Solum* was shortlisted as one of Roadmap Writers' top 25 in 2020, and in 2021, her play *A Saleswoman* was staged by The Bluestocking Theatre Group, Manchester. She was recently a quarter-finalist in 2024's Killer Shorts Screenplay Competition.

Brian Lally is a distinguished artist renowned for his intricate pen and ink illustrations, as well as his colorful abstract oil paintings. With a keen eye for detail and a passion for storytelling, Lally's work captures the essence of both fantasy and reality. His illustrations blend classic comic book aesthetics with the mystical elements of tarot symbolism, creating unique and evocative visual narratives. Lally's artistry draws inspiration from a diverse range of sources including mythology, literature, and personal experiences. His designs are celebrated for their originality and depth, offering a fresh perspective on traditional themes. Throughout his career, Brian has continued to reflect a commitment to pushing artistic boundaries and exploring new forms of visual expression. Based in Sellersville, PA, Lally continues to expand his creative horizons, captivating audiences with his distinctive and compelling illustrations.

Tanith Lee was a British science fiction and fantasy writer. She wrote more than 90 novels and 300 short stories, and was the winner of numerous awards including the World Fantasy Lifetime Achievement Award and the Bram Stoker Award for Lifetime Achievement in Horror. She was well known for her interpretations of fairy tales, weaving in themes of feminism and sexuality. Although she passed away in 2015, she remains a strong influence in fantasy and science fiction today, and received the 2024 Infinity Award for her lasting legacy.

David Kenneth Mitchell is a fledgling author from Cornwall, England. After recently reading Michelle Paver's - *Dark Matter*, and listening to the *SFF Addicts pod*, he was inspired to pick up the pen again for the first time since secondary school. He writes weird fiction, playing with tropes and subverting them into something strange, unsettling, and wonderful.

He's currently drafting his debut novel, a supernatural horror loosely inspired by a recent substantial head injury, and the subsequent fallout from it.

Tiffany Morris is an L'nu'skw (Mi'kmaw) writer from Nova Scotia. She is the author of the Shirley Jackson Award-nominated novella *Green Fuse Burning* (Stelliform Press, 2023) and the Elgin Award-winning horror poetry collection *Elegies of Rotting Stars* (Nictitating Books, 2022). Her work has appeared in the Indigenous horror anthology *Never Whistle At Night*, as well as in *Nightmare Magazine, Uncanny Magazine,* and *Apex Magazine,* among others.

Nico Martinez Nocito (they/them) writes fantasy stories with a queer and feminist bent. They spend their free time running, acting in local theater productions, and posting about fantastic MG and YA books on their blog, *Rapunzel Reads.*

Elizabeth Rosen writes mainstream and speculative fiction. Originally from New Orleans, she now lives in small town Pennsylvania where she has become appreciative of snow and colorful scarves. Her work has appeared or is forthcoming in *North American Review, Glimmer Train, Sanitarium, Dark Recesses, Creepy Podcast, No Sleep Podcast* and numerous other lovely, spooky places.

Erica Ruppert, HWA, SFWA. lives in northern New Jersey with her husband and too many cats. Her short stories have appeared in magazines including *Vastarien, Lamplight,* and *Nightmare,* on podcasts including *PodCastle,* and in multiple anthologies. Her debut collection, *Imago and Other Transformations,* was released by Trepidatio

Publishing in March 2023. When she is not writing, she runs, bakes, and gardens with more enthusiasm than skill.

Liv Strom is an award-winning Swiss-Swedish writer of speculative fiction with stories in *Apex, Hexagon SF Magazine* and *Mystery Magazine*, among others. As a writer with aphantasia (she cannot visualize anything), her magic power is to make her characters live in other's minds. She is currently working on the fourth instalment of her twisted fairytales series *Tales of Bones & Roses.*

Temple (who uses they/them), writes under the name **TT Madden**. They're a genderfluid, mixed-race writer whose work in scifi, fantasy, and horror often deals with the intersections of their various identities. Their forthcoming novellas *The Cosmic Color, The Familialists,* and *Coffin Corner* range from mecha/kaiju, to social horror, and young adult horror.

M. Weigel retells myths and fairy tales and explores science fiction, fantasy, and horror. When not writing, she researches stories in their oldest forms to see how they survive and transform into today's tales. Her work can be found in *The World of Myth Magazine, Partially Shy Literary Magazine, Litmora Literary Magazine, Cosmic Daffodil Journal, Pickle Press Poetry, Pressed Flowers Lit, Carmina Magazine,* and Dandelion Revolution Press.

Jacqueline West is a poet and novelist living in Minnesota. Her work has appeared in *Star*Line, Enchanted Living, Strange Horizons,* and multiple volumes of the Horror Writers Association Poetry Showcase. Her collection *Candle and Pins: Poems on Superstitions* is available from

Hiraeth Publishing. She is also the author of the New York Times-bestselling middle grade series *The Books of Elsewhere*, the YA horror novel *Last Things,* and several other award-winning books for young readers.

Shehrazade Zafar-Arif is a London-based writer who grew up in Karachi, Pakistan, the daughter of a politician and a journalist. Her writing is often inspired by Pakistani folklore and storytelling traditions. Her work has been published in *Fiery Scribe Review, Peatsmoke Journal, Untitled: Voices, FeelsZine,* and *FEED Lit Mag,* and she also writes for *Shakespeare Bulletin, Crayon Magazine, the Croydonist,* and the *Japan Society Review.*

Speculation Publications

Check out the Collections of Utter Speculation
The Lost Colony of Roanoke
The Jersey Devil
Lady in White
The Dancing Plague
Cry Baby Bridge

And our other Books
Incubate: a horror collection of feminine power
Work in Progress: Story Crafting Notebook
Beach Shorts
Yule
Muse

www.speculationpub.com